KV-415-577

Jane Rogers

Body Tourists

WATERFORD CITY AND COUNTY
WITHDRAWN
SCEPTRE LIBRARIES

Waterford City and County
Libraries

First published in Great Britain in 2019 by Sceptre
An Imprint of Hodder & Stoughton
An Hachette UK company

1

Copyright © Jane Rogers 2019

The right of Jane Rogers to be identified as the Author of the
Work has been asserted by her in accordance
with the Copyright, Designs and Patents Act 1988.

All rights reserved. No part of this publication may be reproduced,
stored in a retrieval system, or transmitted, in any form or by any means
without the prior written permission of the publisher, nor be otherwise
circulated in any form of binding or cover other than that in which it is
published and without a similar condition being imposed
on the subsequent purchaser.

All characters in this publication are fictitious and any resemblance
to real persons, living or dead, is purely coincidental.

A CIP catalogue record for this title is available from the British Library

Hardback ISBN 978 1 529 39295 1
Trade Paperback ISBN 978 1 529 39296 8
eBook ISBN 978 1 529 39298 2

Typeset in Sabon MT by Palimpsest Book Production Ltd, Falkirk, Stirlingshire

Printed and bound in Great Britain by Clays Ltd, Elcograf S.p.A.

Hodder & Stoughton policy is to use papers that are natural, renewable
and recyclable products and made from wood grown in sustainable forests.
The logging and manufacturing processes are expected to conform
to the environmental regulations of the country of origin.

Hodder & Stoughton Ltd
Carmelite House
50 Victoria Embankment
London EC4Y 0DZ

www.hodder.co.uk

Body Tourists

WATERFORD CITY AND COUNTY WITHDRAWN LIBRARIES

SFF

ALSO BY JANE ROGERS

Conrad and Eleanor
Hitting Trees with Sticks (Stories)
The Testament of Jessie Lamb
The Voyage Home
Island
Promised Lands
Mr Wroe's Virgins
The Ice is Singing
Her Living Image
Separate Tracks

Non-fiction
The Good Fiction Guide

1.

GUDRUN

Since mine is the fortune that set this ball rolling, and the selection of the players has been down to me, I owe it to you to give an account. I have something of a controlling influence, although all these characters make their own choices: free will is, after all, a basic human right.

I'm old now, with children and grandchildren and more great-grandchildren than I can bother to recall the names of, but my nephew Luke has always held a special place in my affections. Such a clever, awkward, ambitious boy; able to solve the enigmas of science, yet comically poor at fielding human emotions. All intellect, no empathy, is what his sister Hilary says.

Let me set the scene. Recently there have been some magnificent leaps in digital memory transfer. Memory enhancement has solved many problems for the elderly (not me – my memory is still as good as it ever was, thank you). But that has increased the frustration of the old with their frail, worn-out organic bodies. Though they are patched up with replacement joints and organs, a hundred-year-old body is still a liability.

The first digital full-memory transfer into a synth was achieved a few years ago, to great acclaim. But since then there has been a continuing debate about the legal status of such a creature. *Not human!* argue many, due to the absence of organic matter. *Human!* counter the rest, given the presence of a human mind complete with a lifetime's memories and knowledge. The only thing almost all agree upon is that in the eyes of the law, such a synth must have fewer rights than the organic human.

And then Luke comes to me with his own clever breakthrough, solving that synthetic/organic conundrum.

So I give the boy money. What else is it for? Nothing gives me greater pleasure than using my wealth for the benefit of humanity. Am I being vain? I don't think so. I think if anyone's name is remembered it will be Luke's. I'm just the power behind the throne.

It's early days. Lukey is still testing and trialling and has sworn me to secrecy. When he's ready, with enough positive results under his belt and any glitches ironed out, then will come the time to help him steer it through the necessary legal and ethical hoops to put it on the market. He hasn't the charm or patience for that kind of thing. I'm content to wait, as long as I have a ring-side seat.

And that's what I want to share with you, dear reader; a ring-side seat. At the spectacle of Luke's first Body Tourists. Or should I call them guinea pigs? Let me call them *beneficiaries*.

2.

PAULA AND OCTAVIA

First I knew about it was Ryan dragging me off down the clinic queue to get a Fitness certificate. Half eleven and as per usual the queue snaked right across the estate. End of September and sweltering so the towers looked like they was wobbling and melting away in the heat haze. I wish they bloody would. Grey grey grey everywhere you look, grey concrete and flashing windows sharp as knives in your eyes. I had to stare down at my blue leggings for a break. It smelled of sweaty bodies and ready meals, with no wind to shift or even stir it. A few of the oldies were holding up umbrellas to make a bit of shade. I left Ryan keeping our place and went back up the flat to get a towel to drape over our heads.

When we finally got to the medibots they took blood, and weighed and measured for BMI, and made us run on the tread-mills (pouring sweat) then listened to our hearts and lungs, and finally pinged us two good certificates. Which anyone who looked at us could have told without all that. Well, Ryan runs, and I do the dance, and neither of us is into VR. I felt hot and sick and I told Ryan I didn't see the need.

'You will,' says Ryan. 'You'll thank me, Paula, I'm telling you now. We're gonna make ten thousand pounds!'

'You're a bloody optimist!' I said, but he made me smile cos he was always looking forward to something, just like a kid. That's one reason I liked him. He thought there'd be a way out. He went running every morning, right round Coldwater, even though people called him a nutter. He talked about getting work on a farm (which *was* nuts, cos it's all bots, they don't need human muscle) and about being an athlete – which I thought

3

was a good dream. Like me being a dancer. You don't get off the estate but still, you can run and you can dance, and you can dream.

Then he tells me all about it. He's found this online advert asking for help in medical research. All you need is the Fitness certificate and be aged 18–22, and willing to be put to sleep for two weeks. And they'll give you ten grand.

'Right,' I said. 'In your dreams.'

He had to send the Fitness codes and they asked for a load of other stuff digitally, photos, birth certificates . . . I said to him, you know what this is? It's identity theft! What you playing at?

But then we each get a message telling us the time the auto will pick us up, and that we must make ourselves completely available for the next fifteen days.

On the morning, Ryan was going, 'Ten thousand pounds, ten thousand pounds', and my stomach was sloshing like a washing machine. I'd not been off the estate in six years. My mum was still begging me not to go, which I could of done without. I told her hush, I'll be back in a fortnight. The auto they sent for us was cool, retro but silent, and when you're in among a bunch of them shooting along the toll passing and repassing it's fun. But I didn't see those hills and fields you see on TV. The toll was sunk too low in the ground. Never saw London either, not the famous stuff like Westminster, only streets of high old joined-up houses. Ryan said it's where we're gonna live when they pay us. It's ancient on the outside but inside it's all smart. The fridge restocks itself and you never have to take down the rubbish. When we got there the clinic was like that, like a hotel in a film, with real flowers and fruit and wine complimentary in our room and order what you want from the food list. The room glowed and lit up when you moved in different parts of it.

We did another medical, then we had to sign stuff. It was a human doctor, which I was glad about, even if he was a bit odd. Dr Luke Butler, with a posh voice. He was fidgety, like he was awkward with us being there. He looked at Ryan all the time he was talking to us. I thought that was rude. I mean, I know it was Ryan's idea but I was there as well, wasn't I?

So when Dr Butler was shaking our hands, like everything was sorted, I elbowed Ryan to ask him.

'Ask me what?' frowns the doctor.

Ryan's going, nothing, nothing, she's talking crap, so I go, 'What you gonna do with us? While we're asleep?'

The doctor says, 'That's a fair question. I should give you a proper answer, Paula.' So we sit down again and he explains.

When we're back in our posh room Ryan goes straight for the wine and I said, 'Aren't you even gonna talk about it?'

'Why should I? I'll be asleep, I won't even know.'

'But, someone else in your body!'

'So?'

'What if they hurt you?'

'It'll be them that feels it, not me.'

I didn't want to drink. I wasn't allowed to have anything after 8 p.m. anyway cos of the anaesthetic. He fell asleep and snored like a dog and I lay there feeling afraid with all my arms and legs heavy as cement. How could you put someone else's brain into my body? How could you do it without harming me? It was like Frankenstein. I was never even going to wake up again, let alone be me and get paid. I begun to cry and Ryan woke up. He give me a cuddle. 'In two weeks we'll be back here,' he says, 'and we'll be rich.' He told me to take one of the tablets we'd been given, for nerves. I was going first and he was going the day after. 'We only do one per day,' says Dr Butler, 'so we can monitor everything very carefully.' That made me feel better about it, which – looking back – was bloody stupid.

Octavia, Day 1

What?

What has happened to me?

My eyes are half-open and there's light radiating shifting patterns of green and blue, the most piercingly beautiful colours. Into my ears flows the hum of layer on layer of sound: ventilation, voices, distant movement, music, the whole delicious buzz of life. I am warm, sensate, my lungs are breathing, my heart is pumping inside an almost overpowering sense of physical well-being. What is this – wonderful *body*?

Suddenly there is the pink round of a face.

'How are you feeling? Up to talking?' A tall man with a worried face stooping over me.

'I am feeling – magnificent.' I can speak! It takes me a moment to frame the words. My jaw is heavy, it takes longer to operate. And my voice is as deep as his.

He holds out his hand. 'Luke Butler. Doctor in charge.'

I sit up. I extend my arm and he clasps my hand. Skin on skin, warm, dry, firm yet yielding, silken yet grained, with varying degrees of pressure firing my synapses in an explosion of sensation. I have to collect myself. 'I'm – my name is Octavia Harmer.'

'In a younger body.'

It takes me a long time to absorb what he says. It takes me a long time to begin to make sense of it. 'You've brought me back?'

'Yes.' He sits beside the bed.

'My brain—'

'The cloning technique you were working on. It's in the oval capsule in your left axilla.' Now he mentions it, I can feel a soreness in my armpit. I raise my right hand – yes, I can move at will – and gently touch the dressing. There is a slight bulge beneath.

'So how does it actually feel?' he asks.

I don't know. Eventually I manage, 'Intense.'

'Go on.'

6

'I think my senses are heightened. This is a real body!'

'Yes.'

'What year is it? How long ago—?'

'Did you die? Eight years.'

'And in eight years you have . . .'

'I was working on it before you died. I was hoping to talk to you, but you were too ill.'

'I had no idea. I thought we'd use synthetics.'

'Using a host body has turned out to be the most effective option. All the info and updates are on the screen, when you're ready. I thought you'd want to take your time over the research path.'

'How does the connection work?'

'Your brain's connected to the host CNS via a port just below your ear, with the connection tracking under the skin.' My finger tip verifies his words.

He coughs. 'I should explain – the body—'

'You've put me into a male!'

'Yes.' He is ill at ease. 'There were no suitable female volunteers.' I nod, watching with amusement the way my vision leaps from his eyes to the ceiling and back with each head tilt, and then choosing to lock my eyes onto his while I continue to nod, aware of the movement now at the peripheries of vision, and the stillness maintained at the centre. It is my turn to speak.

'I feel like a new driver let loose on a top-of-the-range vehicle.'

'A driver?' He looks puzzled. 'No one really drives anymore. But I know what you mean.' He shifts in his seat.

My ears are tracing a pattern in the distant music – keyboard – the regular rising and shaping, the mathematically satisfying predictability. 'Is that Bach?'

'You've got good hearing. That's playing in Reception. I wanted to talk to you but I can come back later if you prefer.'

'I can talk. Are you the one who did the transfer?' I ask.

'Yes. Supported by specialist bots, obviously.'

'So – can I get up and walk? Can I move like a normal person?'

He laughs. 'Yes. You are a normal person.'

I swing my legs over the side of the bed. Each movement is precise and simple, no obstructions, no impediments, no pain! The muscle movements are so clean it seems I move almost before I think of moving. And when I stand it's glorious. I am the same height as the doctor. Tall! He is watching me critically as I take my first steps, but there's no difficulty at all; these joints are oiled and supple. They hinge with fluid ease. I can bend, I can stretch, I can touch my toes. I extend my arms and tilt my head from side to side. This body is young, and every part of it works. I am suddenly conscious again of his eyes on me, and seat myself decorously on the bed.

'I need to catch up with your research, don't I. You say it's onscreen?'

He nods. 'What I did want to tell you is how much I admire you. It's really your work, you and your team, plus Peter Glazier in New York—'

'Pete Glazier? Digital memory transfer?'

'He made the breakthrough. Anyway, we wouldn't be where we are today if it wasn't for your vision and imagination. I've wanted to meet you – for an awfully long time.' He smiles awkwardly and reaches to shake my hand again. The fact that I know what the sensations will be only makes them the more intense.

A girl brings food. It takes me a moment to realise she's a bot; she's the best I've ever seen. Her features are perfect, and even expressive. Her mouth curves in a smile. She gives me cold sweet melon; a jewel-green Greek salad fragrant with olive oil, scarlet tomatoes, perfumed basil leaves, white bitter-dry feta melting to creamy perfection against the tongue, and pitted black olives. My teeth crush their flesh and it floods my mouth with robust salted earthiness. There's a white roll and a glass of water to cleanse my palate, to allow each mouthful its own explosion of taste. A slice of chocolate cake, its bittersweet flavour as swooningly dark as its colour. A glass of red. I can't bring myself to drink it, only gorge my eyes on the colour. When the girlbot comes back she says, 'Shall I leave the wine?' Her olive-black hair, swinging at chin length, gleams; at her white throat the black top button of her uniform is undone. I see the slender column of her neck. I feel the stirrings of lust.

When she has gone I rise to my feet and pace around my room looking for a mirror. My limbs move not only obediently in response to volition, but also instinctively, as I find when I save myself from tripping over a pair of shoes left for me at the end of my bed.

This body which hums with delightful sensations is all male, from its long bony feet to the stubble on my cheeks. Extraordinary. I approach the one unlit screen in search of a reflection at the very least, but my proximity triggers it and it springs to life with a flood of data. Alright. Awkward Luke Butler will be coming back. I need to get up to speed. I sit and fix my attention on the explanatory female voice, the words and numbers onscreen, the story of the development from Glazier's first ham-fisted downloads to the elegant organic-digital solution which enables me to find myself here today. They've developed a smart neural interface which allows the cloned brain to simply take over when the host brain function is knocked out. I realise that the stem cell / brain regeneration work we were doing back in the day is – as Butler was saying – key; but I'd envisaged robotic embodiment, not living flesh. The firmness of the chair beneath my buttocks relays itself to me, as does the lingering bouquet of the wine. Lifting it to the light, I savour its crimson glow before each sip. The detail of the bio-engineering of the interface is calling for my concentration. But I'm distracted by the golden-brown gleam of the flooring, the tantalising snatches of music from the world beyond this room, and the increasing sensation of . . . of . . . I apply slight pressure to my groin – oh! Yes. The increasing and consuming sense of physical desire. I visualise the woman in the film reading her script in her light clear voice. Naked. I hold my body very still on the hard chair and scan the ceiling. They will certainly have a camera on me. Rising to my feet in some discomfort now I move to the small bathroom. The best chance of privacy is the shower cubicle and a curtain of water. I switch it on and peel off my clothes, the extraordinary creature between my legs bounces up to greet me, and I grasp it in my hand and step under the warm shower.

I am still shocked and shaking when I re-enter the room, but thank god I have dressed myself: Luke Butler is back, sitting on my bed and tapping into his screen. 'Alright?' he says.

'Alright.' He stares at me. The tip of his tongue emerges between his parted lips, before he presses them firmly together.

'You've seen?' He indicates the screen.

'Yes, it's brilliant. Any ill effects for the hosts?'

'It is still early days. I struggled to regain full functionality with the first two hosts – sight in particular. But they're both perfectly recovered now.'

'And me – us – the people you download?'

He shrugs. 'You're digital information. You go back into storage.'

'Extraordinary. Digital memory download into organic material – when you have time will you talk me through the detail?'

'I'd love to.' His face lights up.

'Are you doing this commercially?'

'No. It's still at the research stage.'

'And why me?'

'These are the final trials. Fine tuning.' He glances up into my eyes. 'I chose you.'

The still-damp skin on my arms senses a slight movement in the air; perhaps someone down the corridor has opened an outside door. A shiver passes through me and glancing at my arm I see a miniature forest of fine red-blond hairs rising on the goose bumps. It is hard to tear my eyes away. 'Thank you. I am very indebted.'

He laughs awkwardly. 'Seriously – Octavia – I studied your work at university. It was your research which first got me inter-ested . . . the way you saw the bigger picture, the leaps of faith you took.'

I smile at him and full pleasure in my face is a new sensation; I realise I can't have smiled yet, in my reincarnation. He smiles back. He must be very knowledgeable, yet to my eyes he looks like a boy. The brain behind my eyes, of course, is old. I was sixty-nine. 'Have they found a cure for breast cancer?' I ask.

'Better treatments but no magic bullet. Gene therapy can prevent it of course. But no, no cure.'

'I don't know what I look like,' I tell him.

'You look good,' he says. He glances away, I should say he is embarrassed.

'There's no mirror.'

'No.'

'Why?'

'I don't want to trigger body dysmorphia until you've – bonded – with your new physical entity. I took advice from a shrink.'

A new sound has come into the mix. A distant continuous percussion, a kind of rattling. 'Is it possible to see outside?'

He jumps to his feet. 'I'm sorry. I thought you knew.' He taps the nearest screen once and a bruised mauve-grey light enters the room. Rain streams down the other side of the glass. Beyond it I can make out the blocky silhouettes of other buildings.

'The psychologist was concerned about dislocation, the shock of being old in a young body,' he says.

'I'm not complaining.'

He grins. 'We can only use young bodies, obviously – better able to weather the shock of implantation.'

'And more user-friendly, generally,' I murmur.

'Exactly. But some people have a fixed idea of how they should look.'

'Will you bring me a mirror?'

He nods. 'First I have to ask you something.'

11

'Fire away.'

'My funder wants a client report from someone with a proper understanding of the procedure. She'd like a detailed account of how it feels, the challenges, the positives. I told her how well you write.'

'So I must work for my living.' I'm rather pleased with the pun but he is disconcerted.

'I'm sorry – would it be a burden?'

I put that smile onto my face again, and he blushes. 'Hah. That used to be my sister's favourite game, winding me up.'

'What's the plan?'

'We have the use of a private island, Paradise Island. Unspoiled, five-star accommodation, golden beaches. So we can offer swimming with dolphins, waterskiing, music and dancing, gourmet meals – the best of everything.'

'I'm to go to this island?'

'Yes, there will be six of you.'

'For how long?'

'Hosts resurface after a fortnight.'

There is a silence. I am standing here with blood pulsing in my veins, with every nerve in my body alive and tingling, with the pattering of the rain on the window and distant music calling to me, and the newly released scent of Luke's sweat sharp in my nostrils. I have only got fourteen days.

When Luke has left, I check the other three screens properly. One is rolling news, one offers an endless selection of entertainment, the third, in glowing blues and greens offers 'Your Choices'. The activities he listed to me are revealed; the setting appears to be a sun-drenched island of captivating beauty. I try the door: locked.

The bot, Gemma, returns bearing a cup of tea and biscuits and a large padded envelope. Inside the envelope is a mirror. I am gingery-blond, grey-eyed, a nervy eager-looking face with a wide mouth. I try to place this face. Its pinched look, the sharp nose and wary eyes, the crooked teeth, tell me he is poor. I smile at myself. Now the smile is excellent, despite the teeth; eager, full of optimism. And the physique is surprisingly good. This boy has muscles. He. I. On a weird impulse I lie on the floor and try some push-ups. My body obeys. Sit-ups likewise. The tensing and yanking of my muscles is a good feeling, the deep breaths I pull into my lungs scatter oxygen like stars through my blood. I look at the island onscreen and imagine hot sunshine on this skin, followed by the cool salt wash of the sea. I can see the attraction. After my exercise I take another shower and experiment again with the sensations this body offers. I don't remember anything to equal it. Maybe when I was very young. I estimate the age of my new body. Nineteen? Twenty? I run my hands over it. Me. I feel myself.

Much later the phone buzzes. Luke. 'Sorry, were you asleep? I was just going to call in on you before I head off home.'

'Please do.'

He comes in with his awkward face. 'Are you angry?'

'Why would I be?'

'About the fourteen days.'

'It's not long.'

'I know. But at the moment I've got to convince volunteers there's no risk. It's hard to persuade someone to disappear from their own life for longer than two weeks!'

'Tell me where we are.'

'London.'

'So that – outside – that's really outside?' I nod towards the window.

'Yes.'

'And the place you send the Tourists—?' I gesture at the screen.

'Paradise Island. It's in the Caribbean.' He grins. 'Sea, sunshine, and privacy.'

'There are still flights? I thought air travel—'

'They never really stopped them. The new n-fuels, in particular anaton, have completely replaced fossil fuels.'

'You know what I'd really like to do, Luke. I'd like to go out there.' I point at the glowing darkness which is London.

'I can't let you leave our care.'

'I've got to go to a holiday camp?'

'The problem is the assurances we have to give the body hosts. In a restricted environment we can offer them maximum protection.'

'I'm sixty-nine years old,' I tell him, flexing the muscles in my legs, under my jeans. 'I'm not about to run wild.'

'The other problem is – the hosts are people. I mean, if you met someone who knows your body . . .'

'What's his name?'

'Ryan.'

'And where does Ryan come from?'

Luke meets my eyes and smiles. 'One of the big northern estates. Coldwater, in Yorkshire.'

'Right.'

'I couldn't let you go out alone.'

'Remember, when you look at this callow youth – I'm a respectable old lady on the inside.'

He laughs. 'Alright. I'll take you out for a drink.' He blushes and I wonder if it really was necessary to put me in a male, and whether it was his decision.

The light in here is dim, with swaying pools of colour, reds and golds and purples playing across the upper walls and corners of the room, leaving the drinkers in companionable shadow. As I tune in to the low jazzy rhythms of a live band, I inhale the pleasing aromas of alcohol and warm perfumed bodies. Luke leans close enough for his breath to heat my ear. 'Keep an eye on how much you drink. I don't want you to get ill.'

I note my glass is nearly empty, but I think it's still my first. I have so many questions I don't know where to start. 'How are you recruiting volunteers?'

'The first two were at med school with me. I'd been a guinea pig for their research the year before.'

'And now?'

'The six of you were recruited online. But I won't do that again. Too many time-wasters.' A discreet bot refills our glasses.

'And are there many frozen brains waiting?'

'Well, I suppose there are. In the sense that people have been being cryogenically frozen for decades. But this is still completely under wraps.'

While he checks his phone, I stare around. Everyone here is male. It was my intention to pay attention all the time, but now I am loose and swaying with tiredness, and maybe, the wine. I shift myself and go for a pee (how astonishing it is!) and am slightly more alert, upon my return.

'Tell me how you finance this.'

'The island – and a lot of the money that went to build the clinic – comes from a single wealthy donor. In the long run, I guess she might want to put it on the market. But we're nowhere near that point yet.'

'A scientist?'

'No – no, the world hasn't changed that much, science still doesn't make you rich.' We laugh together. 'Her money's inherited. She lives on Paradise Island.'

'A relative?'

'I don't think you need to know who she is.'

How abrupt he is. Friendly and then rude; I don't know what to make of him. When the bot comes around again, I request coffee. I feel so well! Warm and well and at one with the world, the sensation is very sweet. Slowly I push back my chair and rise to my feet, allowing my body to weave from side to side in time to the music. The rhythm is intoxicating. I begin to dance, the tug and pull of the beat working through me until I surrender to it and am simply moved by it, like seaweed in the ebb and flow of the tide. The music fills me, I am the music, my loose easy limbs are oiled and graceful, the music dances me.

'Hello there,' says Luke, putting his phone away. 'What are you doing?'

'Dancing,' I say. 'Come on.' He stands in front of me, shifting awkwardly from foot to foot. 'Like this,' I say, putting my arms around him. 'Feel the rhythm.' I think of all the years of dancing I have missed – before death, never mind after. What a waste. We dance until the music ends. In the taxi going back, we kiss, and then he takes me into his bare spacious office and undresses me. And since all this is so miraculously new – well, why not?

Day 2

I surface in my clinic room with a thick head and depressed spirits. A touch on the screen reveals daylight outside; Gemma brings orange juice and breakfast. I pace the room. I watch the screens. I wait for Luke. I take a shower, thinking about the girlbot. And, I must confess, replaying what happened with Luke last night. I guess I'm a child again, polymorphously perverse. Or simply enjoying sampling everything on offer.

I tap some notes for the report into my personal screen, I do my press-ups and sit-ups, I wait for Luke. I have lunch: creamy golden scrambled egg, flecked with translucent shreds of smoked salmon; grainy wholemeal toast; radiant grilled tomatoes. Outside now the sun is shining. This remarkable body recovers, my head clears. The sunlight reflects off glass and steel and stirs my memory: New York with Jonathan in 2022, and the sea glinting with promise beyond the skyscrapers.

Time for a plan. I begin to search online. Transport options are limited and pricey. I need money.

Standing on the chair, I scan the room for a camera and find it under the rim of the light fitting. I switch off the sound and wrap a piece of toilet paper round the lens. Luke finally appears in the evening. 'I'm sorry,' he says.

'For what?'

'Last night.'

'Last night was fine. Today is what there is to be sorry for. One fourteenth of my time wasted.'

He is standing awkwardly just inside the door.

'Come and sit down,' I tell him, patting the bed. 'Please.'

'I have to send you to the island.' But he does move across the room, and perches on the bedside chair.

'Listen,' I tell him. 'We can talk. I've disabled the camera.'

'I've been completely unprofessional.'

'I've got twelve days. I need to get out of here.'

'I can't let you out alone.'

'Of course you can. Eventually you will let Tourists out, you'll have to. There'll be too many to fit on your chocolate-box island.'

He is staring miserably at his hands.

'Luke, you can use me for a real report. Not a puff about how lovely it all is in post-life happy-land, but an examination of the experience of reintegration into real life.' He's shaking his head, but I sense a weakening. 'Tourists *will* go into the real world, they *will* interact with ordinary people, you know they will. You can't just keep them prisoner.'

'I can't give permission.'

'Who's your boss? Take me to whoever's in charge here.'

'I'm in charge.'

'Right. Why did you bring me back? Because you know fine well that my research laid the foundations for all this. You don't drag someone back into life for fourteen paltry days, to waste their time. For fuck's sake, I'm a scientist. Let me do what I know how to do – some genuine research.'

He's staring stubbornly at his hands, clenching and unclenching the fingers. 'What if something goes wrong?'

'What if it does? Who's going to have better credentials than me? Who's going to have a greater vested interest in accurately assessing the risks?'

'You'd be lost. You didn't even know how to operate the windows – you're from a different age!'

'Won't that be the case for most Tourists? Given that we're all dead. I'll take this screen, you can check on me anytime. We can quantify how much support Tourists will need in the real world. We can assess the psychological impact.'

'We need to meet,' he says, 'at least once every twenty-four hours.'

'That doesn't give me much chance to get out of London.'

'What? Where d'you want to go?'

'I was thinking, Scotland. Fewer people, and I know the place. London is liable to present many more hazards.'

'That's true.' He twists his fingers together. 'What you say is true.' There's a silence. 'But I'll have to put safeguards in place.'

'Like what?'

'I'll have to tag you.'

I shrug.

'I have to know where you are every minute of the day.'

'If I was alive *I'd* be your boss,' I say.

A sudden laugh escapes him. 'You *are* alive.'

'Right then.' He doesn't say anything. I play my trump card. 'I'm guessing you'd prefer me not to mention last night's "unprofessional" events in my report?'

He continues to stare at his hands as if I haven't spoken. The silence goes on and on. Eventually I break it with, 'Or the disorientation caused by the female to male identity change?'

'I thought you would like it,' he says quietly.

'You thought *you* would like it,' I reply.

The silence lasts longer this time. 'I will come to Scotland next weekend,' he says eventually. 'To monitor you.'

I laugh. After a moment he joins in. I think I have escaped the tag.

He rises to his feet. 'Can you put the camera back on? Before a bot comes to fix it.'

'Sure.'

'I'll unlock the door tomorrow morning at seven.'

'I need money.'

'I'll slip an envelope under the door, with a card and flight booking for you. Where d'you want to stay?'

'Glen Affric.'

'I'll book a hotel.'

I stand and open my arms to him. When we kiss now I am aware of the rasp of stubble against stubble. I am momentarily amazed by the risk he is willing to take.

Day 8

Before Luke came, I was proceeding with a degree of logic. Tidily noting my bodily functions and sleep patterns, my dreams, my mood swings, my activities and desires, as objectively as if I were a lab rat. Eagerly jogging round the loch under a grey and lowering sky, drunk on endorphins; taking my landlord's rowboat out on to the choppy water and gulping in the peaty moisture-laden air. Climbing the peaks of Carn Eighe and Aonach Buidhe, which I thought I'd never do again, savouring each muscle and sinew of my precious new body. Grappling with the fascinating question of whether I am experiencing these pleasures as Octavia or Ryan. Many of them were unavailable to Octavia – male body, obviously. But when's the last time I jogged? Or craved curry and chips? Or drank myself under the table? Certainly I experience them with Octavia's sensibility. But this flesh – the stuff of me – the way it moves, the way it responds, is Ryan. Octavia couldn't defend a goal, as I did very ably on Wednesday afternoon, in a game with some young men from the pub. Un-Octavia-like activity, but I was doing precisely what Octavia was supposed to do – assiduously analysing and recording my state. Until Luke threw me off balance.

On Sunday we cycled to Nairn Beach in bitter bright sunshine and ate fish and chips on the yellow sands. I was checking the stages of the procedure with him. 'Does the host consciousness take over as soon as the connection is severed?'

'If you want to disconnect sooner than the allotted time, yes.'

'What d'you mean?

'Length of Tourist stay is inbuilt. The neural interface inside the portal is programmed to self-seal at fourteen days.'

'I'll be cut off automatically, you mean?'

'Yes. That's how it's designed.' His expression is hidden behind his oversized dark glasses. I turn away from him and face into the blast of the wind. It provides some cover for the water streaming from my eyes. I gulp the air. I was confident of persuading him I needed more time to complete. I was counting on extending my deadline. Dead. Line.

When my face is under control I ask, with careful casualness, whether the cloned brain capsule can be reused in another host?

He shrugs. 'Why would we?'

In the evening, when we are lying in a sweatily sated heap on my bed, I ask him lightly if he would consider sending my brain somewhere for a longer trial. He laughs as if I am joking.

'Nah,' he says, 'they'd never find a body that suits you as well as this.'

'I think I'd suit a lot of bodies.'

'Seriously,' he says, 'don't you think this is the most perfectly bitter-sweet way to experience a sexual relationship? No time for it to fade or go sour – every moment heightened . . .'

I lift myself off the bed and begin to pull on my clothes. 'Good selling point,' I tell him. 'I'll mention it in my report.'

He's like a schoolboy when he leaves. Fumbling and unhappy. He wants me to forgive him, he wants me to like him. I point out to him that the affection of a person who will be dead in six days has scant value. He presents me with my return flight ticket for day twelve, and says we will talk then. And discuss my report. He says he knows he's not great on emotions, that his high expectations in meeting me have been fulfilled ten times over, that he will never forget me. And that I should remember that I am only here thanks to him.

I reply politely that his generosity will be obliterated from my memory, along with all the rest, in under a week. I also mention that since my reincarnation, I find myself more attracted to girls. Once he's gone, at least it is only my own terror I have to deal with. I put the plane ticket in the fire.

Paula

I woke up like I was dragging myself from the bottom of something and I was really scared it was too soon. I tried to speak and this smiling nurse-face was there going, 'It's all right, welcome back, just relax.' Everything took a long time – moving my hand, getting words into my mouth, turning my head – like remote control or something, for a few minutes I had to force myself to do each movement. 'You're OK,' she kept saying, 'you're drowsy. Take it easy.'

I lay still and I could feel my senses coming back to me. She gave me a drink of water.

'Did I do it? Has the Tourist been?'

'Yes. And she was very happy.'

'She really got up and walked and everything?'

The nurse nodded. Her badge said *Gemma*. It hit me she were a bot and I felt thick cos I'd been talking to her like a human. There's no bots as good as her on the estate. 'She left a card for you.' She passes me a fancy silver envelope. Inside it's handwritten but I can read it. *Thank you for the loan of your beautiful body. I have enjoyed every moment. Are you a swimmer, like I was? You have a swimmer's legs. But you need to take fish oil for the dry skin. It's a bit better now, and I've used plenty of sun block. Enjoy your precious, precious life! Melanie.*

The nurse goes, 'Mr Butler says she was a famous swimmer. Olympic. About twenty years ago. Of course, she was old when she died. He says you made her really happy.'

When I go to the shower I can see the ghostly outline of a bikini. My finger- and toenails are done with a classy pearl varnish. There's a nice smell, lemony but sweet, reminds me of flowers. Posh skin cream, I would say. And when I look in the mirror my complexion's better too, brighter, she's had some kind of a facial. There's a plaster over the place in my armpit where they put it in. Melanie. When I think of her being me and then being dead, I feel a bit weird.

My clothes are on the bed plus a printout telling me the money's been transferred to my account. Ten thousand pounds. Genius Ryan! I'm thinking, I bet we can do this again. Say every other year? We'll be rolling in it.

Gemma brings a tray of fancy stuff but I'm not hungry. 'Is Ryan done?' I ask her.

'Not yet. He's due to resurface tomorrow.'

Octavia, Day 13

O for a life of sensations rather than of thoughts. I have abandoned the report. There's no percentage for me in laboriously chronicling my state. Why should I waste hours of my brief life for the benefit of others?

The memory of all the days, the weeks and months and years of my life, when I lived as if my body counted for nothing; feeding, watering and resting it mechanically, engaged only with my intellect, my *research*, my *big ideas*; the memory of that waste sickens me, as much as the knowledge of insensate death to come.

The only thing to do with my precious store of days is to cram them as full of experience as possible. I have sampled and indeed relished many pleasures. A dram of whisky by the fireside. Speeding along winding lanes on a motorbike. Venison, fresh raspberries with clotted cream, bacon sandwich, pot noodles, freshly ground coffee. For the past four days I have visited, on a nightly basis, the massage parlour above the shop on the corner. Sex is the most reliable release, and they have some interesting sexbots along with two very sweet girls. I have swum in the icy North Sea and the ache in my flesh overpowered thought.

Yesterday, I went hang-gliding, and that, the giddy swoop of it, the cold wind scouring my eyeballs, the soaring lift of the updraft, the adrenalin-filled crash-stumble of landing, occupied me fully. My strength and my physical control are a source of continuing delight. Tonight, I was back in the massage shop; my prowess gives me deep satisfaction – I begin to understand the male need to boast!

But I can't sleep. I've found a company who will take me white-water rafting tomorrow. I watch their activities online and try to imagine fear, excitement, the rush of terror. I am listening to Beethoven's Ninth on my headphones, Scots pine is glowing in the fireplace and giving off its clean resinous scent, I am alternating sips of peaty Laphroaig with nibbles of oatcakes laden with Stilton, my feet are buried in the sheepskin pile of the rug, yet all my senses are faint – insipid, distant, as if through glass. Has something inside me already closed down, a day early? I break into a sweat. There *are* sensations. The foremost are heat, panic, fear. But rather than overwhelming thought, fear spawns a torrent of ideas and images, it makes my brain hyperactive. I am frantic, appalled – which way to turn? On an inspiration I tap my whisky glass against the fireplace. Light glints on the broken edge. I apply it to my wrist. And cut. Yes. Oh yes. The rich blood swells, beads, and drips onto the hearth; the sharp pain releases me. My breathing slows. Red blood drips hypnotically. I am flesh, and blood, and pain. I am body again. Thank god.

Now I can hear the weather lashing outside. The vast crashing of thunder overhead, the stand-still brilliance of sheet lightning, the sudden downpour of a storm all urge me out of doors and I stand in deafening strobed darkness with the water drilling into my skin. When I ache all over with cold, I take myself into the scalding shower. The stinging of soap in my wound is a sharp star.

Paula

I'm in a daze staring at something trashy onscreen when I imagine there's a noise at the door. It's 2 a.m. I mute the sound, there's a little knock. The doctor. 'I didn't want to wake you,' he says. He can see I wasn't asleep. He's in a state. 'I'm sorry,' he says.

'I have to tell you the truth. This is my fault.' He tells me this story about a famous old scientist called Octavia who he put in Ryan's body.

'Why d'you put a woman in Ryan's body?'

He stares at me like a maniac, then just carries on. When he gets to the end I'm puzzled more than scared.

'He must be in Scotland then. Phone him. You can send someone to pick him up.'

'I don't know where to look,' he says. 'He – Ryan – when he resurfaces, he'll be very disorientated.'

Well I should think he could cope with being in Scotland, it's not like it's the dark side of the moon.

'I shouldn't have allowed her to go,' says the doctor. 'I shouldn't have allowed it.' He says he checked up on her by phone every day. He went to Scotland last weekend to do monitoring in person, she was safe and well, she was writing a report for the other scientists.

I'm not getting why he's so upset. OK, Octavia missed her flight back to London. But there's something Dr Butler isn't telling me. Eventually I ask the right question. 'When did you last speak to her?'

'Five days ago.'

'Five *days*?'

'She stopped answering. She left the hotel. I've been trying to trace her since Tuesday.'

'You think something's happened to him.'

'If it was possible for her to come back, I believe she would have done.'

'You think he's dead.'

The doctor and I sit in horrible silence.

Octavia, Day 14

In the morning the river is high and swollen. The bot at the rafting company states it is too dangerous. We look out at

24

the white water boiling over the rocks. There's no one human working here. I've never had to persuade a bot; are they programmed to be rational? 'I've been in worse than that,' I tell her firmly. 'I'll take a kayak.' I invent past expeditions, in South America, in Australia; 'I'm a fully qualified instructor,' I tell her. Only in the water and the rocks might I find enough sensation, enough physical terror, to subdue the mental. I know how an addict feels. I struggle not to be grotesque, a thousand thoughts jostle in my head more violently than the racing torrent of the River Orchy. I imagine tearing around this wooden shed howling like a dog and dragging oars, wetsuits, life vests, helmets from their tidy piles into a chaos on the floor. I imagine lifting the counter and bringing it crashing down on the bot's head. I imagine biting myself, biting through the top joint of each finger and spitting it out, blood and gristle and bone, hunting, hunting, hunting the blessed relief of pain.

The bot's glistening eyes examine my face minutely. 'You are agitated,' she pronounces. 'You could get hurt.'

'I know what I'm doing. I take full responsibility.' For god's sake. There must be a way to turn the wretched thing off. I tell her to show me the hazards, and she calls up a large-scale map onscreen and indicates the rapids, the waterfall, the triangular black rock I must keep to the right of. I stare at her neck, that would be the obvious position for an override button. No! A remote – there will be a remote. As she drones on, I lunge behind the counter and sweep my arm over the shelf behind the card reader. Yes. She's already turning back towards me. Press *pause*. Again. She freezes.

I am digging my nails into my palms, I am sinking my teeth into the soft insides of my cheeks. The taste of blood revives me. I don helmet and life jacket, and drag a small red kayak from the shed. Outside the blessed wind whips my face and the cold spray splatters me, knocking at my senses, trying to rouse them from their deadly slumber. In the water the boat bucks and shudders like a live creature. I scramble in and the current takes me, slewing me round the first bend, engulfing me in its thunder, drenching me in spray. The kayak is juddering and swinging, plunging under and rearing up. We hit something and the kayak rolls. I take in a lungful of water. I am choking, gasping, bleeding, rushing, freezing, roaring, living. I see the black rock and the spray of the falls. Oh yes! By god, I am alive!

3.

MARY

For what shall it profit a man, if he shall gain the whole world, and lose his own soul?

Eh-eh, that Bible saying was written for my boy. Right now he is walking God's earth with his strong healthy body that I laboured to produce in sweat and tears and another man's soul is peeping out his eyes. You know what you will ever be? I asked him. A night-dancer. Yes, *possessed*. It's the worst thing a person can be, to be not his true self. He laughs at me because what do I know? I'm his mother, just. I'm a foolish old lady whose work can be done by a machine, a robot, a nursebot. Oh yes, I'm on the scrapheap.

He never even set foot in Uganda. Not since he's a baby. But as though he knows it all, about the country we come from. He's a black boy but he thinks like a white, eh, a real mzungu, though I hate my mouth for saying so. 'Night-dancer!' he says, 'Whoo-hoo, juju! Call for the witch doctor!'

'Eh-eh. You know nothing,' I tell him. 'Shame on you. You know nothing about your own people's past.' But as though he doesn't care.

OK. I have nothing to do but tell my story now, because he's lost. He's swapped his soul for cash and soon his empty body will be eating money.

We come here to London sixteen years ago, when they were crying out for doctors and nurses and tempting us with citizenship. A kyeyo woman and her man Kibuuka and baby Joseph. Kibuuka left me and I somehow broke my heart for one–two years. Then I come to my senses and thought, 'But this life is kawa, it's good.' Kibuuka paid the rent because he's guilty he left me a single mum. I have my Balokole friends at church, and my boy growing up vigorous and tall, I can even save some small little part of my wage from the hospital to pay for holidays. Banange! Even me and Joseph, we visit the seaside! I am ever a good-looking woman so yes, I have gentleman friends, but none of them can tell me what to do. Eh-eh, if they try, I send them packing!

Zibbs began when Joseph hit the teens. He cut school and he stopped to work. He join some kind of gang, I don't know even. I ask him if he's on drugs, but he laughs at me, just. I can't catch him wrong-doing, but I know he's not doing right, he's gone astray. And then he have a huge bust-up with Kibuuka. His daddy was seeing him every two–three weeks, I know he's proud to have such a fine clever son. But now he tells me he's not paying for a whole boy who's off the rails, and when Joseph reaches eighteen he will stop housing us. I'm not so surprised at that, somehow more astonished he already pays so long.

Then the hospital tells me thank you for twelve years of hard work and your job is finished. We knew about the nursebots, they been running trials with them in A&E for years. The best jokes in the hospital are ever about the nursebots. Someone programmed one to empty bedpans in the tea urn. When you take your tea – pah! You flick their language switches, they go round chatting Russian to the patients, or print out their notes in Arabic. But we nurses could see which way the river was flowing, just. They brought ten nursebots in Oncology and they made twelve of us redundant. Eh-eh. The new broom sweeps better, but the old one knows all the corners.

So, then we're in a bad place: no money coming in, and when Joseph gets his eighteenth birthday, no roof over our heads. 'We're on the scrapheap,' I tell my boy. 'We better pack up and leave town.'

'Where we going live?' he asks me but the boy's not stupid, he knows as well as me where we going live. You got no income and no one to pay your rent, you move to the estates.

'Even me I don't like it,' I tell him. 'But look how we're fixed, bambi. You got some bright idea to make your fortune? You got a magic money-tree?'

He's even more scared of the estates than me. True, you hear bad tales. And with his build and muscle he will stand out as if the crested crane in a lake of mud. 'But look here,' I tell him, 'they're people there like you and me. Poor people, not bad people, just, and Jesus loves them. At least you get a roof over your head and a card for your food. We have no choice, my son – your taata dropped us. You going to live in a cardboard box?'

At first, you know, this pressure does him good. I see him turn himself around. He stops drinking, drugging, whatever trouble he was up to – and don't ask me how he could even afford that in the first place. For me I gave him nothing. He fires off a string of messages to his daddy begging forgiveness and asking to be given another chance, and can he go back to school and take his papers. Kibuuka never even replies to the boy. He just ignore. I try to cheer him up and tell him, 'You are fine, you can get schooling online when we're at that estate. You can ever follow courses, you can study.'

He pulls a sneery face then, a face I don't like to see on him, a face not his own. 'They only use online for two things up there, Ma: porno and VR. You take us there and we gonna be VR zombies like all the rest. Cos the life there is shit and ain't nobody can't stand it.'

'Eh-eh. I brought you up to have more self-respect,' I tell him. 'Why you don't pop to church with me this Sunday and ask the Lord for help?'

He laughs. 'I'm fixing to help myself. You'll see. You can pray for the both of us, and I'll find a way to make some money.'

'What? If you're thinking of turning detoother, my boy, you better think again.' I remember saying that to him and lying awake fretting over him all night, wondering if he couldn't find no other route to getting money if he would turn into a crook. Sweet Lord, now I think to myself, somehow crook wouldn't be so bad. There's worse things than crook, just.

So, here it is. He come home Monday last, big grin on his face, and tells me, 'I done it!' I'm happy to note he's putting on that snug red puffa jacket I bought him for Christmas, even though he told me he won't be seen dead in it. But I know better than remind him of that.

'Take off those wet trainers now-now. Why you don't put on your boots, this cold weather?'

'You hear me? You will ha-ha when I tell you how much!'

'What you done, boy?'

'Got us ten grand.'

I sat down so hard on the bench my backside still paining me. 'No,' I whisper. 'Please God, no.'

He's laughing at me. 'I'm earning it, old lady. It's all legit.'

'Eh-eh. What you can do to earn cash like that?'

'Medical volunteer. Two weeks' medical volunteering.'

'What? You selling your organs?' I heard tell of that trade and even my friend Lavinia she sold one of her kidneys when her daughter caught with a baby and no money to pay for the abortion. But you don't get ten grand for a kidney. More like £500, just.

'No ma'am. All I gotta do is sleep for a fortnight.'

'For a fortnight? How you plan on staying asleep so long? Is it drugs you testing?'

Then he shakes his head and grins and purses those lips of his as if he's holding back the world's greatest secret. 'I can't tell you, Ma, I signed a paper. It's gonna be fine, they won't hurt me. I had a medical and everything.'

'Stop cowardising, boy. It can't be a secret ever from your own mother. That's against law and against nature.'

He cut a wire then, telling me I don't know jack shit and I always think I know best and why can't I be grateful, just.

'Eh-eh. Even me, I will be grateful if I hear you are not volun-teering for any danger or harm to your person. But that sum of ten grand tells me somehow there *is* danger and harm, cos why else you demand them so much?'

It takes me two days, but I worm it out of him in the end, and it's a story to make your hair stand upright on your head. Can you imagine they call it science? It's meddling in knowledge the Lord did not intend us to have. It's putting one man's spirit in another's body. 'Your body is sacred,' I told him. 'Sacred to you, just. You are ever the Lord's vessel, made in His likeness. This thing you propose goes slam against His teaching, it disrespects your body and it disrespects Him.'

Joseph takes me seriously when I say that. 'I don't want to hurt your beliefs, Ma. But this is science. It helps people. It helps us cos they will pay me. It helps the dead man who wants two more weeks of his sweet life. Nobody is pained in this, only good comes from it.'

'What? This is the devil's work. Your soul and your body are united, one being, until the day your body dies and the Good Shepherd takes your soul up into Heaven. It's the devil's work to put another soul into your living body.'

'Stop going on about souls, will you? It's a brain, a digital brain. It's like a memory stick, right?'

'But your body is going to stand up and walk with that other man's brain telling you what to do, just? As if a zombie. As if a night-dancer. Eh-eh, he could be evil, he could do the devil's work. Is he mzungu? What kind of a man is he?'

'Why you always fearing so much! They got doctors watching that body twenty-four seven, there's big money tied up in this. Plenty of people done it already, nobody suffered harm.'

I try to persuade him to talk to Pastor Jenkins. I show him pictures online of poor individuals who are possessed, and when I have tried every way I can think of and no result, I tell him about my jjajja.

'You heard the story of your great-grandfather?' I knew he never had because it's not a tale I like to tell. He's fed up with me by now, rolling his eyes like I am some foolish village idiot.

'He was a big man, my jjajja and an important man in the village. He was schooled and he passed every paper. He went away to Kampala teaching in a school there. And with a wife and family in that city, he had a little boy who grew up to be my taata. He left the pagans in the village behind him. But he come back when his old maama got sick. She was at the end of her life and dying, and he stayed in the village all summer tending her. And he got help from Sanyu, the Headman's daughter. She was sixteen years of age and she looked as if an angel.'

I only knew her when she was an old lady, when I was growing up and went back visiting in that village. She was a fierce old lady then and wouldn't speak more than two–three words to me.

'Back when my grand-daddy met her, she was a beautiful young girl. She helped by cooking posho for my ancestor, sitting by her when my grandfather went to sleep, washing her, helping with all those little chores. And my grandfather was sweet on her. Eh-eh, too sweet. When his mother finally died, he stayed a long time sorting her affairs; he was lost in the village even when they were calling for him at his Kampala school. And when he did return to his city wife and family, the Headman learned that Sanyu was with child.

'Well, the news it travels. So, my grandfather comes back to the village one more time, very distressed. He asks the Headman can he take Sanyu for a second wife? The Headman cut a wire. "You're not worthy to be her husband even if you don't have a wife and child already! You stole her innocence and now the devil himself will repay you!" And he calls down juju, witchcraft, on my grandfather's head.

'That very night, after the Headman's curse, my grandfather left his bed and crawled through the village. He went on all fours, can you imagine, bambi, howling as if a dog. The villagers watched from behind their doors. They said his yellow eyes were staring from his face and his tongue hanging out as if a wolf. He was possessed. Oh yes. Possessed by an evil spirit called down by the Headman's curse. And that spirit takes him round the huts and on his hands and knees all along the dusty track to the well. And he crawls up the stone wall and drops right down into the well, ever howling as he falls.

'The villagers went with ropes to fetch him out, but he was drowned. I tell my boy, when you are a night-dancer, you cannot save yourself. Night-dancing is like madness, a man has no defence against it. And you are telling me, you will be a night-dancer for money.'

I knew he was listening good because he never took his eyes off me. But when I finished that story he said,

'OK please,' and stretched and yawned, like I made him sleepy, and he wandered off into his room. Eh-eh. Nothing I could do but pray to God to change his mind.

Now ten long winter days have passed. Ten cold dark days where I wake every morning with my guts knotted and my dreams are haunted by a mask of my Joseph's face with crazy yellow eyes behind it. I have lost my appetite and drift around like even me, I am a ghost myself.

And bad news comes soon, as if Heaven is trying to admonish me for my boy who is so unnatural. It happens the very day after he goes into that clinic. It concerns the soul of my dear friend Namakula from church and I get a beep from her daughter Winnie. I tell her, 'Sorry, I'm sorry, Winnie.' But poor Winnie is breaking her heart.

So, I will tell you what happened. Namakula died last August in a terror attack. She and twenty-one other innocent folk got blown to bits on a trans, right in front of the Houses of Parliament. Can you imagine, how is it possible a man could board a trans with a bomb in his backpack? We all know a trans is ever fitted with a scanner. Well, the News told us someone switched off the scanner on the trans. And because that scanner was switched off, the bomber could do his evil work.

It turned out the bomber sent a message to MPs but nobody read it till after the blast. He was from the group NOBOTS and he lost his job to a securibot, just. Eh-eh, then he lost his wife and kids. They say he asked MPs how they will feel when bots come to replace them. Well, bots replaced me and most all the nurses I knew, but we don't go around blowing up innocent people.

So, then Transporto, the company that runs all the trans in the city – or the whole world, for all I know – they tell the relatives of the victims, *we are freezing your loved ones so they can come back to life one day when the technology is in place.* Well, Winnie's very troubled. She's grief-stricken for the loss of her dear maama, but at the least she wants her mother's remains for Christian burial. It breaks her heart to imagine Namakula in some half-dead-half-alive-style limbo, instead of folded in to the loving bosom of our Lord, as the scriptures promise.

But when she asks the release of the body, Transporto refuse. They tell her all the victims are cryogenically frozen already and if she wants to bury her mother she must talk to their legal team, just. Poor Winnie tried every wise to get advice and it took months. In January she told me at last she'd found a lawyer who would challenge them, and it came to court last week. I clean forgot all about it due to Joseph's antics. But like I say, the very day after he goes into that clinic, I receive a call from poor Winnie, to tell me her lawyer lost the case. Ah, bambi, I am sorry. So, Namakula, who had a kind word for everyone, must stay in that unnatural frozen state in the hope of bodily resurrection on earth, which is a travesty of the everlasting life of the souls of our dear departed in Heaven.

OK please. I grieve for poor Namakula, robbed of her sweet life, and now her soul. And I grieve for my boy, who must also be in some kind of purgatory, halfway between life and death and not even knowing where his own beloved body is.

4.

PAULA

When it sunk in Ryan weren't coming back, I went mental. I wanted to go and look for him in Scotland, but Dr Butler locked me in my room. I remember screaming at them to let me out, banging on the door and chucking stuff at the locked window – the bowl of fruit, the bedside lamp. They smashed to bits without even cracking the glass. I remember great globs of snot and tears sliding down my face.

Then I got frightened. I called softly and said please, and Gemma opened the door. I asked for my phone. I wanted to talk to my mum. She told me I'm not allowed to talk to anyone, and locked me in again. I thought, they're going to keep me prisoner. They'll kill me like they did Ryan. And no one will even know what's happened to us.

I went and sat on my bed very quiet, trying to work out how to escape, and I was shaking so hard my teeth were chattering. At last a human woman came in, Jeanette on her name badge, and she was kind. She brought me a hot drink and she put a blanket over my shoulders, then she sat on the bed and put her arm round me. She wasn't mad about the mess or trying to tell me what to do, she just hugged me till I stopped shaking, and whispered, 'Hush, hush, darling. You'll be alright.'

They must've put summat in the drink cos I reckon I conked out then. I don't know how long for but when I woke up, I was tucked in my bed and Jeanette was gone. My room was clean and tidy, like nothing had gone wrong, and everything felt very far away. Like it had happened to some other little people way off in the distance.

Gemma brought me food but I wasn't hungry. Then Luke

Butler came back. He said, 'You can talk to your mum, Paula. But I need to have a serious conversation with you first. Is that alright?'

I remember lying there staring at him and it was like he was on TV and I could go to the bathroom and he'd just carry on talking whether I was there or not. But he moved towards me and that got me up and yelling, 'No! No! Keep away from me!'

He lifted up his hands like I was going to shoot him or something, and went backwards till he was leant against the door. 'Paula, I'm not going to hurt you. I'm not going to touch you. Will you listen?'

Didn't have much choice, did I?

So he starts on about how sorry he is Ryan's gone and it's a tragedy, but now we have to be practical.

'I want to go home,' I told him.

'Yes. This afternoon, I promise.'

I said, what am I gonna tell Ryan's dad? And he says, well, as you know you've signed a silence clause about all this and lots of other people stand to benefit from this scheme, so we don't want to mess it up for them, do we?

I thought about Melanie the Olympic swimmer and her nice little thank-you note, and I thought how shit it was for Ryan. Butler wanted me to tell his dad he died of an aneurism.

'What's that when it's at home?'

'It's a weakness in the wall of a blood vessel. It causes the artery wall to bulge outwards and if it bursts, the patient suffers internal bleeding.'

I didn't understand, but he showed me a letter for Ryan's dad, telling him Ryan would have died anyway, wherever he was, cos this aneurism was in his brain since the day he was born. 'He was never ill,' I told Butler. 'Not once.'

'Exactly. That's how it is with an aneurism. It's an invisible weakness. Some people live with them all their lives and never know. But if they burst, they can be fatal.'

'But why should it burst right now?'

He shrugged. 'They burst without warning. At any time.' The letter said the clinic would cover all costs. Which made me ask, who gets Ryan's money? Cos he bloody well earned it.

He went quiet for a minute. 'Look,' he says, 'I'd give anything to bring him back, but I can't, Paula. I'll give Ryan's money to his dad.'

I suddenly thought to ask, 'Have any others died?'

'No. The technology has never had the smallest fault, up till now.'

Hah, I thought, I bet that'll be curtains for his research. Then it hit me it could've been me. I could be dead as well as Ryan. 'Are you gonna stop doing this?' I asked him.

'I'm going to make a hundred per cent sure that what happened to Ryan never happens to another host.'

I could tell he was bullshitting but at least he were taking me seriously. 'What now?' I asked.

'When you're ready, the auto will take you home. I should never have told you about Octavia, just forget all that. What you've got to remember is that Ryan died from an aneurism.' He went over to the window. It had reverted to screen but when he touched it we could see outside. It was grey and raining. 'Paula?' he said.

'What?'

'I need you to sign something, please. A guarantee promising never to tell another living soul what really happened to Ryan.'

Same as he'd said before only now he was being nice and treating me like an equal. I *am* his equal, I thought to myself. I am his equal only he's got money and power and I haven't. What's he giving me? Ten grand, to keep my mouth shut. I bet ten grand is peanuts to him. 'I want a dance studio,' I said. It come out of my mouth without me even thinking.

'I'm sorry?' he said.

'That's what my ten thou was for. To get a dance studio on Coldwater. But it's not enough.'

He was staring at me like I'd grown two heads. 'You teach

dance,' he said, like it was news to him, like I'd never put it on my application form.

'Yeah. But the community hall's a wreck, the roof leaks and the floor's all splintery—'

'I know. I – I've visited one of the northern estates. I know the infrastructure is very poor.'

Whatever. 'Well, will you give me money for a dance studio?' I couldn't believe I was bargaining with him, but there was a little voice in my head telling me, *Go for it, Paula! Ryan's not coming back so at the very least make Butler pay dear.*

You might think, what a hard-hearted cow. But I wasn't. I was sadder than I'd ever been in my life. He had to give me something. He had to give me something big, to make him realise how bad I felt.

And he agreed. Not in so many words, but he said yeah, he knew about a builders who done work on another one of the estates. Blackrock, he said. He would do his best to help me. And I said – can you believe this? – I said, I'll sign to keep my mouth shut about Ryan if you sign a promise about the dance studio. And he said, done. And that was it. I went to London with Ryan, and I went home without him.

My mum was the first person I had to tell the aneurism story to. She knew what it was, she said she knew someone who died of an aneurism, the woman who set up the bots at Parks and Gardens. She was sitting at her screen one day and then she just slumped down in her chair and that was it. A burst aneurism. 'It was instant,' Mum said.

She were distressed. Not that she ever liked Ryan, but to be fair to her, she knew I did. Also she was the one person who told me beforehand not to go to London, and that there were bound to be a catch with 'Medical Research', so called. But she never said *I told you so*. She was proper kind to me. I guess if one good thing did come out of poor Ryan dying, it would be that my mum and me stopped fighting.

She'd been mad at me ever since I started going with him; she said I was neglecting my dancing, I wasn't getting enough sleep, I was throwing myself away. Every sad old cliché you can think of. I told her, you're jealous, aren't you? Cos I've got someone to cuddle up with and you haven't. I felt bad after I said that, but she never let up. And now he was gone, she was sweet again.

After my mum, I had to tell Ryan's mates, and then I had to crack on and tell his dad before he heard about it from anyone else. When he read the letter he cried, and that made me cry – properly, for the first time, I should say. There was something so unreal about it, with me not seeing Ryan's body. I couldn't even believe it'd happened. I told his dad about the money, his £10,000, and I know he didn't really take it in. But next day he come round to say it was in his account and then I think he was relieved cos it meant he could stay in his flat as a single. They downscale you right away when someone dies, unless you pay extra.

Everyone knew I had money. They didn't know how much, but right from the day I got back they began to hit on me. For a loan. To pay a debt. To get a kid's birthday present. To buy some teeth. At first I was like, yes, of course. But then more and more came, people I didn't even know stopping me in the supermarket and asking for cash. My mum had more sense than me. She said, your money'll melt away if you carry on like this.

I was rich, but I felt like shit. Kids from Dance who knew Ryan came and told me how sorry they were and what bad luck. Plus I was bone-tired. Maybe there was some side effect off the Body Tourist swap. Stands to sense a thing like that might wear you out. There was a lot of nosy parkers too, wanting to know what the scientific research was, and if they needed any more volunteers, and could they put their names down? I got sick of all the questions; it got so's I didn't even want to poke my head out of the flat. I couldn't be bothered to eat, I just took the supplements.

You got enough money to move away, girl, I told myself. But the only place I'd want to go would be back where me and my mum used to live when I was a kid, in the flat above the bookies in Ashton. They demolished all that when we moved. There's a deliverybot centre there now. I lost touch with all my mates and I know they bulldozed the Methodist hall where we used to do our dancing. So what'd be the point in trying to go back? Besides, Butler was gonna build me a spanking new dance studio. Be a bloody waste to walk away from that. Nobody in their right mind wants to live here. But I never saw anyone move off the estate, I don't even know if you can.

And the money – OK, it was a lot, but it wasn't like I could earn any more. So I stopped giving it away. And I looked at the estate and thought what a bloody miserable dump it was. Coldwater Estate. Five hundred towers, twenty floors each, little boxy rooms. Population 100,000. Just like all the other northern estates. We're packed in like baked beans in a can. Some towers are rougher than others. Some have working lifts, some don't. Some have functioning domestibots, some don't. The druggies hang together in Thatcher and Major and Cameron, and people try to keep their kids away from there. But all the druggies are old, now. Youngsters go straight onto VR, they don't even want to try the drugs.

The place is quiet, you know? Considering the noise 100,000 people could make, it's a ghost town. They're all plugged into VR, with their glasses and drink packs and nappies, that's it. Each high-rise with its 200 inhabitants all quietly stashed in their rooms and plugged in to virtual. Having wild times. Splatting bad guys and jumping off cliffs and racing through fires and blowing everything up and shagging porn queens. Sitting there quiet and still with just their eyes flickering, or maybe jerking off as they watch. Yeah, that's about the only exercise most of them get. And then outside, trailing like ants from each tower to Lianhua supermarket and back, older people dragging trolleys full of nappies and cans and the frozen shit we eat.

Sometimes there are kids, tearing about smashing things. Sometimes there are young mums with babies, that's quite sweet, down in the little play park that's inside a locked monkey-cage and only the mums get the code to go in. That is just about the only bit of the place that don't get trashed. Once a week they unlock the clinic and then you do see a bit more life, there's a queue right round Blair and Mandelson and Brown, people coming down to get their meds. And there's the primary school, run by bots, behind a two-metre-high razor wire fence. Oh, and the Bin, where they put people who've lost it. You know, the old ones too daft to feed themselves or use the bog. That's run by bots as well. It's the place where you go on a one-way ticket.

There was the community hall and a gym, even then, but it was horrible – proper scruffy, they always said kiddy fiddlers went there and I never set foot in the place. Grey cement with no windows, like a place for torture. It's different now of course.

It's different now. And I suppose the dance studio was the start. Well, I know it was. It was the start of all this. Luke Butler done what he promised. He sent a contractor to talk to me. Big Brian told me he converted the community hall on Blackrock into an athletics facility. And now Luke Butler was gonna pay him to do the same here, only make a dance studio.

'Well good luck with that,' I told him. 'The community hall's stuffed. Even though it's got barbed wire round it like a sodding prison. Some lads knocked out the CCTV then they piled rubbish against the main doors and set it on fire. It's smouldered right through.'

'No problem,' said Big Brian. That was his mantra. No problem. 'All I need from you,' says he, 'is specs. Is there owt special you're after? I've got bots can build it in three weeks flat, but you might want a say in how it's done.'

So I started checking out studios online, looking at sprung flooring and mirror walls and changing lockers and sound systems – the works! My mum was over the moon. It was good to have a project and it stopped me moping about Ryan all the time. Plus I liked working with Mum. She made lists of things I never thought of, like light fittings and ventilation. We looked together at pictures of famous studios. She worked out the best sound system for the volume of space in the studio. She sits there and knits and I swear it makes her brain speed up, clickety-clicking along with those needles.

When Big Brian came back we had a good design all planned out. A bit of me thought we wouldn't be allowed. How could anyone just make over a community building, even if they had the cash to pay? Then I come to understand that no one gives a flying fuck what happens on Coldwater. Long as you don't start killing people, you can pretty much do what you want. Nobody's even going to notice building work going on. I worried about the security though. I told him forget CCTV, I wanted it in a cage, like the kiddy play park, with bolts and padlocks and only me holding the key.

Big Brian and his bots cracked on at a fantastic pace, *no problem*. Well they never stopped, day and night. There was always a crowd of kids watching. First the cage, then all the materials piled inside it, scaffolding up, old roof off, new roof on, channels for new pipes, new walls for the changing room . . . Those cute little beeping bots doing the electrics. I never knew how much went into a building. It was early spring and the nights were getting lighter. I was still waking up sweating over Ryan, and crying myself back to sleep. But the studio was real and it did cheer me up.

Mum started me dancing aged three. And when we moved to Coldwater, when I was thirteen, she ran dance classes herself in the community hall, and got me teaching there as well. Kids liked to come, but it was proper ramshackle cos no one had any money. Mum started selling her knitting online. She knitted all the time and when I was little she dressed me in jumpers and hats that made me look like a freak. When I got in my teens I told her straight I wasn't wearing weird home-made stuff anymore, and she got into knitting fancy clothes for sale; Fair Isle, Shetland, lacy things for babies. So then she could buy an old speaker and plug her phone into it, for music. It wasn't great in that big echoey hall, but it did give you a tinny kind of a beat. And she got a couple of full-length mirrors which we had to lug back to the flat after classes cos anything you left in the community hall would walk.

And it just grew. Mothers used to crowd into the tiny kitchen and make tea and chat, or sit on the old gym benches near the door and watch. We couldn't do competitions cos there was no money and no transport, so we did shows instead. The mums rigged up fantastic costumes out of next to nothing, old clothes and cut-out bits from food packets. Skirts from yoghurt pots strung together. They used to raid the recycling bins and dig out all sorts.

Mum was the main teacher but over time we switched roles. I was more flexible than her – well, I was younger. She hurt her left leg a long time ago, in some accident at work, and with all the dancing it started to make her knee ache. Except what was weird was, the pain was in her right knee, not her left. Anyway, she was always best at choreography and she used to work out routines for me to do with each group. And then came the trip to London and poor Ryan's vanishing and the awful time that followed. The classes stopped. Of course they did. I didn't care about dance, I didn't care about anything at all.

But now I had a studio all of my own, right there in the middle of our grim-as-fuck estate. The first class I taught in there was Advanced. The looks on their faces as they come in! Mum and I had painted the non-mirror walls shocking pink, and the sprung floor was glowing golden wood. They knew to take their shoes off when they come in, but now they each had a purple locker to put them in, in a changing room with hot showers. I got them warming up to Abba cos you can't beat those old songs for pounding rhythm, and I watched them all stretching together and bending together and jumping together and starburst! Starburst! Staring at themselves in the mirror with their eyes practically popping out of their heads. I had a remote for the music, so I could watch myself demonstrating in front of them, stopping at the end of each sequence and replaying for them. It was so easy and it saved so much time – honestly, I kissed that remote. And the music – you could hear every note, not just *one* two three four, *one* two three four, and it didn't have to be deafening. I'd say my teaching and their dancing both improved a hundred per cent in the first week.

Everyone wanted to come to the studio. I could run a full timetable, with kids I'd taught way back as littlies now big enough and good enough to run classes themselves. Charmayne and Meghan were both good teachers. It was like being in a palace! Different classes in turn helped me clean it once a week and we kept it spotless. It made your heart beat faster just to walk in the door. I did my own practice there every morning on my own, and I felt like a queen.

It was always a hassle over money, though. *Can I pay next week?* My mum said I was hopeless and she took over the finances. But they didn't get any better. The studio was the best thing that ever happened to me, and people started showing me respect. Not just the kids who came dancing, and their parents, but I was a known person on the estate – the woman who made the studio. I s'pose it gave me confidence.

So when Paul turned up at the studio for lessons . . . well! He were new on the estate. He'd been a drummer with a band in York. The band folded and after that he couldn't get work. The usual story. So he come to the studio to learn to dance and to make some friends. And he made friends with me! He had a great sense of rhythm but two left feet. He'd never been to a dance class in his life.

I really fell for Paul. Look, I hadn't forgotten Ryan, and I still loved him. But that didn't make me a nun, did it? I was head over heels with Paul. The first time I stayed over at his, we had the best time ever. We played at being honeymooners, and we only got out of bed to eat the fantastic meals he cooked.

Golden days. He was fresh enough on Coldwater to remember real cooking, and he bought ingredients instead of ready meals, which even my mum didn't do anymore. The food he made was out of this world. Spicy lentil curry, and pasta sauce made from real tomatoes and garlic. He moaned about Lianhua and their crap range but what he made tasted heavenly to me. And he played me amazing music. It wasn't classical or pop, but strange tinkling clanking singing music, full of sudden changes of rhythm and little runs of tunes. It made me want to invent new dances to it.

We talked. We talked about everything. He told me about a girl called Adele who he was in love with, who left him. And I told him about Ryan. But not how he really died of course – I couldn't tell anyone that. Paul was a couple of years younger than me, tall as a giraffe and somehow gangly. Yeah, like a young giraffe or a foal. He had beautiful brown eyes and when he laughed his whole face lit up. We couldn't keep our hands off each other, the sex was like a drug.

So although we were taking precautions, neither of us were really surprised when I fell pregnant. In fact, we were happy. Because we knew we wanted to be together. Paul and Paula – had to be! And this was Paul's idea, but I loved it – if we had a boy we'd call him Ryan, and if a girl, Adele. We talked about getting a flat together, for our own little family. But it felt mean on my mum so I held fire on that. I thought there would be time enough once the baby was born.

But then everything went tits up.

5.

LUKE

The smells on the plane are sickeningly distracting; not just the warmed-up food and chlorinated cleaning fluids, but a hint of menstrual blood and a blanket layer of 'floral' hairspray. Nevertheless, Luke has solved today's advanced puzzles and scored 100 per cent on *Flash Anzan*. He flicks at his screen, but it was the highest level; there's nothing above. He sighs and looks up. The engine sound has changed, they'll be landing soon. Through his porthole the brilliant green of the island is set in an improbably blue sea. Paradise Island always gives him a headache.

Should he tell Gudrun he has lost a host? He considers Ryan/Octavia's pale pointed face and eager smile. It was bad to lose the boy; unforgivable. Luke has not yet recorded that loss in his research data. It would destroy his unblemished success rate and necessitate a longer trial period of a larger sample of volunteers. And this wasn't a technical glitch; Luke knows nothing went wrong with the body/Tourist interface. It was human error, pure and simple. For this reason, it would be inappropriate and counterproductive to enter it into his stats. So, it's safer if no one else knows.

Besides, can anything be served by telling his aunt? She has backed his research from the start. She is Body Tourism's generous benefactor and its greatest enthusiast. Ryan's death cannot be reversed. And if Gudrun is told, might she become more cautious? Or even demand safeguards which he can't furnish? In future all Tourists must come to Paradise Island; Luke has already promised himself this, and it's the only safeguard possible. Therefore, it would be pointless to tell her. She will be keen to see Octavia's reports, and fair enough, since she asked for them in the first place. But he has the complete set, up to Day 8, and he's perfectly able to emulate Octavia's style and furnish reports for her second week. Favourable reports. It's fortunate that Octavia was not one of Gudrun's buddies.

He's here today for her to make her suggestions for the next batch of Tourists. Since almost everyone she knows is both loaded and dead, there's no shortage. The landing is faultless. Before Luke leaves the shelter of the tiny airport terminal, he carefully adjusts his shades. The light here is fierce. He rejects the auto and walks along the coastal path for the two miles between the landing spot and her home. To his right the gently undulating sea produces a wide, unbroken swell which spills onto the beach in a whisper of creamy froth. His path is lined by the ubiquitous coconut palms and shaded by occasional breadfruit and sapodilla. Entering her garden from the beach he sees his aunt is sitting under a gaudy parasol, facing away from him. Her white head bobs up and down as she argues with her phone.

'No, you must come here!' she shouts. 'Lally will cook for everyone. No, no bots. I'll decide . . . lobster, certainly.' Listening for a moment she turns her head and spots Luke. 'I'm going now, Luke's here. Yes, bye.' She waves the phone at Luke in greeting and extends her neck so he can kiss her withered cheek. Her skin is unlike any he has ever seen, unnaturally soft to the touch and so finely creased and wrinkled that it no longer really adheres to the shape of her face, but hangs in loose folds as if a soft duster had been draped over her skull. He has always wondered why she doesn't have cosmetic surgery, or use fillers like everyone else. But Gudrun has never been interested in pleasing anyone other than herself.

'You look terrible,' she says. 'Have you been ill?'

'No, have you?'

'Certainly not. I'm in the pink.' She gestures at her shocking pink skirt and rocks with laughter. An unfamiliar type of bot approaches and extends a small flashing screen to him. 'Oh, tell it what you want to drink, will you?'

There are names of three drinks onscreen. He taps *Freshly crushed pineapple with lime, tamarind and chilli* and the bot emits a series of small mechanical/organic sounds before its dispensing arm uncoils and squirts delicious-smelling liquid into his glass.

'Cute, isn't he?' says Gudrun. 'I've told Simon he should make the next model with a clear panel in his tummy so we can watch the fruit being crushed.'

Luke gets up and walks around the bot. 'What does it do with the skin?'

Gudrun laughs. 'Compacts it into neat little pellets in that compartment in the bottom. Like an owl. Lally empties it once a day.'

'And your grandson made it?'

'For his tech project at school. I think it's delightful.'

'It's clever.' Luke sits and sips his drink, relishing the chilli.

'Guess who I've got for you!'

'I don't know.' Luke understands that Gudrun needs to dramatise everything, but not how much he disappoints by failing to play her game.

'As a Tourist. Guess!'

He shrugs.

'You remember Richard K, the rockstar?'

Oh, but he does. Richard K was the gyrating dervish who convinced teenaged Luke that he really was gay, even though there was a great deal of evidence that the man in question was himself irredeemably hetero. Richard K was the singer Luke met in his dreams, whose lyrics he knew by heart, whose rhythms set his young pulse racing. 'He's not dead.'

'Of course not. It's his father.'

'You knew Richard K's father?' Luke is aware that the super-wealthy move in a rarefied world almost solely restricted to their own kind, and he knows for a fact that Richard K's father was a plumber.

'No, silly. I've met Richard himself. The girls knew I liked him so they invited him to sing at my ninetieth, and we've kept in touch.'

'You've told him.' Luke's voice is flat. Gudrun should not have told Richard K, or anyone at all, about his research. He has explained to her, and she has agreed, that Body Tourism is not yet ready for the prying eyes of the world. It is Luke's intellectual property but so far there's nothing in the public domain confirming that, and he knows only too well how easy it would be to steal.

'Luke, don't sulk. I mentioned it in the vaguest possible terms. We were chatting about our parents and he said his dad had died too young, and he regretted that, so he had him frozen.'

'What did you tell him?'

'That there have been new developments in digital memory transfer from cryogenically frozen subjects. I gave him the clinic number.'

Luke imagines getting a call from Richard K. It makes his palms sweat. He touches them to the sides of the glass of iced pineapple.

Gudrun goes on to suggest three other candidates, passing the contact details of their families to Luke. The only other name he is familiar with is Chloe Esterhazy.

'Why do you want to bring that creature back? She tried to shoot her husband!'

'Under severe provocation, Lukey. General Ted dumped her for a girl who was of an age with their grandchildren.'

'People split up. People have affairs. They don't have to shoot each other.'

'Well Chloe was brought up with guns, her parents' place was full of them. I remember staying there when we were in our teens, and she showed me the semi-automatic she'd been given for her birthday.'

Luke shakes his head. 'It's no excuse.'

'Well, I'm sorry for her. Her older son and the daughter contacted me. The last few years of their mother's life were really wretched, she simply couldn't get over Ted's betrayal. They wanted her to have a little happiness, and I agree.'

Luke sighs. Gudrun always gets her way. A standard bot comes trundling over the well-watered lawn, bringing an array of lunch dishes, and as they eat, Gudrun asks him about his sister. 'I haven't heard from Hilary for months. Is she better?'

'Yes.'

'Completely?'

'No.' Hilary was an athlete. She'd got onto some sort of international team – not Olympic, nothing as grand as that, but respectable – and then at some games in Stockholm she'd fallen, hurdling. It was a trimalleolar fracture of the right ankle and now it had healed she had been advised she would not reach international standard again.

'Luke, for goodness sake, I wish I could train you in the art of conversation. How is she? What's she doing?'

'She can walk normally. She's decided to become a coach now she can't compete.'

'Excellent. Where?'

'One of the northern estates – she's got a thing about helping the disadvantaged.'

'Right. Is she enjoying that?'

Luke has visited Hilary once, at Blackrock Estate. He found it quite horrible; her claustrophobically tiny flat in the dull grey tower among a forest of other towers that looked exactly the same; the obese zombie-like residents; the vandalised communal areas. 'I don't know. She's put all her compensation into an athletics centre, for high jump and long jump and stuff like that. It's well equipped.' The centre had seemed as out of place on that nasty estate as a state-of-the-art MRI scanner in a remote African bush clinic.

'And she's teaching?'

Luke nods. Hilary had met his questions with amused contempt. 'You know how many sports teachers are on the scrapheap, thanks to bots? I've had more volunteers than I can find classes to run. We're going to turn the kids on this estate right around.'

'Is she still living with that Mark what's-his-name? The runner?'

Luke has no idea. Gudrun sighs, and makes a mental note to contact Hilary. Luke is her favourite, of the siblings, and Luke is the one her brother asked her to look out for when he knew he was dying. Luke is different and sometimes needs a person on his side. Hilary has always managed very well on her own, but this sounds like an odd move.

'Now, the other thing I wanted to tell you is that I've got a new doctor.'

Luke nods. Sometimes people say the most irrelevant things. He understands that they can't help it.

'Mehmoud Koubaji. I want you to meet him.'

'Why?'

'Because you could use a human doctor here on Paradise Island.'

'For the Tourists? But the medibots are more than adequate.'

'Allow me to know better, dear boy. How many times did you fly back and forth from London when your first batch were here?'

'That's different – that was the first batch, precisely, I had to be careful. Now I can afford to relax.'

'Maybe so. But for the Tourists themselves, a human doctor on site is reassuring.'

'Medibots have been proved to be more efficient.'

'That's not the point, Luke. We're talking about Tourists who're even older than me, who grew up with human doctors, and trust them.'

'Medibots are secure.'

'And so is Mehmoud. You'll see. He's coming to meet you this afternoon. And his bedside manner is a vast improvement on yours, I can tell you.'

Luke looks up at a sudden squawking. A flock of Jamaican Amazons have landed in the high acerola bushes behind Gudrun. They're bending the woody branches with their weight, squabbling and jostling over the bright-red fruit, making an appalling racket. It would be a relief to come less often, to this too-bright, too-loud island.

'What have you told him?'

'That you send patients here to recuperate. I haven't said what from.'

'But I'd have to tell him everything, if he was to be any use at all.'

'Of course. *You'll* tell him. *I* wouldn't presume. I thought you could show him the report from that scientist, Ophelia? Octavia? – assuming it's positive. I'd like to see it myself, by the way. She must have completed by now.'

She's a manipulative creature, Luke thinks angrily. The fewer people who know about Body Tourism the better. And now he's got to spell it all out to some ignorant quack. 'What's his background? Does he know the first thing about digital to organic?'

'Yes, he does,' says Gudrun triumphantly. 'You think I'd employ a stupid doctor? He's been working as consultant physician and geriatrician at King's College Hospital, and he's had first-hand experience of digital memory download into synths.'

'And he's your doctor? Why?'

Gudrun's creased face creases further, in a smile that momentarily hides her twinkling eyes. 'Money, dear boy.'

Despite himself, Luke warms to Mehmoud. He's reticent and laid-back, and asks good questions when Luke explains the details of his work. He also agrees with Luke that medibots will handle any medical issues more skilfully than a doctor, and suggests his own role should be more that of an observer, living with the Tourists in the hotel, on hand to answer questions and resolve anxieties. Luke has had CCTV recording in all the rooms from the start, to cover his back and so that any unusual developments can be analysed. But he is forced to admit he's not watched any of that at all, and probably never will. If Mehmoud keeps a careful eye on everyone then he can alert Luke to potential problems, and provide a daily summary.

'Were you expecting this?' Luke asks. 'Did my aunt offer you this work when she asked you to be her doctor?'

Mehmoud glances at the door, which is closed. When she left them together, Gudrun announced that she was going to take her siesta. 'Not in so many words,' he replies carefully. 'She hinted that there might be more patients here than just herself, but didn't go into detail.'

'You do understand that this is confidential? It's still at the research stage.'

Mehmoud smiles and Luke suddenly sees how attractive he is. 'My lips are sealed,' he says. 'I can understand you being jumpy. If it's any help, I had personal reasons for wanting to leave King's. Gudrun came knocking at an open door.'

'Thanks.' Now he feels safe, Luke relishes describing his research path to a well-informed equal. It's a rare treat – in fact, it hasn't happened since Octavia.

Mehmoud gets the point of Luke's work. He tells Luke, 'You're like a present-day Robin Hood. Only you're dealing with time instead of money. Taking from the time-rich young—'

'—and giving to the time-poor dead,' Luke finishes.

'Exactly.' The two men are still deep in discussion when a bot comes to tell them Gudrun is expecting them for afternoon tea on the terrace.

6.

RICHARD K

My dad died when he was sixty. It's no age, is it? I was only thirty-two, and to me, back then, he was old. But now I'm sixty myself I can see he should have had another twenty years. He hadn't even retired. He should have played with his grandkids and been to see the Great Barrier Reef like he always wanted. He was robbed!

It was a heart attack. But he wasn't one of your couch potatoes. Never had a day's illness in his life. Then – blam! He was DOA. I had him frozen because, hell, I could afford it. And I couldn't really cope with him being dead right then; having him frozen seemed more of a compromise.

It doesn't seem to be hereditary, the dicky heart. I've been having checks these past ten years. It was just pure bad luck.

So, when Gudrun told me about this body-swap thing she's got money in (*top secret, never tell a soul*), well, it struck a chord. As we say in the trade.

You change, don't you? Over time. Obviously you grow up. But not till older than you'd expect. I mean, at thirty-two I was still a pretty callow youth. I'd got a name for myself in the music industry and I was making more cash in a night than Dad earned in a month doing his old plumbing. And frankly, he got on my tits. He worried for me – I can see that, now, but at the time it was nuts. Such a string of tedious crap; was I in a pension scheme? Was I paying tax? Why didn't I apologise to Emily and try to make a go of it again?

I understand where he was coming from, now. And I have a bad conscience, because he really wanted to see Emily's baby and I just – I didn't – it was too fucking hard. I mean, it was over

54

between me and Em before she even had little Charlie. She knew I wasn't ready for a baby, and she went back to her mum and dad and they did all the nappy changing and puke-wiping and hand-holding, and I sent money. It was an OK arrangement. Apart from the poor kid's name, of course. I told her, you can't call him Charlie! She said not everyone's a drug-obsessed pillock like you, Richard. Maybe she had a point. But Dad wanted to see his grandson. He was soft on Emily, anyway.

Now, I can understand him wanting to see his grandson – course I can. Because now Charlie's grown up and married, he's got back in touch with me. And the best thing that's happened all year (all year? All decade!) is Charlie's own crazy little kid; *my* grandson! Derren's two, he's the cleverest kid on the block. Two years old and he speaks like an old fogey. Yesterday he tells me, very solemn, 'Gampy got a smart jacket!' And then he claims he's got an owl in his pocket. 'An owl?' I said. 'A bird that goes *too-whit too-whoo*?' That confused him but he digs in his pocket (which is not easy when said pocket is as small as a teabag) and he does indeed fish out a tiny plastic owl. He cracks me up.

Look, I've got the money. That's one thing the old man need never have worried about. Money loves me. Those early songs are still going strong, and so are the royalties. I could do another world tour tomorrow if I wanted – not that I do. What I want more than anything is to bring him back and show him: no need to worry, the boy done good! Show him the grandson, so he can enjoy the kid like he wanted to enjoy Charlie. Show him the house and the pool and the recording studio. Show him my Meryl and her beautiful baby face, show him the good life. And say, sorry, Dad, I was a dick.

Well, I turned it over for a few days then I told Meryl.

'Would you like me to go stay in New York?' she said.

'Why would I like that? I want him to meet you!'

'But Richard, honey, this is about you and your dad. I don't wanna gatecrash.'

'You won't. I want him to see my life. Sweetheart, *you* are my life. Not to mention my wife.'

'You sure, honey?'

'Hon-eee, yes.'

She laughed, I can always make her laugh when I mock her accent and then her eyes shine and she looks like a little girl on Christmas. 'OK. But it will be seriously weird. You planning on telling people he's your dad?'

'Why not?'

'In a young body he's gonna look like, I dunno – a college kid?'

She was ahead of me. 'Yeah. I guess it's too weird for Derren. Better just say he's a cousin or something.'

'Right.'

There was some pretty heavy legal stuff. My lawyer didn't like it. 'They'll have you over a barrel,' he said. 'If your dad fucks up, if the host body gets damaged in any way – it's your name on the contract. You sign this, they can charge you with GBH, manslaughter, even murder.'

'I'm not planning to take him skydiving. I'll look after the old bastard, that's the whole point.'

'But he won't *be* old. You gonna be able to stop him getting pissed? Or taking off on a motorbike?'

'Can't you insure him?'

'It's confidential, dickhead. It's still classed as research.'

'He's my dad, for Chrissakes. It may be a young body but it's my dad, not some teenage rebel.'

'I'm just doing my job, Richard. This is new technology, there could be all sorts of cock-ups. Bottom line, I wouldn't sign a contract like this myself.'

'Noted. Now pass me the pen.'

It ground on for weeks. They said he couldn't stay with me, I was only allowed to meet him at the clinic on day 1, then they were gonna fly him off to some exotic island. Well that was beyond stupid. I put in a call to Gudrun. She was slurping her way through her breakfast cereal, which made one hell of a soundtrack.

'Luke's a control freak,' she told me. 'And this is his baby, Richard. He's not keen on me interfering.' And she chomped her way through another mouthful.

'Why would I pay for my dad to go away?' I asked. 'There's nothing in it for me.'

She leaned closer to the screen. 'How about you come and stay with me, while your father's here?'

'*What?*'

'Here. Paradise Island, my island. The Tourists come here and stay in my hotel. You can visit him, it's a beautiful spot.'

Took me a moment to process that. What a cunning old bird! How long had she been plotting a way to get her scrawny hands on me? I looked at her, with her wispy white hair and her bright little eyes fixed on me, and I thought, Madam, I salute you! Never say die! But what I told her was the truth. 'No good, I'm afraid. I want him here with the family, Gudrun. I want him to meet my wife and son and grandson.'

She pressed her lips together in an ugly little line. 'Luke won't agree.'

'Deal's off then.'

We both sat and listened while she slurped up the last of her milk. She wiped her mouth on a snowy napkin. 'Alright. I'll tell Luke he must make an exception.'

'And let my dad come to me?'

'Yes. It'll cost you, though.'

'How much?'

She named an eye-watering amount, at which I nodded. And then she made some comment about us both knowing how to get our own way. I was already laughing and waving goodbye, so I didn't have to point out to her that actually, she hadn't got hers, I had got mine.

They wanted guarantees that I wouldn't take him further than a twenty-K radius from the clinic, that I or a member of my family would be with him at all times, that he would check in daily with their doctor . . . I started to think they would be giving me a cripple. No no, they assured me, but we have to safeguard the host. I mean, how would you feel about someone borrowing your body? There's no reply to that, is there.

At last the magic date arrives: the Return of the Daddy. A cold bright February morning. The receptionist walks me down to meet him – Jeanette, a sexy brunette. I remember her name from the phone calls. 'How does this usually go?' I ask her. 'You witnessed it before?' I'm feeling like maybe we could slow things down, I'd appreciate a coffee and a chat before I have to see him. Jeanette could give me some tips on how best to make a revenant feel welcome. But she just grins and opens the door. 'You'll be fine,' she says. Only one person in the room, and she shuts me in with him.

He's black! What the fuck? He's black, and he knows me straight away. 'Richard! My god, Richard!' He's hugging me and pressing his cheek against mine and it's all I can do not to push him off. I never saw any man on earth less like my scrawny little Yiddisher dad.

'What's going on?' I say. 'What the hell?'

'I don't know. Thank god you're here, Rick. I woke up and—' He bursts into tears. You never saw anything more incongruous; a strapping handsome young buck, maybe twenty years old, crying like a little boy.

'Are you alright?' I ask. 'Does it hurt?'

He shakes his head and I locate a handy box of tissues. 'I'm fine,' he says after a minute, 'but I just don't get it. Look at me!' He holds out the backs of his hands to me, long fingers spread, the ebony skin supple and elastic over the bones. Jazz piano, blurts my stupid brain. 'Why have they done this to me?'

'I – I asked them to, Dad. I mean, I asked them to bring you back to life.'

He pulls himself together. 'The doctor told me. I can't seem to take it in.'

'Well it's quite a lot to process.'

'He said I'd died.' He says this so sadly I'm floored. I mean, don't you notice when you die? 'Years ago,' my dad continues, 'and that you paid them to do this.'

'Dad, I just need a word with the doctor, OK? Wait for me here?'

'Of course, Ricky.' He smiles sadly and steeples his fingers together in his lap, like he always used to.

I barge into Luke Butler's office and he looks up from his screen, startled. 'Something wrong?'

'I'll say.' He's on his feet and heading for the door but I stop him. 'Not medically. But he's black!'

'And?'

'Why the hell d'you give him that body?'

'Because Joseph was the healthiest, strongest volunteer host I could find, and I wanted you and your father to have a good experience. I've been a fan of yours since—'

'But he's black!'

'Are you racist?' Like he's politely asking if I take sugar.

'Of course not. But my dad—'

'Ah. I didn't think of that.'

'He's not *racist*, he's not exactly racist, but don't you think it's shocking enough coming back from the dead, without the whole trauma of different skin colour?'

'*Trauma*. I see.' Like I'm a different species and he's studying me. 'Would you like me to restore the host?'

'What d'you mean?'

'If this is going to be a problem, shall we terminate?'

'Stop him? Stop my dad?'

He nods.

'Is there another body he can have?'

Butler pulls a weird face. Maybe he thinks it's a smile. 'No. I can't accommodate a racist. You think it's easy getting volunteers to host?'

I don't know. I don't give a monkey's if it's difficult as all hell.

What I do know is that if this is my poor old man's one bite of the cherry then it can't be snatched away. 'We'll have to make the best of it then.'

Butler nods calmly. 'I suggest you go back to your father, he'll be feeling disorientated. I'm here if you need me.'

Smug little prick. 'It wouldn't have hurt to warn me.' I go back to this stranger, aka my dad. He's sitting in exactly the same position, and gives me a grin as I go in.

'You're so *old*, Ricky! I'm not sure I'd have recognised you in the street.'

'You can talk!'

That cracks us both up, and suddenly everything feels possible. I explain to him about the young healthy body thing and he does seem to take it in. 'I'm not complaining. Well, I suppose I am. But it suddenly seemed so much worse when I saw you. Because you know who I am, and how wrong it is for me to look like this.'

'To be honest, anything would be wrong. Cos it's someone else's body.'

He nods. 'It's quite a lot to absorb.'

'That's the understatement of the year.' Which makes him smile cos it's one of his old favourites. He used to say it to me all the time. When I staggered in at midnight and admitted I'd had a pint or two – *that's the understatement of the year*. When I told him my exam results weren't that great – *that's the understatement of the year*. When I told him I wasn't cut out for a 9–5 job.

'D'you feel up to going home, Dad?'

'Home?' There's a sudden note of hope in his voice.

'To my home. Where I live with my wife Meryl.'

'Did I ever meet that one?'

I shake my head. He must have thought I meant *his* old home. Poor bugger, there's a lot of catching up to do. The bot gives him a hideous red puffa jacket which he puts on without a word of protest. 'The auto's waiting.' When I actually look at him I can't bring myself to call him 'Dad'. It's too weird. 'Anton? You good to walk?'

He laughs. 'My boy, I have the body of an athlete!'

'OK, follow me.' Maybe I should take his arm. I can't tell. In the car park he squints at the light then stops and stares. 'Good lord!' Now that *is* my dad. I can hear my dad's astonishment.

'They're all electric now, Dad. And self-drive, obviously.'

He grins. 'They look like Noddy cars.' Noddy's some ancient kiddy book they had when he was young, so I laugh.

'Mine's the purple one.'

When we're sitting side by side the size of him hits me all over again. His broad shoulders are wider than the seat. The young guy who owns this body must work out regularly. Weightlifter? Basketball player? He's talking. I can hear my dad talking again, not this young man.

'I really can't remember, Ricky – can you tell me . . . how?'

'How what?'

'I died. I mean, I don't even remember being ill.'

'Oh. Heart attack. You were in the Co-op. You collapsed at the checkout, they told me.'

'Really.' He ponders this for a while. 'The Co-op on the corner?'

'Yup. You had frozen peas and mincemeat in your basket.' Don't ask me why I remember that detail. I guess it struck me as pathetic – in the true sense, full of pathos. He'd paid for them so the manager gave them to me next day when I called in to thank them for trying to help him. They'd kept the peas frozen.

'For my tea,' he says. 'Well, I never felt a thing.'

'I guess that's good,' I offer, and he nods.

'You sure I won't be in the way, Rick?'

'What?'

'At your house.'

'Absolutely not, you daft creature. I *want* you at my house, I've got a family for you to meet.' And I tell him all about them; Meryl, Charlie, Derren.

When I'm done he sideswipes me with, 'Where's your mum?'

'Mum?' Why's he asking? She left him. They divorced, way back when I was in my teens. 'Um, she died, Dad. Quite a while ago. Ten years after you, actually.'

'Did you have her frozen too?'

'No.' He doesn't ask why and that's a relief because the honest answer is I was too busy with my own shit at that stage and forgot to think of it.

'So – all my generation – have gone.'

'Well, nobody's immortal!'

He laughs and it's weird because it's a warm deep laugh, not my dad's wheezy chuckle. As the auto crawls along he's craning his neck at the buildings, the traffic, the bots. Twenty-eight years he's been dead – I wouldn't have thought it had changed that much, to be honest. 'Some of these people,' he says, gesturing to a couple of nannybots waiting to push their charges across the road, 'are they . . . ?'

'Bots. I guess they only really came in in the last twelve years or so.'

'Those are real children?'

'Yeah, the kids are human alright.'

'People trust them with their children?'

'Sure. They've taken over a lot of the caring roles. I'd be surprised if they didn't have them in the clinic.'

'Yes, the nurse. I wondered – I didn't want to be rude.'

I laugh. 'We've got a couple, Kay for kitchen and Gary for garden. You'll see, they're great.'

'The ones that aren't robots – might they be like me? Old wine in new bottles?'

I gawp at him. 'It's early days yet, for this research, Dad. I don't think they've done more than a handful of awakenings.'

'So why me?'

'I asked for you, you eejit! I wanted you back.'

'Ah.' When we pull off the Euston Road and arrive at my pad he wants to know where we're going.

'Here. This is where I live. Eleven Park Crescent.'

'But—' The door swings open when it sees me coming, and he follows me in, gaping.

It's an old trick in London now, but I thought it might be a new one for him. The outside is olde-worlde historic (designed by John Nash for the Prince Regent in 1806) and the inside is spanking new. Atrium, moveable walls, five floors, fully automated. He's shaking his head in amazement. 'You paid for all this with your music, Ricky?'

'Yes sir! All this, and a condo in New York, and a little cottage near the beach in County Cork.'

'You must have been pretty successful.'

'We went platinum seven times. Played the O_2 arena and Madison Square Garden; headlined Glastonbury. Five world tours.'

He's nodding and smiling, at last he's looking properly happy. And when he meets Meryl I am proud. Because he can see what a doll she is, and she gives him a real lady-of-the-house welcome. His change of ethnicity doesn't phase her for a second. She can always banish awkwardness; for the first time that morning I relax in his company.

'Anton, we're just going to give you the time of your life! Ricky's been telling me about you since the day we met, and I'm going to get your side of all those stories and shoot them right back at him.' She gets Kay to bring us coffee and cake, and we settle in the atrium. He confides to me that Meryl looks more like my daughter than my wife. Yes daddy! That's the way I like 'em. She starts quizzing him about his favourite food, what music he likes, what kind of clothes he wants, and suddenly the day is taking shape. We've got Buddy Holly pumping from the speakers and an order of shepherd's pie followed by sponge pudding and custard for his dinner, and an expedition to buy clothes and shoes planned for the afternoon. I never even thought – he must be wearing the original guy's clothes. I mean, the clothes of the Host. My dad used to wear these brown trousers, the baggy ones with a crease down the middle, and check shirts and a pullover. And a dark-blue boilersuit for work. But he won't be putting garments like that on his handsome new body. Hell, he won't even be able to *find* garments like that. I guess Meryl will sort him out. He was never any great shakes as a follower of fashion.

He's asking her about her childhood and her home, and I can sit back happy and watch this strapping black youth who has my old man's speech patterns and his old-fashioned politeness and hesitation, and all his funny little ways. When I'm watching and not trying to talk to him, I can start to see where the host ends and my dad begins – in the way he cradles his mug in both hands, and sits forward in his chair so's not to miss anything she says. He had trouble with his hearing, in his fifties; now I'm wondering if he remembers he's a bit deaf, or if the new body is also slightly deaf. Unlikely. He probably has perfect hearing, to judge by the perfection of everything else.

The conversation moves on to what he'd like to do on his 'holiday' as Meryl calls it. He turns to me. 'I'm in your hands, Rick. What did you have planned?' Then he shakes his head and grins. 'How old are you, exactly?'

'Me? Sixty.'

He laughs. 'Every time I catch sight of you, I get a shock.'

Meryl is delighted, of course, she always finds references to my age hilarious. She claps her hands. 'OK guys, I'm off to the gym. I'll see you at lunchtime. You going to show Anton round the house, Rich?'

And so I do, conscious again of a slight awkwardness between us once she's taken her leave. He's almost pedantic, as we trail from room to room. 'Is it a sensor, bringing these lights on? Where is it?' and 'How's the place heated? I don't see any radiators.' He wants to know who designed it and how much it cost and if all the 'normal' houses are like this inside? He wants to touch the screens and once he sees the picture quality and hears the sound he's transfixed, in front of a cookery programme for Chrissakes. 'Dad, you've never been in VR, have you?'

He doesn't even know what it is. And the screen has filled his head with thoughts of food. 'If that – that bot in the kitchen—'

'Kay.'

'If she makes different dinner for each of us, won't there be quite a lot of waste? I'm more than happy to eat the same food as you and your wife.'

'It's fine, Dad, we have different meals all the time.'

'But I don't want to create extra work.'

'It's a *bot*! Listen, I was talking about VR. After I've shown you round, I'll set you up, I've got some old glasses you can borrow. Virtual Reality? You've heard of it?' I have to do a lot of explaining, and when I tell him I've got an implant so I can do Virtual Reality and Augmented Reality without the faff of glasses he stares at me like I've sprung wings. 'It's not that weird, Dad. It's pricey, because they had to do massive security moves after some people got hacked. But it's getting to be the norm.'

'Is it for games?' he wants to know. 'Like *Space Invaders*?'

'Um, it's moved on a bit since then. You can get into another world, you know? On top of a mountain, looking round 360 degrees and admiring the Himalayas. Or fighting the Battle of Waterloo.'

'Well I wouldn't fancy that,' he says with a real Dad-ish prissiness, and we both laugh.

'OK. You're in for a treat, I promise you. The first time in VR is like losing your virginity.'

That popped out without me thinking and I can see there's a disjunct, between the hip young guy I said it to, who should laugh, and my old dad who's a bit shocked.

'Sorry. All I meant was compared to 2D on a screen, it's realistic. Immersive.'

The windows fascinate him, and he stands there like a kid making it transparent/foggy/black and wants to know if you could have one that did colours too. I'm tetchy now. Did I bring him back just so I could show off to him?

I remind myself he'll enjoy meeting Charlie. The presents he sent that boy! Em would call me and go, *Guess what your dad sent this week! A Lego garage . . . a tricycle . . . a rocking horse . . .* Grist to her mill of course, since it was my poor old dad who was generous, and rich bastard me who forgot his own kid's birthday. And he'll see young Derren, who actually *could* keep him amused for hours, with his favourite books – which were, as it turns out, Charlie's – *Fireman Sam* and *StickMan* on repeat, and his solemn questions and pronouncements. Not to mention his singing. Other kids go 'Baa baa black sheep' but I'm training my little star in the greatest hits from my back catalogue!

The stuff about showing off is bull. The thing that matters to me is what used to matter to Dad – the kids, the next generation, and the one after that. My present to him is his great-grandson, which is pretty neat because my grandson is also – if you think about it – his present to me. Considering he sired me before I could sire Charlie, and Charlie, Derren. We're a nest of Russian dolls but he's the Big Daddy. Now the Big Daddy gets to meet Daddies 2, 3 and (with any luck) 4.

Still, we also need some plans. Outings and activities. Thank god for Meryl, she'll know what to do.

I show the old man everything, and we spend nearly an hour down in the studio, so's I can explain the process of recording to him. He's sweet and polite but there's a sneaking bit of me that says he's only showing interest for my sake.

We don't really have the conversation till that evening. Meryl's taken him shopping and he's kitted out with sleeker smarter clothes than he arrived in. The red puffa is consigned to a wardrobe, in favour of a decent black wool coat, so he won't be an embarrassment. He looks distinguished, actually – a young academic, a TV pundit. We're on our second bottle of wine and I'm feeling mellower, and Meryl's gone to her Italian class. (I know, I know. Why can't you just get a language implant, like a normal person? I asked her. For half the price! But she put me to shame cos she's so sweet and serious. She likes to be in a real place with a human teacher and classmates, she likes to learn with her own mind. I know exactly where she's coming from on that. It's another reason why Derren's so important to me. A kid knows the real world is *it*, and everything's amazing. The cloudy sky, a muddy puddle, a face, a dog, a shoe. I dread the day he starts to lose himself in digital.)

Anyway, Meryl's Italian class leaves me alone with Anton, and at the end of his first proper day that's a good time for both of us to take stock. I refill our glasses and sit back. 'So how're you feeling, Anton? It must still be a helluva shock.'

He hesitates. 'It's all very new, of course it is. But I actually feel very well. I mean, as if I could take it all in my stride.'

'That's good.'

'I believe it's to do with this body.'

'How d'you mean?'

'I remember how I used to feel, you know, about technology. About all the new gadgets. Mobile phones, for example.'

'You hated them.'

He nods. 'I wouldn't let you have one, would I?'

'I nicked one off a lad at school but I didn't have a charger so I ended up selling it back to him.'

'There we are. The firm bought me one in the end, but it made me tired. My fingers were too clumsy for the little buttons. I didn't like calls interrupting my jobs. And computers – the way you started having to do everything online, paperless billing and suchlike – it would take me longer fiddling about on the computer trying to pay the electric than it would have done to write a cheque and walk to the post office with it.'

Write a cheque. Walk to the post office. 'They don't even exist anymore. Cheques and post offices.'

'I'm not surprised. But I used to think, I'm past it. If this is how they want to live now, I'm well out of it.'

I know how he feels. When I see Charlie onscreen it makes me giddy. Five or six windows up at the same time and he's chatting in one and banking in another and catching up with the news in the third and replying to work messages in the fourth and maybe updating his music streaming preferences in the fifth and gaming in the sixth. Why not focus on one thing at a time? I ask him. But he just laughs.

'Here and now, the situation is very different.' My father props his hands together, fingertip to fingertip, a gesture I can remember seeing when I was a kid and he was trying to explain something complicated.

'The situation?' I ask.

'Everything has moved on, of course. But I don't feel so – daunted by it. That weariness, that feeling overwhelmed, must have been down to my age. Now I'm young again, I've regained my appetite for learning.'

'So are you feeling better about it now? That beautiful black body?'

He laughs. 'It's the ultimate fancy dress, really, isn't it?'

'I guess.'

He gazes at his hands, turning those pink palms up and stretching the long fingers. 'I don't know what I think,' he says slowly. 'I'd never have imagined being black. Not in a million years. I'd never have chosen it. But I feel . . . I feel like me. I feel just like myself.'

'Well that's a relief,' I tell him.

'Black people . . .' he says, and I'm tensing up for something racist. But he just shakes his head in puzzlement. 'I used to think they were different. I guess I'm learning a lesson.' There's something wistful in the way he says it. I'm thinking, what's happening to him is really fucking *hard*. It's not a holiday, like Meryl says, it's a weird hard thing, being himself and not himself, getting his head round it all.

'You're doing great,' I tell him. 'Good body, hey?'

'Excellent.' He flexes his muscles. 'Sensations are more intense, too. Maybe,' a deep soft laugh here – 'because I've had what you might call a *rest* from feeling anything at all, for twenty-eight years.' Which is as close as he comes to admitting he's dead. 'I mean, what time is it now? Half past nine. In my old life I'd have been thinking, a spot of telly then bed. But right now I'm good for hours. I could get out there on a bike and cycle across London. I could run a half-marathon!'

This is not good news to me, since I am, like his former self, thinking more along the lines of a spot of screen and bed. Having a father in a younger, more athletic body is actually an unlooked-for burden, like getting a dog who needs walking every day. Suddenly I remember; 'We've got a swimming pool in the basement, Dad. I forgot to show you that. It's pretty cool, Meryl uses it most days.'

He stares at me. 'Ricky. I don't know how to swim.'

'You don't know how to swim?' A body like that, it's impossible it doesn't know how to swim. I start to laugh and he joins in. 'Well, Anton, I guess you could learn. Now you've regained your appetite for learning.'

'I imagine I could. Yes, Rick, I probably could. May I take a look at it tomorrow morning?'

I tell him to do that. When I can't keep my eyes open any longer, at his own request I give him the VR glasses and show him how it works. For a first go I let him choose and he plumps for the Amazon rainforest which is a damn fine choice, I'd say. I still get a kick out of watching someone in glasses jumping and peering and twisting round to see a whole new world which isn't really there. The rushing and dripping and weird calls of birds, the thick green light, the flicker of sunlight through the leaves, the red flash of a parrot's wing; it's brilliant. After five minutes I bring him out of it and he's speechless. 'Ricky! It's so real!' I put him into a light aircraft flight across the Pyrenees, and say goodnight. He's peering down to left and right alternately as I go, happy as Larry, and with a catalogue of other journeys to choose from.

But as I am trying to get to sleep the full implications of him

and his young body start to hit me. He is twenty, for Christ's
sake. Of course he's full of curiosity and energy. He's in his prime
and if he's anything like I was, randy as hell. He must be
wondering when he'll get to meet some cats his own age. And
once I start thinking about what I liked to do in my twenties,
drink and sex isn't the half of it. Coke, heroin, LSD, I used to
imbibe my own weight in pharmaceuticals on a daily basis. What
if he does stuff like that? He won't, I tell myself, of course he
won't. For Chrissakes, he's your *dad*. And I remind myself how
cautious and polite he is – like a little boy, really. Timid. His
character hasn't changed a jot.

Well, the next day is a roaring success, I'm glad to say – aside
from the fact that I'm so tired I can barely function. Charlie
comes over with Derren in the morning and he and Anton really
hit it off. Anton asks Charlie hesitant, modest questions about
his work ('I'm sorry if this seems a bit simple, but can you explain
to me . . .?') And Charlie opens up to him in a way I've not seen
before. Soon they're onto politics and international affairs – my
dad diffident and deferential, and Charlie glowing with the attention.

Meanwhile Derren and I happily build and knock down towers,
and read *The Quangle Wangle's Hat* six times. I guess I'm a bit
disappointed that my dad doesn't really notice Derren. He nods
and smiles when the kid speaks to him, but his attention is all
on Charlie. Maybe I need to get Derren over here without his
dad next time.

In the afternoon Meryl offers for Anton to go to the gym
with her, Charlie puts Derren down for a nap and gets on with
some work, and I have a nap too. Everybody's happy! And
dinner that night is quite a jolly affair. Charlie's much better
at getting my dad talking than I am, and asks him about his
own childhood, back in the 1940s, about what life was like in
London just after the war, all that. Meryl's fascinated, like he's
talking about another planet – bombsites, wounded men

begging on the streets, smog – and once he gets going my dad's on a roll, telling them all about his primary school where one teacher was in charge of sixty kids and the Head used to hit them with a cane for answering back. The three of them are getting on like a house on fire and by eleven I've had enough and leave them to it, and I'm so sound asleep I never even hear Meryl come up.

In the morning she's a little hung-over and I make her tea and bring it back to bed. 'I really like your dad,' she says. 'But didn't he have a terrible life!'

'Terrible?'

'Well, the aftermath of the war! The hardship and all, when he was a kid. Then a whole lifetime in the same boring job with – Thames Water, was that it?'

'It was.'

'Plus your mom walking out on him. That must have been so tough.'

Aren't the kids supposed to be the ones that suffer most? But what the hell, I'm glad she's taken to him. 'How was he at the gym?'

'My god, Rich, he's strong – you should see the weights he lifted! And I'm pretty sure he ran six K in the time it took me to run my three.'

'Well honey, I'm glad. The gym's the ticket for him, he's got energy to burn.'

'You should come along too, lazybones.' And she pokes me slyly in the belly.

'Right. I'll consider it after he's gone.'

She laughs at me. 'But I do feel sorry for him. He's so unconfident. Even at the gym he was hanging back, asking me if it was OK for him to try the cross trainer – as if he doesn't have the right to anything.'

'Yeah. Obedient and law-abiding, that's what I had to rebel against.'

'In the auto coming home he asked me if I mind him being here.'

'What did you say?'

'Of course not! Dope! But don't you think it's sweet he asks? All he's got on this earth is two weeks, and he's worried about being in the way.'

'He and my mum never went anywhere except maybe a B&B one week a year.'

'Oh Rich. It's so *sad*.' She's sipping her tea then she suddenly says, 'He wanted to know where to buy toiletries, so I was like, *It's all in your room for you, Anton, toothbrush and shaver and products, just help yourself*, thinking he was too shy to do that. But he wanted something else.'

'What?'

'He was embarrassed so I was thinking, OK, it's a man-thing, I have to get Rich to ask him. But then he blurts out, *I don't know what to do with this hair!*'

Of course. He's gone from limp strands of grey to thick luxuriant black curls.

Meryl laughs. 'He broke the comb in his room.'

'You get him what he needs?'

'Yes, but even then – oh honey, he's like a little boy! He was afraid the barber would think he was weird not knowing what kind of comb to ask for, like he'd never combed his hair in his life before.'

We laugh and I give her a cuddle. He *is* like a little boy, and we're his mum and dad.

When I go down for breakfast Kay's already provided a fry-up for Anton and he's tucking in like a starving man. But when he sees me he stops with his fork in mid-air. He looks positively guilt-stricken. 'Rick, I apologise. I've just had a swim and it really gave me an appetite.'

'Hah! So you *can* swim?'

He chuckles. 'Turns out I can. I should have waited for you. But Kay here was already cooking before I realised you weren't up.'

'No sweat, Dad. There's no protocol, you have what you like when you like.' I order smoked salmon scrambled eggs and sit myself opposite him. 'I told Charlie we'd take Derren out today – just the two of us, somewhere for kiddies. D'you fancy the zoo?' He and the old lady took me to London Zoo once, when *I* was a kid. The only time I can ever remember a family outing. They must've had a row and been trying to play at happy families, cos I remember they both mainly chatted to me and were strangely polite to one another. My dad said we should go to the aquarium, he was always keen on fish. When we went in I was amazed cos it was all dark and mysterious with these brightly coloured windows of fish and coral, and Dad talked about the Great Barrier Reef and how everything there is brilliant. He'd seen a David Attenborough programme about it.

He nods. 'The zoo, good idea. Charlie's asked me for a drink with some of his mates tonight. Would that be alright by you?'

The way he says it makes me realise I'm not invited. Charlie has asked his grandfather but not his father. Except it's obvious why, it is a young dudes' drink and I am his dad, for Chrissakes. And no one would know Anton was his granddad. In fact, Charlie himself has probably forgotten. This is just his new mate Anton. But when did Charlie ever invite me out for a drink? I'll admit I'm a little stung but I haven't got a leg to stand on. And it does give me a night off.

'I wanted to ask you about the VR,' Anton says, carefully wiping the egg yolk and grease off his plate with a slice of bread, just like he always used to.

'Oh yeah, I meant to tell you, go for it whenever you like. No one even uses those glasses anymore.'

'Can you believe, I went swimming with whales after that flight finished?'

'So *that's* where you learned to swim.' We both laugh.

'But, Ricky, can you actually *do* anything in it?'

'How d'you mean?'

'Can you affect anything? In that flight, for example, could you crash the plane?'

'Why would you want to do that?'

'Well, I wouldn't. But I got curious about how much reality there actually is in the situation.'

'OK, I know what you mean. You can be in those places and see and hear everything, and smell it and feel it too, with the right gear – but you can't make anything happen. You're basically a spectator.'

'Which means you can't have an adventure. You can't really have a story.'

'No.' I'm impressed. He's worked out in a day what must have taken me weeks. 'It's why people mainly go into VR for games, because you *can* do things in games; kill enemies, overcome obstacles, win credits. In a game your avatar does have agency.'

He nods.

'Shall I set you up in a couple of games, later on?'

'Thanks, I'd like that.'

The zoo's kinda disappointing. It's a chilly grey day and most of the animals are taking a kip. Nothing to be seen in the lion pen, and only half of the back of a sleeping tiger behind a tree. The aquarium is a dead loss. My dad seems to have forgotten he ever gave a tinker's for coloured fish, and looks a bit vacant when I raise the Great B Reef. And Derren has to be lifted up to see into the tanks. He's bored with them because he thinks they're screens and the fish should be fighting or telling a story, not just hanging out behind a clump of weeds. In one, where a couple of turtles are comatose on a rock, he asks me what to press to start them. 'They're real,' I tell him. 'It's not a game. These are real turtles!' But he's not impressed.

Derren gets most excited about a robin that's tucking into a leftover sarnie under a picnic table. I guess zoos are a bit advanced for two-year-olds. My dad is amiable but – I dunno. Am I being unfair to the guy? He's just not that interested. He does carry

Derren on his shoulders for a while and the kid clearly loves that. Anyway, I'll stop carping.

When we get home Meryl suggests taking Derren in the pool. She's bought blow-up armbands and some other inflatable shit, and my dad's well up for it so I agree.

'Come in too, Rich,' she goes. 'It'll be fun!'

'I'll see.' To be honest the pool isn't my thing. I had it installed for her, and if it's good for young Derren too, then so much the better. It's well designed; turquoise and green tiles with dolphins, underwater lighting, decent showers – but it's underground. Down in the basement I get a weird vibe of the weight of the whole house pressing down on me. I had a bad trip back in the noughties, where a great blue water-monster rose out of a pool and dragged me down, down to where I couldn't breathe. Sometimes just the whiff of chlorine or the slap of water against the tiles is enough to get me panicked. Meryl doesn't know that of course. She thinks it's part of my whole anti-exercise thing. It's the only time she really pisses me off, when she's nagging on about exercise. Compared to a lot of guys my age I'm fit as a fiddle, and when you take into account the quantities of chemicals I've imbibed, I'm a walking fucking miracle.

Anyway, I went down to the basement with them but when my dad came out of the shower room where he had modestly gone to change, and I saw his fully ripped torso in all its naked glory, I thought, *Forget it, Ricardo; comparisons are odious.* He stopped to quiz me about whether the pool water was recycled, and the type of pump we used, about which I knew sweet FA. Meryl poked him in the ribs and told him to quit being such a plumber, and dragged him into the pool. I watched the pair of them with Derren between them, laughing and splashing fit to burst, and I was happy to see the kiddo enjoying himself. But, frankly, I was a spare part in this scene. So pretty soon I took myself off back upstairs.

In the evening I'm thinking Meryl and I might get up close and personal together while the boys are out, but she has a date with some passing American girlfriend. So I end up in the studio teasing out a little number that's been at the back of my mind all week, and I'm still in there fooling around when Meryl and Anton come home.

'Is it that late? Where's Charlie?'

'We went on to a wine bar and he wanted to stay longer.'

'But he was meant to be looking after you, Anton. You know I'm not supposed to let you out alone.'

'*I* brought him home,' says Meryl.

'You?'

'Sure. It was dumb luck. These guys turn up at the wine bar where I'm meeting Kylie. So we join them, and when Kylie's ready to leave I'm ready too, and Anton decided to come along with us.' She's looking at me wide-eyed and I suddenly get it. Charlie and his mates must have been pissed. And my old dad has always been a two-pints-are-plenty kind of guy. She rescued him.

I smile at her and she smiles back like the sun coming out. I've never seen her playing Mom before, and it kind of makes me ache. 'Sorry, guys, let's have a nightcap.' I pour them some bourbon. 'I probably didn't explain to you, Dad, the legal shit I had to agree to at the clinic. If I obeyed their instructions I'd be keeping you wrapped in cotton wool and never allowing you out of my sight.'

My father nods. 'Fair enough.' He stretches out his hands. 'No scratches or bruises. All in good working order.'

We laugh, and drink. When Meryl comes to bed, well after me, she's shattered and says can we leave it till morning? And she is asleep in five, breathing her little whistling sleep-breath. So I snuggle up to her and replay the evening in my head. She brought Dad home. And I know she would have done it lightly, without making Charlie feel like an irresponsible dickhead, or making Dad feel a wimp. She would have made a great mother.

She used to want a baby but I stalled on that for as long as I could. When Derren came along I thought he'd plug that gap.

But I guess she hasn't seen as much of the kid as I imagined she might want to. Now I'm thinking, would it have hurt to let her have a kid?

Well, that's a conundrum I can't answer, but still, it goes round and round in my dumb old head half the night.

7.

ELSA

In the weeks after Lindy's death, Elsa is beset by memories, and by the disjunction between these memories. She remembers the young, diffident Lindy from their teacher-training days, with her long coppery hair and intense gaze. When Lindy stood up in the lecture theatre to disagree with their lecturer, her cheeks flushed pink with embarrassment and it seemed she would not be able to get the words out. Elsa remembers thinking, my god, why does *she* want to teach? She'll be crucified. But what Lindy said in her soft low voice was far more thoughtful and critical than anyone, including the lecturer, had anticipated. Elsa remembers her own desire to enfold and protect Lindy's vulnerability; until it dawned on her that Lindy could defend herself perfectly well. That Lindy would always do and say what she believed to be right, paying the price in nervous energy and near-crippling self-consciousness, but that she was actually the strongest and most idealistic student on the course.

Elsa remembers the admiration she felt for this clever yet somehow defenceless girl, this young woman who did not seem to have developed any kind of protective shell against the knocks of daily life. And how, in the rapidly changing group dynamics of the students, Lindy transformed from socially awkward outsider to the person whose good opinion everybody valued. She was the only one on the course who admitted to a nerdy fondness for old video and computer games, and she was enthusiastic about using them in teaching. They were being trained to work with edubots, but all the lecturers were dragging their feet. They were suspicious of the edubots, and frightened for their jobs, disliking what they perceived as soulless cost-cutting. Lindy's gentle insistence on trying out the new, and on frankly revealing her love of games (for which everyone else was maintaining a snobbish disdain) was very endearing.

To begin with Elsa loved her because she was defenceless; then she loved her for her openness and her strength. Lindy existed, the Lindy she loved and who, amazingly, loved her, so that they moved in together in the second year of their course. The loopy Lindy who joyously declared, 'The last Metroid is in captivity. The Galaxy is at peace!' when they woke in their own bed in their own flat for the first time.

That Lindy existed.

But so did the one who died in the bomb blast on the trans; closed, bitter, angry, dead-eyed. A person Elsa can't reach, an evil-doer, her lovely hair cropped into a severe bob, her skin ashen.

Before and after the fall: Elsa can't make sense of what has happened.

Begin with Jade.

Jade F came to their school in New Cross as a highly disturbed eight-year-old. She could not – or would not – read, and didn't engage with any of the elementary reading programmes, although she knew her numbers and did occasionally complete some maths tasks. She was sometimes passive and silent all day, causing no trouble but refusing to follow any programme onscreen. It was in group activities that she became disruptive, calling out during story time ('This is for fucking babies!' and 'Bor-ing!') so often that she broke the other children's concentration. In sports and dancing she always made an exhibition of herself, moving off in the opposite direction to that required, or parodying the actions she was supposed to be making, or simply hurling herself at other children so that they dodged away shrieking. They were all afraid of her because she fought viciously, biting and eye-jabbing. When she was excluded from class she sat in the corner of Elsa's office sucking her thumb or making tiny congested drawings of ant-like people and animals.

Elsa tried to talk to the parents but they would not divulge any information about her previous education and claimed that her behavioural problems were the fault of the school.

'I think we may need to expel her,' Elsa told Lindy. 'She's too disruptive. It's not fair to the other kids.'

'Well she's not stupid,' Lindy replied. 'I would say she's highly intelligent. She's just very, very angry.'

'Yes. But we haven't got the staffing or resources to deal with that.'

Edubots had replaced all class teachers in their little primary school by this stage and were responsible for ensuring that kids followed their onscreen programmes and lessons, and joined in group activities. Edubots monitored trips to the toilet, play-times and lunch break, and flagged up problems to the human staff – now reduced to Elsa and Lindy. Access to extra help, tuition or child psychology had to be requested and paid for by parents.

Elsa was head teacher, in charge of testing, progression, finance and admin, while Lindy circulated around the six classes helping individual children, tracking the effectiveness of new edubot programmes, and paying particular attention to the infants. Thanks to her love of computer games, they were often given new ones to trial.

'Can I try working with her for a couple of days, Else? Let me see if I can break through.'

'Like I said, Lindy, it's not fair to the other kids. Why should that little minx get two days of your full attention, when there are other perfectly well-behaved kids who *want* to learn, who need your input?'

'Two days, OK? If I don't get anywhere then I agree, we'll have to ask them to move her on. But it will be the same story in another school. What she's doing is a cry for help.'

'Cry for help, bah. I'll cry for help. You great softy.'

Elsa remembers patting Lindy's cheek, across the big desk where they were seated, and Lindy swiftly turning her head and pretending to bite Elsa's fingers. She remembers the smile they exchanged.

When Lindy came home after the first day with Jade, she was exasperated. The girl had blocked her every move. She did not want a human teacher, she wanted to sit in her normal class. She didn't want to read, it was stupid. She thought the special interactive VR games Lindy attempted to play with her were boring, she didn't want to talk about anything she ever did at home, and when asked about her favourite activities she replied 'resting' and 'watching telly'. She would not identify what she watched.

Lindy made progress the next day. She started reading a story aloud. Jade responded in her normal way, 'This is fucking boring' and 'This is shit'. But Lindy persevered in a louder voice. After fifteen minutes Jade stopped commenting and put her fingers in her ears. 'But loosely,' Lindy explained to Elsa, grinning. Around forty minutes in, she removed the fingers, and after an hour she was so hooked that she reacted angrily when Lindy broke off to take a sip of water. Lindy read aloud for a good part of the day, and she and Jade made a pact that Lindy would teach Jade to read for herself. There would be real reading lessons with nobody but Jade and Lindy, no screen, and Lindy would bring special big-girl real books which the other kids never saw.

Lindy had to pick up with her classroom duties the following week, but she worked with Jade regularly after school, and unsurprisingly, Jade made swift progress. Within a month she was reading and her behaviour had improved. A jubilant Lindy high-fived Elsa and told her, 'Your quest is over. Job's done.'

But Jade had developed a crush on Lindy. She did not want her private lessons to end, and demanded extra maths help as well. Elsa had to explain to her that the online programme taught maths far better than Lindy could, and that Lindy was responsible for many children, not just Jade. But Jade would hang about waiting for her after school and tried to follow her home. There were long and serious talks from both Elsa and Lindy, and calls to the parents, explaining why she must not do this. Then she was absent from school.

Three days into her absence, a policebot came to school and took Lindy in for questioning. The girl had made an accusation of child abuse. Lindy had been alone with her after school on several occasions. There were no witnesses.

'But this is mad,' Elsa said, when she got home. 'What are you supposed to have done?'

Lindy didn't know. She was unpacking her school bag, item by item, onto the table.

'Why on earth did her parents go to the police? Why didn't they come to me?'

'The police asked for a record of the dates and times I saw her, and a list of what we did.'

'Reading.' Elsa slumped onto a chair.

'Uh-huh.' Lindy laid her purse, remote, headphones and three pens in a row. 'But they wanted specifics. Screen or paper, titles, how many pages, if we sat side by side or facing.' Lindy's voice was sharp.

Elsa realised belatedly that Lindy was very angry. 'I'm so sorry, love. They've told me I've got to suspend you, pending investigation.'

'*I'm* sorry, Else. It's rubbish timing, with the reports—'

'Sod the reports. They can make do with edubot reports. What I don't understand is why the child's accused you. The reading went well, didn't it?'

'It went fine. I would say she enjoyed it. Why else was she pestering to carry on?' A water bottle, a charger, an e-reader and several folded bits of paper were laid on the table.

'What are you looking for? D'you think it's because you wouldn't carry on with the reading?'

Lindy shrugged. 'I wonder if her parents put her up to it.'

'But why?' Elsa laughed humourlessly. 'They'll get their own punishment, having her at home all day.' She was rewarded with the ghost of a grin.

'I'm looking for a note she gave me.'

'Jade? Written by her?'

Lindy nodded. 'She gave me a little note, after our last reading session. "THANK YOU FOR TEECHING ME" in big spidery letters.'

'OK.'

'It wasn't a card or anything, it wasn't from her parents, it was just a scruffy little bit of paper she'd got hold of. I thought it might be useful to show them, you know, that she wasn't complaining at that stage.'

'You told them she tried to follow you home?'

'I – I don't know, Elsa. D'you think I should?' A dull red crept up Lindy's throat and coloured her pale cheeks.

'Why not?'

'Because it's not appropriate behaviour. And they might think I had encouraged her to behave inappropriately.'

Elsa pulled off her shoes. 'I think you should tell them everything because it all adds up to a picture of a silly spoilt child. You can't honestly imagine they'll believe her word against yours?'

'Well they *should*. They should give the child the benefit of the doubt, in cases like this. And since it is me that's accused, I am obliged to think about it seriously and not be so high-handed.' She held her bag upside-down over the table and shook it, and assorted paperclips, coins, safety pins and used tissues fell out. She began to unfold and smooth out the crumpled bits of paper.

'Have you got it?'

'No.'

'I wasn't being high-handed, I was just—'

'Yes you were.'

'Lindy—' Elsa reached across the table and clasped Lindy's arm. 'It's hard for me to take it seriously because I know you and I know how ludicrous this is, but I'm sorry you're upset.'

'Wouldn't you be?'

'I – perhaps I would. Yes.'

'Well then.' Lindy glanced up and met Elsa's eyes.

'Sorry. Look, shall we go out?'

'Where?'

'I don't know. A meal, a drink?'

Lindy was methodically replacing the items in her bag. 'Out is good, but not a meal. I feel – I don't know – grubby. Claustrophobic.'

'A walk? It's not raining. Down to Greenwich?'

'Yes, along the river, that would be good.' She closed the bag.

'I'll tell you one thing. Once this has blown over I'm expelling that girl, no discussion.'

'Yes, that's come back nicely to bite my bum, hasn't it.'

'Well. Let's not talk about this anymore.'

Lindy smiled. 'Thank you.'

The next afternoon Lindy phoned Elsa at school. 'I'm sorry Else, but they've arrested me. Do we have a lawyer?' A medical examination had revealed that Jade had been subjected to sustained sexual assault. Lindy was bailed on condition that she did not leave the house, and their computers, tablets and phones were confiscated, to be scoured for child pornography.

Elsa remembers that evening clearly. She took an auto to the police station to pick Lindy up. She remembers Lindy's bewildered, appalled expression; she remembers the way misery lodged in her own chest like a stone. The charges had been fully explained to Lindy in the presence of her lawyer. Jade's accusations were detailed and revolting.

They finally got home to New Cross after nine. The house felt invaded, desecrated. Missing screens left yawning gaps. Items left strewn on the sofa and table seemed peculiarly significant, as if testifying against them; evidence of their perverted lifestyle. The food in the fridge, the medicines in the bathroom cabinet, their unmade bed, the dirty washing in the clothes basket, all offered silent witnesses to lives which were capable of being suspected of such a crime. All were tainted.

Before the police called, Lindy had been preparing a lovely old-fashioned dinner of slow-roasted lamb and vegetables, the type of cooking neither of them normally had time for. She had switched off the oven when she left the house, and now she opened the door and took out the still-bloody meat surrounded by its congealed vegetables. There was a strong smell of raw flesh and garlic.

As Elsa stolidly tipped the contents of the roasting pan into the bin and scraped it clean, she listened to Lindy vomiting in the downstairs toilet. When they were both done, she poured them a drink and they sat at the table.

'D'you want anything to eat?'

'No.'

'We should have something or we won't sleep.' It was a ridiculous thing to say, neither of them were remotely likely to sleep. But Elsa cut bread and put it in the toaster, which was worth doing for the smell alone. She buttered it while it was warm and slid a slice across the table to Lindy. Lindy stared at it but did not move to pick it up. When she spoke her voice was a near-whisper. 'What are we going to do?'

'I don't know. What *can* we do? What did the lawyer say?'

'He said they have to get a child psychologist to interview Jade.'

'Fair enough, but what about you?'

'I have to think about character witnesses and anyone who can attest to seeing me teaching her after school.'

'Like who?'

'Kids in detention with an edubot? I don't know.'

'If only we had CCTV in every room.'

'But we opposed that, didn't we.' They had both fought a rearguard action against more and more technology in the school; it was expensive and their budget had already been cut to the bone. The edubots were a local authority contract, and all schools got two for every twenty-five kids, there was no choice. But CCTV surveillance, automatically locking door systems, bulletproof glass and defence shields, Lindy and Elsa had argued against. What was the point? If a terrorist really wanted to attack a school, he/she would do it anyway. Doors were constantly opening to admit teachers and kids; CCTV footage of a person shooting children was not going to stop it happening. The governors, on their ever-shrinking budget, were persuaded. No one had considered that CCTV might be useful in their own – in their teachers' – defence.

Elsa grasped for a positive. 'When it comes down to it, it's her word against yours. The word of a very disturbed eight-year-old against a teacher of sixteen years' experience, with a spotless reputation.'

'But it's not, Elsa. The medical evidence shows that someone has assaulted her. That's why they've got a case.'

'OK, who?'

'Has she got a brother?'

They didn't know. Maybe a babysitter? Maybe an uncle, or a family friend, someone so close she couldn't be disloyal and accuse them? Maybe a parent? Impossible to know, but surely up to the police to find out.

'Will they question other people? They can't just assume it was you because Jade says so. There must be other suspects.'

Lindy shrugged. 'I have no idea. If a psychologist is any good, he or she will quickly find out what a flake the child is. But still—' Her face contorted and she began to sob. Elsa got up and went to put her arms around her. She had to stoop to do it, and she can still feel the hot stickiness of Lindy's wet cheek against her own.

'Hush, hush, my love. It's alright.'

'But still – what's happened to her is awful. She's only a little girl. It will ruin her life.'

Elsa pulled out the chair next to Lindy and sat beside her, taking her hands. 'It is awful, I agree. But she shouldn't have dragged you into it.'

'Maybe she was trying to talk to me. Maybe that's why she kept hanging around – she wanted my help—' Fresh sobs.

'Lindy, stop this. Don't torture yourself. Whatever has happened to that child, you showed her nothing but kindness.' Elsa lowered her head to kiss each of Lindy's hands in turn. 'Game over. New start. OK?'

That night in bed Elsa lay curled around Lindy's back trying to work out how to cover Lindy's absence at school. The child's anonymity had to be preserved. Convincing and entirely separate reasons for Jade's and Lindy's absences had to be found. There was nothing in the budget to pay a supply teacher, edubots were supposed to be able to provide cover. A prolonged absence would cause real difficulties. Did the governors have to know? If word of this got out it would be terrible for the school. Then she remembered that it would go to court and everybody would know, and she had her first pang of fear for herself.

She was Lindy's partner. If Lindy stood accused of such an unspeakable crime, Elsa might well come under suspicion of – what? Aiding and abetting? Condoning? Creating the conditions to make it possible? She would be tarnished by association and the governors would need to get rid of her.

But it was absurd, the whole thing: how could Lindy, of all the people in the world, stand accused of such a crime?

It was impossible but it had happened, had happened to others before and would no doubt happen again, and no amount of twisting and turning could make it unhappen. The next few weeks took them deeper into the mire. The lawyer forbade them any contact with Jade's parents and somebody – Elsa remains convinced it was the parents – leaked the story online. Nobody was named, the school was identified simply as being in New Cross, but that was enough. The governors held an emergency meeting and assured Elsa of their continuing support for her exemplary work as head teacher. And then began a stream of parental messages and visits to Elsa. The first few were innocuous, seeking reassurance: 'We know there's been a problem with one of the little girls. We've got absolutely no complaints, this is a lovely school. But Sam/Ahmed/Nate is a bit upset about it and so are his friends. What advice do you have?' Elsa bounced that one back to the governors and a trauma counsellor came into school and talked about how important it is to tell a grown-up if anyone does anything to upset you. There were an increasing number of absentees. When Elsa contacted a couple of parents she had always felt she could count on, they offered vague reassurance: the children had colds, or were unsettled, or were simply sad that Miss Lindy was off. They would be back next week.

Then came a different kind of message. It stated that the writer's child had told her that the teacher had touched his bare bottom with her fingers. In view of the seriousness of the allegation the child was being withdrawn from school and the matter was being taken to the police. The ones that followed made this charge seem mild.

At first Elsa knew exactly what she thought, and told Lindy; 'It's a witch-hunt. It's *The Crucible*. Hysterical children are being egged on by stupid, evil-minded adults. Sweetheart, don't worry. We'll get through this.' Thinking about how wretched it must be for Lindy to be confined alone in the house while she was at work, Elsa suggested asking friends round, and inviting Lindy's sister Beattie to stay for a few days. Lindy was absolutely against it.

'You think I want *anyone* to know about this? What am I going to say to people? Elsa, I beg you, don't tell anyone I'm off work. I can't bear it.'

'You've done nothing wrong. This is turning you into a prisoner, it's not fair!'

'It's not fair but I'd feel ten times worse with Beattie buzzing round trying to cheer me up. It's OK, Else – thank you. I know you're trying to help but I really don't want to see anyone. I've got books to read and music to listen to, I'm fine.'

They agreed that Elsa would tell friends that Lindy was off work with stress and had been advised to rest and sleep as much as possible. And that her phone and laptop were switched off, doctor's orders.

Then two windows at the school were smashed. The head of the governors called Elsa and told her, with the greatest regret, that he was anxious about the safety of the school being compromised and it might be best if she took a few weeks' leave. He had a replacement head lined up to start on Monday.

'But there'll be no one here who *knows* the kids, Jim. They need continuity—'

'Elsa, either you go or we close the school till this blows over. Continuity is the last thing on people's minds right now. As you know, there are schools on the estates which are allegedly working perfectly well with no staff but second-generation edubots. That's what I want to protect our children from; the loss of all their human teachers.'

Elsa cleared her desk and went home. Lindy wept. 'It was bad enough when it was me, but now you're being dragged down too . . . it's so unfair. If I moved out, might that make a difference?'

'Don't be ridiculous, it would make things ten times worse. The best way for us to behave is completely normally.'

'Don't be cross with me, Else. I can't bear it.'

'Look, Lindy, crying isn't going to fix anything. We have to ignore them.'

Lindy retreated to her study, where Elsa could still hear her sniffling. Elsa knew she was being harsh. But Lindy had been the victim for days, and now that Elsa was also in danger of losing her job, the best Lindy could offer was more tears.

The days at home were long and strained. Elsa bought them both new phones, since the police still had theirs. She arranged a meeting with the lawyer to get a better sense of the time frame.

'We've got to wait for all the other children in that class to be interviewed by the psychologist. These other allegations are bad news for Lindy,' he told her. 'I have to be honest with you. Some of the other children will be called to testify – via a CCTV link – and that always sways a jury. I mean, there's usually no smoke without fire in these cases.'

Lindy was sitting in the dark when Elsa got home, although it was a sunny afternoon. She had closed all the blinds. 'What's going on? What are you doing?' asked Elsa.

'There's a drone. They've been around the house a few times before but this one is more precise – I don't know, better controlled. It comes right up to the windows.'

Elsa listened. 'I can't hear anything.'

'Well you will. It'll be back.'

'But Lindy, we can't hide. You can't sit in a darkened room all day.'

'What d'you want me to do?'

'Act normally. Ignore it. Once they realise there's nothing interesting going on they'll soon get bored.'

'It's an invasion of privacy. It's against the law.'

'So we'll complain to the police.'

'I have. Twice last week. They said they couldn't do anything about it.'

'Then you need to get on with your life.'

'How am I to get on with it? My laptop's gone and I can't leave the house. *You* can wake up in the morning and think, aha, I'll go out in the sunshine today.'

'Indeed. My life is a bed of roses.'

'Where have you been, anyway?'

'To talk to the lawyer.'

'Derek? You've been to talk to Derek?'

'Isn't he your lawyer?'

'Yes, but why are *you* talking to him? Why are you talking to him without me?'

'Lindy, I just wanted to get an idea of how long all this might go on.'

'Why didn't you ask me? Why are you going to him behind my back?'

'It wasn't behind your back—'

'Yes it was. You didn't tell me you were going to see him. Why not ask him to come here so that I can be part of the conversation? What are you saying to him that you don't want me to hear?'

'You're being paranoid.'

'Right, I'm paranoid. I've been stopped from doing the job I love, arrested, accused of child abuse and confined to this house like a criminal, and my phone and laptop have been confiscated. How paranoid of me to notice when my partner has a private chat about me with my lawyer.'

'It wasn't about you.'

'Well what was it? Conversation about the weather?'

'For god's sake.'

'What did he say, then? What words of comfort did he have to offer you?'

'He said there's no smoke without fire.'

In the claustrophobically darkened room, with sunlight creating bright bars around the edges of the blinds, there's a sudden silence. Into the silence comes a buzzing; the drone is at the window. 'Aha,' says Elsa, turning to the distraction in relief, 'yeah, I can see that it is annoying. I'll complain as well, two complaints are stronger than one.'

Lindy does not reply. Elsa digs in her bag for her new phone. 'Lindy? You alright?'

'There's no smoke without fire. That what *you* think?'

'Of course not. Of course not. I didn't say it to—'

'There's no smoke without fire. Right.' Very quietly she gets up and goes to the bathroom. Elsa stands suspended, phone in hand. The drone buzzes at the window like an insistent bluebottle. After several long minutes Elsa moves cautiously to the bathroom door and listens. Nothing. She goes into the dim kitchen and opens the blind and puts on the kettle. In an instant the drone is at that window. She jabs a V sign at it then makes a pot of coffee. Going back to the bathroom door, she listens again. Nothing.

'Lindy? Want some coffee?'

Nothing. Elsa goes back into the kitchen, where the drone

continues to buzz inquisitively, pours her own coffee and slumps at the table. Lindy is right, the persistent buzzing is intolerable. Angrily she closes the blind. What a stupid insensitive thing to say. But the lawyer's words; it was more of a warning, to alert them to the danger of what other people would be thinking. Other people – the *jury*, what the jury might think. And if they find Lindy guilty, and she goes to prison, what then? Could she really be found guilty if she's innocent? Why? Why has all this happened? There's no smoke without fire. For the first time, a sliver of doubt enters Elsa's head. This must have come from somewhere. If half the children in Jade's class think their teacher is a paedophile, there must surely, somewhere, under all the exaggeration, be perhaps a grain of truth? For a flicker of a fraction of a second the question flares: what if Lindy is guilty?

It is a hateful disgraceful treacherous thought and Elsa stifles it. This is how lives get trashed, through false accusations and victims' friends and loved ones failing to stand by them. Lindy is her partner, her wife, her beloved. Lindy could no more harm a child than – than cut off her own right hand. There's no smoke without fire is the wickedest thing she has ever said.

Lindy cannot forgive her. She keeps herself aloof and silent, she makes her bed in the spare room. She maintains the pretence of being busy when Elsa attempts to talk to her. There is no getting through. 'Game over. New start!' is entirely ignored.

Impasse. Outside, the drone buzzes. Gradually, with what seems like glacial slowness, there are developments. Jim calls to see how Elsa is and to reassure her that her job will still be there for her when this is all over. Only a week till the summer holidays now, thank goodness. Derek comes round to brief Lindy on her case and is concerned that she is becoming depressed. He says that now the case is longer and more complex than originally thought, he will raise the issue of the conditions of Lindy's bail. A few days later a bot comes to tag her and tells her she can go out as long as she stays in London, and keeps at least a kilometre away from the school.

Lindy goes out and Elsa breathes a sigh of relief; breathes freely, it feels, for the first time in days. Then she appals herself by bolting the front door and closing the blinds and going through Lindy's study like a detective. What does she imagine she will find? The police have already looked anyway. She hates herself. But she has to know. She has to know if there is, anywhere in the house, a single shred of evidence to support the accusation. She works hastily and in terror of being interrupted, but Lindy stays out all day. Indeed, she stays out so long that Elsa is later afraid something has happened to her, and wonders if she should call the lawyer or police. It's unfair of Lindy, after all she's put Elsa through, not to realise that she might worry. Then Elsa remembers all that *Lindy* has been put through, and not one jot of it her own fault, and hates herself with such a vicious contempt that she bites her hangnails till they bleed. Lindy returns at 10 p.m. and retires immediately to the spare bedroom.

And more days pass. Elsa tries to discuss the issue of character references but Lindy says it's under control. Elsa does not believe her because Elsa is the one who keeps old phone numbers and addresses in her little book, retaining the quaint old-fashioned custom of writing things down. Lindy is poor at synchronising her digital info, and Elsa knows, because she has checked, that she has very few contacts on her new phone. Since the police are showing no signs of returning their confiscated phones or tablets, it is impossible that she would know how to get in touch with teachers from her former school, or parents of children she taught three years ago. But if Elsa calls Derek, she is going behind Lindy's back.

Suspicion worms its way into every thought and observation. Lindy has stopped speaking to Elsa because she is so insulted by the insinuation behind *there's no smoke without fire*. But equally, if she were guilty, that's how she would react if she thought Elsa really suspected her. She wouldn't be able to brush it off and forget about it, she wouldn't be able to carry on pretending nothing had happened. Is Lindy behaving like a guilty person?

The drones are driving them both mad. Who is sending them? Lindy hasn't been named by the media, she can't be, with a trial pending – so how do they know who and where she is? The police aren't interested; an automated voice tells Elsa that there is insufficient person-power for trivial and neighbour-feuding incidents. Patrolbots are not sophisticated enough to trace drones back to their point of origin.

Elsa scours her memories of their sex life for signs that Lindy may have been overly interested in the young. Not only does it make her feel disgusting, it also breaks her heart to remember how warm and happy and easy they used to be with one another; how a look or the lightest touch could suddenly alert one to the other's desire, a swift flame leaping between them. How intent and focused they were on giving and receiving pleasure. It's gone. But surely not just recently, because of all this? No, it was going before then. Hadn't sex become stale, dull, routine? If she felt that, then so must Lindy. All the more reason, then, for her to look for satisfaction elsewhere.

Could that be possible? Another woman, perhaps? A younger woman, someone with more time and imagination than Elsa, maybe. But a child?

No.

The lawyer rings to make an appointment to discuss her testimony. Elsa insists on it being at the house, for Lindy's sake, although that horse has only too obviously bolted. When she tells Lindy that Derek is coming, she replies that she personally does not need to see him. Derek still knocks at her study door to ask if she'd like to join them, since the conversation will be all about her, but she thanks him politely and declines.

Elsa makes coffee and sits opposite him at the kitchen table. He's a small, kindly man with a big chin which makes his face look upside-down. As he opens his laptop and retrieves information, Elsa imagines Lindy in her room, ear pressed to the door to hear whatever Elsa might say about her. Except she won't do that. She would have contempt for the very idea, she won't care what Elsa says and has probably put on headphones to save herself the annoyance of overhearing a single word. Derek looks up. 'I want to call you for the defence, obviously.'

'Yes. Have you got many witnesses?'

'Character witnesses – three. No actual witnesses, it goes without saying.'

'D'you mind me asking who they are?'

He gives her the names of a teacher from Lindy's previous school, a parent whose daughter moved up last year, and Jim, the head of the governors.

'There might be . . . I could probably get others,' she offers.

'Only if they can add something significant. And Lindy has asked me to contact as few people as possible.'

'She doesn't want anyone to know.'

'Which is understandable.' He types then glances up at her. 'OK? I'll start by asking you to fill in the background of your relationship; where you met, how long you've been together . . .'

Elsa nods.

'That's straightforward. But I'm afraid I will have to ask you some questions about your intimate life together.'

'Intimate?'

'Your sex life.'

Of course. Why hasn't she seen this coming? How prurient and hateful. 'Do you – will you ask Lindy the same questions?'

'It depends on your answers. If there's anything that needs clarification, then yes.' There's a small silence. He is regarding her steadily. 'If I don't ask, the prosecution will, and I hope I can do it more kindly than them.'

Elsa nods. 'What—' her voice cracks. 'What sort of thing will you ask?'

He looks at his screen. 'If your relationship is open or monog-amous. How often you have relations. How you would describe those relations.'

'Describe?'

'For example, games, role plays, sadomasochism, use of dildos or objects . . .'

'I really have to *describe*?'

He finally looks up at her. 'Because of the detail of the child's accusation, the court will be looking for any pattern or similarity of – of sexual predilection.'

'Right.'

'I'm sorry, Elsa. That's why I thought I should give you the chance to prepare yourself. Bear in mind that the child won't be present.'

'I bet her parents will.'

He shrugs. 'If you can be as clear and brief and unemotional as possible, that would be good. Do you want to practise now?'

'Give me a moment.'

'Of course.'

Elsa locks herself in the bathroom and looks at herself in the mirror. She has to talk about what she and Lindy do in bed, which used to be joyously inventive and, for the past year at least, has been almost nothing. Which will in itself assume the aspect of a damning piece of evidence. She can't lie, she can't soften anything. Because Lindy never will. She stares at the stolid fleshy face she will present to the jury and realises they will pity her at best, and at worst feel disgust and contempt. If she could talk to Lindy, if Lindy would listen, they could try to work out at the very least how to make this sound less incriminating. Except that even if Lindy would listen, she wouldn't agree to massaging the facts. Elsa can hear her honest hesitant voice already, saying, 'We have not had sexual relations for the past six to twelve months', and giving them all the detail, all the rope they need to hang her with, about the games they used to play. This is Lindy's fault, this public parade of their private life. No, not

Lindy's – Jade's fault. But Lindy will not help herself or Elsa, and for that Elsa can blame her and be furious. How can she support Lindy, how can she help her, how can she *like* her, when Lindy's behaviour is so judgemental and stubborn and self-destructive? Does she think for a moment about how Elsa is feeling? No. Her selfishness cannot be excused.

Elsa returns to Derek in the kitchen and answers his *practice questions* fully, grateful for his quick nods, his matter-of-fact typing, his quiet efficiency. When she asks if he'll do the same practice with Lindy he hesitates. 'May I ask a personal question?'

Elsa raises her eyebrows. 'Personal?' And he starts to laugh. After a moment she joins in, and it is the first time she has laughed in so long that she can't stop until tears are coursing down her face. When she has wiped her eyes he asks,

'Have you and Lindy fallen out?'

It must be obvious. 'I'm afraid so. But – but I still completely support her. I mean, I still want to do everything I can to help her case.'

'Naturally. You're both under a lot of pressure – a case like this always takes its toll on a relationship. It's very common, believe me.'

Elsa nods.

'But for that reason it might be better, easier, for Lindy, if I talk to her on her own. Sometime when you'll be out, maybe?'

'OK. Just tell me when you want to come and I'll leave the field clear.'

'Thanks.'

Lindy alternates between staying in her room and going out for the day. Elsa writes her notes, leaving missives on her desk, texts her, and lies in wait for her return and begs her, implores her to talk. But Lindy is impervious. The relief when she goes out is tremendous. The house is still semi-dark, with the constant buzzing outside, but at least it is Elsa's own space. It is bizarre to have no schoolwork to do, but that was all on the computers they have taken. Swathes of unexpected time open up. Elsa finds herself on her new phone, trawling the internet for whatever images the drones are relaying back, and for references to the case. She can't find any, so she surfs details of other child-abuse cases. Then she wonders if the police might confiscate this phone too, and interpret her search history as corroboration of a perverted interest in children.

She is sickened by herself. It is time to get a grip, and find something positive to do. She takes up painting, which she enjoyed as a teenager and has always imagined she could be rather good at. She buys some decent watercolours and paper, and practises still lifes of fruit. But it is close and hot in the house; the August sun beats down outside and anyway, watercolour was invented for landscapes. She should go out somewhere where it's green and she can enjoy the light and sunshine on her skin.

But increasingly, going out is hard. There's the gamut of the drones to run. And other people are staring. The neighbours, with whom they've never been particularly friendly, often seem to be lurking at their windows or doors. On the semi-detached side, the family who used to play hideously loud rap seem to have fallen silent, and Elsa imagines them listening, ears pressed to the party wall, for her and Lindy's brief, shrill exchanges. People on the street who she knows say hello and ask when they're going on summer holiday, rubbing her nose in the fact that they are going nowhere. Briefly she considers going away on her own. But could she leave Lindy behind? Of course not. Her place is by Lindy's side, and no one must get the slightest inkling of the wedge that this has driven between them. Like Lindy, she no longer wants to have to deal with other people. The line of least resistance is to stay in the gloomy stuffy house and paint terrible pictures of apples and bananas.

Then comes the night when Lindy doesn't return. She left at lunchtime, and is generally home by ten at the latest. The longer she stays out the better, but Elsa is aware of her absence, and when it gets to 11 p.m. she is concerned. She phones; it doesn't even ring. Lindy must have switched it off. As she tries to think who else she could contact she realises how effectively they have cut themselves off, not only from everyone else but from each other. She has no idea where Lindy goes or what she does. Might she be at a friend's house?

Hesitating with the phone in her hand she touches her thumb to *NEWS*. An image of a smoking mangled trans. *London bomb outrage, 22 killed. Terror attack in Westminster.* How could there be a bomb on a trans? They all have scanners. Twenty-two dead? She stares.

Not possible. How could she even imagine it? But simultaneously she is swiping to find out the details. Because there's a tiny bit of her, a tiny pulse in her gut, which is already quite certain Lindy has died. *You and your friends are dead. Game over.*

Elsa makes herself wait, through the long hours of the night, willing Lindy to come home. She will not allow herself to report her missing, or to try to discover the names of the dead. The knock on the door comes at 7 a.m., with the sun pouring down on what will be another lovely summer's day. Lindy's tag has been found. She died in hospital without regaining consciousness; massive injuries to chest and spine. At the request of Transporto's insurers, the dead have been cryogenically frozen.

8.

RICHARD K

Day 5

I wake up alone in bed in the morning, with a thick head. My dad's onscreen with three busy windows open and he tells me Meryl's gone out but she didn't say where. He's had a swim and breakfasted and he's already checked in with the clinic. It's 11 a.m. After I'd lain awake for hours last night I took a sleeping tab and now my groggy brain's the price to pay.

I crank myself up with a couple of double espressos, and ask him what he'd like to do. Dumb question, I tell myself, because he doesn't even know what there *is* to do. But he comes back with, *Please can we visit the old house?* He would really like to go for a wander round where he used to live. I offer to take him in VR, damn sight easier for both of us, but he says if I don't mind he'd much rather see real bricks and mortar.

'I think it might have gone, Dad. We can drive over there and take a look, but you know London – always redeveloping.'

He nods. 'I don't want to put you to any trouble, Ricky. It's a shame I can't go there on my own. For old times' sake, I'd love to walk around there and see what's become of it.'

I haven't got anything better to offer so when I'm ready we head out in the auto. He stares at the streets like a little kid, his eyes constantly distracted by new sights. He's playing 'can I spot the human?' 'Bot,' he says, 'bot, bot, human.'

'If they're walking around here they're probably all bots,' I tell him. 'But the ones on bikes are human alright.' Health freaks. When we get to Spitalfields he wants to get out and walk. It's one of those cold grey early spring days with a nasty biting wind that whips round corners and makes your eyes water. I'm putting my best foot forward but I can see he has to slow his pace to mine, and he's better at avoiding the hazards too. A couple of times he has to yank me out of the way of a deliverybot as it mounts the sidewalk. There's nothing left of the old place – I was right – not even the name of the road. I call up AR for the year 2000 and he's chuffed with that. We can position ourselves on the exact spot where the old place stood. It's now the lobby of a multipurpose tower block, office and residential with a restaurant on the top floor. It's good to be in out of the wind and I take him up for lunch. He turns a few heads, in his handsome new coat, but I'm not sure he notices.

Needless to say, he's rapt by the view through the 360-degree glass, so that's cool, and we spend a happy half hour checking out various landmarks and tracing the line of the river between towers. He's miffed that he can't see St Paul's and wants to know what happened to London's protected skyline. I laugh. 'Money! Money's what happened to it, Dad!'

We sit down with our coffee and he suddenly asks, 'How long have you been married to Meryl?'

'Eight years.'

'You were married to someone else before, weren't you?'

'Zoe. That ended badly.' So badly I never want to see or hear her or her squalling brats ever again.

He nods. 'Your life – three wives—'

'Four. Don't forget Brenda. She's the one that got away.'

He rolls his eyes. 'It's been very different from mine.'

I laugh. 'Better, you reckon?'

'Maybe so. I think we were very – my generation was quite constrained. If you were married, it was for life. If you had a job, you stuck to it.'

'But Dad – you got divorced!'

He nods. 'Oh yes. But it was rather shameful. To me, at least.

And I never – after your mum left, I never had anybody else.'

He must have been what, forty-five? Christ, I met Meryl when I was fifty-two. 'But you could have done? If you'd wanted?'

He shrugs. 'I didn't think I had any right. I'd had a good marriage and a son and then she left. I didn't feel I was entitled to more.'

'But, Dad,' I laugh but my heart is aching for him. 'You were still a handsome young dog.'

Now it's his turn to laugh.

'You could have got a girlfriend easily enough.'

'Maybe. I don't know. I don't think I wanted that. I wanted your mum to come back.'

'That's really sad.'

'Yes. For a long time I thought she would. *It's just a fling*, I told myself. *We married when she was too young. She never got to sow her wild oats.*'

'You were waiting for her.'

'I was waiting for her. And I suppose life was passing me by. I got cranky, didn't I?'

'Well you did when I'd been to stay at Mum's.'

'I was jealous. I wanted you to tell me what was happening, and naturally you wouldn't.'

'Look – fathers and sons have to fight.'

'That's true. But I wish I could have been, I don't know, more open? More able to understand what you were up to. I mean, all that band nonsense – that's what I thought it was, nonsense. That you'd have to grow up and see sense and get a job like everybody else. And I was wrong.'

I'm thinking of the stroppy beer-swilling dirty little stop-out I was and how I despised him. 'I might not have tried too hard to help you understand, Dad.'

'No. But I – ah – loved you.' Oh Lord, he's embarrassed. Embarrassed to use the L word. My poor old dad. 'I loved you more than anyone in the world and all I did was tell you off.'

'It's one reason I wanted to bring you back. I don't think either of us saw the best in each other. We were at really different places in our lives, weren't we?'

He nods. Smiles. 'Yes. And now the tables are turned.'

In our touchy-feely chat this hits a rather creepy note. Still, I guess this is the conversation we needed to have. 'Are we all done here? Where next?'

He wants to carry on exploring but I've had enough of walking. I suggest we take the auto for a more extended trip around central London, and drive past some of the old places he wants to see, like Westminster and Trafalgar Square. I don't tell him how much it costs per minute to take an auto through central London, and frankly I don't even care. He's happy staring out at it, and I'm happy he's happy. The only bum note is when he asks to go to the place in Clapton where he used to have his allotment. 'Spring Lane, by the river,' he keeps saying; 'near Walthamstow Marshes.' It's an estate, of course, and he's disappointed. And it brings us both down.

When we get home late afternoon, he tells me he'd be into catching up with the world onscreen and, yes, he's figured out how it all works, so I head back into my studio. I'm tired but I want to fool around with 'London Bridge Is Falling Down', I had a cute little idea while we were driving. It's a relief to shut the door on him. No one can be sociable 24/7. But you know what? This is how he's *always* made me feel; like I want to escape. That's why I didn't get on with him in my twenties, even when I was supposedly an independent adult. He's too particular. Too thorough. He has to check out all the old things exactly, he can't just take my word that it's all gonna be different. I mean, finding the location of the old house was OK, but the allotment was definitely de trop. And he can rabbit on about being open, and not thinking the band's nonsense, but he's really not into music. Which is even more of a bummer than it used to be. I'd imagined playing some of my best tracks to him but it'd be embarrassing. It wasn't his thing back when I was twenty, and it isn't now either.

I poke my head above the parapet at 6.30 because it's time for a preprandial and everything works better when I'm oiled. Nobody in though. Kay reports that Anton and Meryl have gone to the gym. Perfect. I can enjoy my G & T in the company of Muddy Waters and Little Richard on the headphones.

When they get back he comes and throws himself into the corner sofa. He's already moving differently – less like my dad and more like the strapping youth, his body. 'Have you been to that gym?' he asks me.

'Why?' I say cautiously. I know how keen Meryl is to get me there.

'What they wear!' he says. 'Especially the women. I mean, it leaves nothing to the imagination.'

I have to laugh. My poor old dad, lusting after an array of fit young things in lycra.

But he carries on. 'They're all so friendly. It's wonderful.'

'Friendly to you?'

'Yes!'

Can he really be so naive? 'Dad, haven't you looked in the mirror? They're flirting with you. You are one handsome guy!'

'Oh.' Now he's embarrassed. 'I hadn't thought of that.'

'Enjoy it while you can,' I joke, 'you sexy beast!'

'Ah well,' he says, leaning forward to fiddle with the scented candles Meryl has just placed on the coffee table, alongside our drinks. 'You know why I wanted to go to the allotment this morning?'

'No.'

'You don't remember the bonfire?'

'What bonfire?'

'Our November the fifth. On Walthamstow Marshes.'

Suddenly I do. Christ, I haven't thought about that for years. The bonfire!

I was just a nipper, eight or nine maybe? Desperate for a proper Guy Fawkes night. I remember him telling me how it was when *he* was a kid, how they made a guy out of his dad's old clothes stuffed with newspaper, and dragged him round the streets getting money off people for fireworks, and built a bunty in the brewery yard. I was jealous as fuck. But none of my mates wanted to do it; the stupid arses said it was too cold, and the miserable old git at the newsagents wouldn't even sell us bangers. I tried Jimmy and Mick and the people who weren't even my friends, but no one was having any of it. Mum said, 'NO fireworks! You'll blow your bloody hands off.' And that was that. I was having a major sulk when Dad asked me to go to the allotment with him. Why would I? It *was* cold and it's not as if there was anything to do there. Then he winked and said, 'I'll make it worth your while.'

So I went. I remember sitting on the bus glaring out through the condensation dribbles on the window, thinking it wasn't fair, and when I was grown up I was going to have a MASSIVE bonfire with a hundred rockets all going off at once.

The allotment was bleak and empty, with dead brown plants tied to canes. They had tiny wizened green tomatoes on. Dad's plot was neat but nothing special. I remember rows of Brussels sprouts. Why anyone would want to eat stuff that smells like that is still beyond me. And at the far end was Mr Watkins's falling-down shed, that Dad hated with a vengeance. The roof-covering, which was black tarry cloth, was ripped and flapping in the wind, and there were gaps in the walls where planks had slipped or were hanging skew-whiff on one nail. Dad blamed that shed for his veg being later than everyone else's, because it shaded them. He blamed it for being bang on the border of his plot, so he lost six inches of cultivation because he couldn't dig right up to it in case it collapsed on him.

The place was deserted. No one else was mad enough to go gardening on a freezing foggy night in November. But the old man's buzzing. 'Right then, Ricky my son,' says he. 'Here's the plan. We're going to demolish that bastard shed plank by plank and drag it over to the marshes and build a bonfire.'

I remember gawping at him. I was only a kid but I already knew he was the most law-abiding guy I would ever meet.

'You want a bonfire, don't you?'

'Yes, but—'

'But nothing. It's rotten, it's an eyesore, it's dangerous. We'll be doing the man a favour.' Then he opens his rucksack and takes out a hammer and a hacksaw and the little axe Mum uses for kindling, and we're off.

First he kicks in the door, and we can see there's nothing inside but some mouldy sacks and a heap of flowerpots. 'The trick is,' he tells me, 'to get it to collapse on *his* side and not onto my soil. Stand back.' Then he whacks the corner posts with his axe, and pushes with all his weight against the end wall.

Well it went down like a house of cards. He gave me his gardening gloves which were massive and thick and grey like asbestos, and said I had to wear them cos of splinters, and we started bashing and dragging the planks and panels off the frame.

Weird how I'd forgotten it. Cos it was a big day for me and my dad. Grinning like maniacs, with great clouds of steam billowing out of our mouths, heaving and ripping that old shed to bits. Glancing nervously over our shoulders to check the coast was clear. And then piling everything onto a tarp he had stored in his little locker, ready to drag down to the marshes. That was down the big footpath and over the bridge and I was petrified someone would try to stop us. But he shook his head. 'It's rubbish, son, we're just clearing some rubbish. Two loads should do it.'

It was bloody hard work dragging it over the allotments and along the footpath. When we got to the bridge he had to pull some of it off and leave it by the playground. His face was dark red and his hand was bleeding from a nail, and he looked so mad and funny I couldn't stop laughing. 'It's alright for you,' he grunted. 'Here. Give me a hand.'

There was mist all along the River Lea, and it was getting dark. Up ahead I could see scraggy black trees and bushes silhouetted against the dark blue sky. 'I can't see,' I told him.

'We need to get further away from the park. What's up? You scared?'

'Course not.' But I was. On the other side of the river the mist was thick and low to the ground so you couldn't tell where the bushes ended and the mist began. And the water there was deep and black. Not that I could see it but I knew it must be somewhere about; they wouldn't call it the Marshes for nothing. He kept going, heaving and grunting and hauling the tarp over the bumps in the path and me not pulling at all, just holding the corner so I wouldn't get left behind, until finally he was satisfied. Then we had to tip the splintery wood off the tarp and head back for the bridge, to do the whole operation all over again.

By the time we were done I was knackered and starving and cold as a witch's tit. He heaved and kicked the timber into a heap, and held his cigarette lighter to the end of a plank. It wouldn't take, of course, and he had to dig in his rucksack for his newspaper to get the fire started. He passed me a packet of chocolate digestives. Never has a biscuit tasted so good. He kept one panel out of the fire for us to sit on, and told me to watch out and not get any nails up the bum. We squatted on the panel, chomping on the biscuits and staring at the flames as they began to creep and then leap over the wood.

And that was it. Me and Dad in the pitch black, with the dancing heat of the fire blasting our faces, and the yellow and orange flames roaring up at the sky, and the wood spitting and crackling and throwing off thousands of red sparks that glittered and then died in the smoke. Better than fireworks. The smell of the smoke was strong and dry and grey, billowing up, and underlit to a sinister orange by the flames. When you followed it up with your eyes you could see sheer blackness above, with just a handful of pale winking stars impossibly far away. I looked at Dad and his eyes were shining in the firelight and watering with the smoke. It was the bonfire to end all bonfires.

'Thank you,' I say. 'I do remember, now you say. It was fantastic.'

He nods. 'Sentimental, but I thought it was worth revisiting – if it had still been there. Your mother would have killed me.'

'What about the shed man? Watkins?'

'Dunno. Nothing was ever said.' We laugh.

Meryl joins us and we move to sit at table. His eyes are shining now, in the candlelight; well so are Meryl's, and I guess, my own. We are all bright-eyed. I'm a lucky man. I love my wife and I love my father. They're both cheerful and expansive if not a little tipsy, and with good food and animated chat the evening passes in no time and I roll into bed very happily at 11. I'm shattered, and I never even hear Meryl come up.

Day 6

But next morning when I wake and she's already up and dressed, I start to feel a little tetchy. I find her at breakfast. 'Hey, babe, feels like I haven't exchanged two words with you since the old man arrived.'

She laughs. 'I thought you wanted to spend time with him one on one? And then, I was watching you, and I thought what you *really* wanted was for me to take him off your hands!'

She's the sharpest knife in the box and that's half of why I love her. And the other half is definitely not anyone's business but mine. 'Spot on.'

'So, I've arranged to take him out for the day today.'

'For the day? Where to?'

'You want to come along?'

I'm thinking she is going well beyond the call of duty here; and anyway I don't mind going if she's there because she makes chatting with him seem easy. But it turns out she's been quizzing him about what he likes and found out about his old allotment and how he's really into plants. So she's gonna take him to Kew where they have a botanic garden and an arboretum and a tropical house. 'There's millions of plants,' she enthuses, 'which is great for him and great for me because as you know, honey, I'm on the lookout for some inspiration for the Cork garden.'

The Cork cottage has a decent-sized garden. I didn't pay much attention to what was there last summer, because I was busy fixing up a studio in the stables. But I do remember her saying she wanted it landscaping. 'Aren't we getting a gardener to do that?'

'No! No, Rich, I want to plant it myself. It's my project for the summer, don't you remember?'

I don't remember but I don't want to sweat it, there's an ever-growing list of shit I don't remember, and if she wants to be inspired by plants then who am I to stop her? They can't sing, they can't dance, and worst of all, they're green. 'Sure. Sure thing, ho-oneeee.'

'Right. You would never in a thousand years come and look at plants with me. Anton's cool with it. Relax! You got a day off.'

I get Kay to bring me Buck's Fizz and a mushroom omelette, to celebrate. I have to run it all past the clinic, give them Meryl's ID and the destination and route, but it's under twenty K so they're alright with that. My dad emerges damp and glowing from the pool, where he's swum an outrageous number of lengths, and Meryl tells him to be ready in an hour. Then she trots off to have her nails done. He and I settle down to some serious eating.

'You're a lucky man,' he tells me, when he pauses for a sip of tea. It's an uncanny echo of my thought at dinner last night.

'You mean Meryl?'

'Everything. I look at you and I think, what was I doing in my fifties? Feels like I gave up on life.'

'Come on! You did your allotment, didn't you? You used to go for a pint down the King's Head. And you must have watched every game Arsenal ever played!'

He laughs. 'You're scraping the barrel, aren't you, Rick? Or maybe taking the Mickey.'

'It's different times,' I tell him. 'We're not comparing like with like, are we? I mean, the way you kept a flame alight for my mum – well that's impressive.'

He shrugs. 'Or stupid. I mean, I look back on how strait-laced I was and I ask myself, why? Why didn't I let myself go and have a bit of fun?'

'The moral code you were brought up with. It's hard to chuck away your parents' values.'

He bursts out laughing. 'Well you should know!'

Touché.

'Seriously, Rick,' he leans forwards, his fingertips pressed together in that steeple shape he does with his hands. 'Seriously, do you regret any of the bad-boy things you did? Do *any* of them keep you awake at night?'

I have to ferret about for something. 'I regret not seeing Charlie when he was Derren's age. But I wasn't ready to have a kid then. I wasn't living a child-friendly life.'

'No. And you don't regret leaving his mother? Or all the – relationships – you had?'

Relationships is a bit of a coy term for my six-groupies-a-night phase, but I can get behind his sentiment. 'Hell, no! Freedom rocks! What's that Blake poem? *He who binds to himself a joy/ Does the winged life destroy/ But he who kisses the joy as it flies—*'

He's nodding. '*Lives in Eternity's sunrise.* Well there we are.'

'So do you . . . ?' It's not fair to ask him. But he's already on it.

'Regret? Yes, Ricky, I do. I regret being so strict with you. I regret not talking – more honestly – with your mother.'

'I'm sorry, Dad. I didn't – I don't want you looking back and regretting. I want you to have a ball and enjoy every single minute.'

He smiles. 'I am, don't worry. I am enjoying every minute. I'm *grabbing* life by the throat!' He makes a comical awkward grabbing gesture.

'You do that, Dad. Go ahead and grab all you can and stuff it into these two weeks. I'm only sorry it's not longer.' That's not strictly true, though of course it is when I imagine myself in his shoes for a moment.

'You have nothing to be sorry for, Rick. This is a wonderful opportunity you've given me – seriously son, I can't thank you enough. You and Meryl have both been so kind . . .'

I put on a little girly voice; 'Aw shucks, Paw, now you're embarrassin' l'il ol' me.'

He rises to his feet and clasps my shoulder as he passes me on his way out of the room. The warmth and firmness of his clasp shock tears into my eyes. This is my dad; he can *touch* me. And I'm going to lose him all over again. Poor bastard, poor son of a bitch. For the first time I think how hard it will feel when I have to take him back to the clinic on day 14.

My day is quiet and slow. I lay down the couple of tunes I've been tinkering with, to run past my agent, Tony. I connect with the housebot in Cork and get some pics of the garden sent over for Meryl. I check my royalties; I get a new spring jacket delivered. I'm waiting, with a fresh drink, for the happy wanderers to return around 7 p.m. when Meryl calls to say they've walked miles today and they're starving so they're stopping off to eat en route.

'You doing OK? He hasn't bored the pants off you?'

'He's fine. We've been doing serious botanical research.' There's a laugh in her voice.

'OK, hon. Catch you later.'

'By-eee.'

I eat dinner on my lonesome and settle down to some serious listening. When I open my eyes with a jerk (yeah yeah, I drifted off) it's gone 11. Those cats are still out. I'm reaching for my phone when I hear auto doors slamming and laughter from outside. They roll in on a blast of cold air and alcohol, rosy-cheeked and full of cheer, giggling over some guy in the pub who wanted to know their life stories.

'Anton's is really interesting,' Meryl starts to tell me. 'He was born in Sudan—'

'I think we said Somalia,' he interrupts.

'And he was in their youth Olympic team for – for jumping?'

'Hurdling. But sadly for me I sustained a serious leg injury while pursuing a lout who had robbed my grandmother of her hearing aid.' They both collapse in giggles; clearly drink has been taken.

'Sounds fun,' I say.

'Nightcap?' asks Meryl, and she's pouring the cognac before I can get a word out. And we sit there and drink and the pair of them are gabbling so fast I'd need to drink three bottles straight down to catch up. The cautious dad I had seems to have vanished. Meryl is here with a handsome, humorous young stud. We sit there for the best part of an hour and I can't get a word in edgeways. I drain the bottle and blow me if Meryl doesn't open another.

'You abandoned your health regime, honey?' I could bite my tongue out for saying that, like some shitty old killjoy. So I try to laugh it off, give her a peck on the cheek and head for bed, ignominiously bumping into the door on my way out. Sourpuss, I tell myself, miserable old fart.

Day 7

And when I wake up at 2.30 and she isn't in bed I am stone-cold sober. I crawl out of the bed and creep to the top of the stairs. They are still talking. I catch the lower rumble of his voice, and her quick light replies. They aren't laughing like hyenas anymore, but there's no law against talking. I stand there feeling cold and ashamed, then take myself off back to bed.

In the morning Meryl *is* in bed, snoring and deaf to the world. I reckon it'll take her till midday to sleep it off. I get a reply from Tony thanking me for the tunes and saying he won't have time to listen properly till the weekend, which is bullshit and means he doesn't like them. I could kick myself for not running them past Meryl first; she's got a good ear, and I generally do. But when the hell could I have played for her, in the last week? I still have the aftertaste of that sick jealous feeling in my mouth, and

I tell myself I'm being a jerk. My dad's having fun with Meryl because she's always wanted a little boy to look after. He's *my* responsibility for Chrissakes, not hers.

I call Charlie and ask to take Derren out for the day again. We'll go someplace the kid has never been. The seaside! That's where you go on family outings, the seaside. I'll take him and my dad to Brighton. The kid has never seen the real sea. And if the sun deigns to shine we can collect a bucketful of pebbles on the beach. And if it doesn't, we can still walk down the pier and visit the olde-worlde amusements that will be right up my dad's street and will likely amuse a two-year-old as well.

My dad looks a bit peaky, but to be fair to him, he is up and about well before Meryl. 'I'm sorry,' he says, 'we really hit the bottle last night. I'm afraid I'm not used to it. But we had a great time. Thanks for lending me Meryl for the day.'

Weird. He isn't even talking like himself anymore. He's picking up some kind of trans-Atlantic mash-up, from Meryl. 'I don't *lend* her,' I say. 'She's a free individual. She chooses how to spend her time.' It comes out heavier than I intended so I laugh like it's a joke, and the poor guy looks a bit bewildered. His head must be banging. I tell Kay to give him a big fry-up, best cure for a hangover.

We pick up Derren at lunchtime. I sit in the back with him and we play peekaboo behind our hands, then I pretend to hide under my coat and after he's pulled and poked at the coat for a while he starts to call, really worried, 'Gan-pa? Gan-pa?' I suddenly pull the coat down and he absolutely roars with laughter, like it was the funniest thing a man ever did. God, that kid can turn your mood around on a penny, I love him to bits.

My dad is pretty quiet in the front so I motion to Derren to keep schtum, and reach out my fingers like a spider creepy-crawlying up the back of Anton's seat towards his head. When I tickle him he swears and swats at my hand, and Derren chortles.

'Sorry.' Anton does not turn in his seat. 'Sorry, I didn't know what that was.'

'Just look at this kid, he's splitting his sides.'

'I can't turn round just now. Actually, do you mind if we stop?' His voice is pinched and I realise something's wrong. I tell the auto to pull onto the hard shoulder and Anton shoves the door open only just in time. He is sick as a dog. Poor little Derren has the best view in the house and it frightens him badly, the sight of his great-granddad's fried breakfast and cognac and red wine all spouting out in a great Technicolor yawn. I pass Dad some baby wipes and the kid's water bottle and he wipes his shoes and swills his mouth. 'Sorry. Sorry, I've never been much of a drinker.'

'Hey, Dad, no sweat. I seem to remember pulling a stunt like that when you picked me up at the Red Lion, about forty-five years ago.'

He smiles forlornly and edges back into his seat, slams the door and we drive on. I give Derren a kiddy fruit bar to cheer him up, and in the peace and quiet I suddenly think, shit. This is not my old man's body. What if he's done some damage? What if it's not just alcohol poisoning, but something worse, and this beautiful black body is starting to crash and burn?

'You feeling better now?' I ask him, and he mumbles that he doesn't know. 'Is it motion sickness? You want us to stop a while?'

'Yeah. Maybe.' I instruct the auto to pull off at the next service area, and we take a little walk. Derren loves *one-two-three-whee!* So we take a hand each and walk and swing him between us. We do a couple of circuits of the picnic area then I ask Dad if he'd like a cuppa.

'Oh dear no, that would set me off again.'

Shit. 'You check in with the clinic this morning?'

'Lord, no, I forgot.'

Great. I've paid enough for this joyless experience without lining up penalties for him breaking the rules and making himself sick. 'OK, use my phone. Call them now.' I take Derren off to buy a drink, but my dad catches up before we can reach the dispenser. He's holding out the phone.

'They want to know where I am.'

'That's ridiculous. The phone can tell them where you are.'

'Yes but they want to know where I'm *going*.'

I swear, he's addled his brain. I take the phone from him. 'Hi, yeah, we're going to Brighton.'

'Sorry sir, that's not permitted. We need the Host and Tourist to stay within a twenty K radius of the clinic. It's in the agreement you signed.'

'But it's just a day trip. We'll be heading home this evening.'

'Sorry sir. Twenty K is the limit.'

Great. I take a look at Anton. His black face glistens with a sheen of unhealthy sweat; it's probably best to call it a day. Take him home and put him to bed. 'OK, message received. We'll turn around.'

'Thank you, sir.'

It's little Derren I'm sorry for; he was gonna see the sea. 'I'll take you on the boating lake at Regent's Park,' I tell him. 'While Anton has a nap.'

And that's what we do. I tried to take Dad on a fun day out but there you go. It was not to be. *I* have a fun day out, with Derren. We feed the ducks, we splash about in a pedal boat, I change his pants when he has an accident, and we celebrate with ice cream. He falls asleep all sticky and content in the auto going home. I hand him back to Charlie at teatime, and head for home myself.

Meryl is out and my dad's asleep and I'm knackered, so I doze in front of an old film till it's time for dinner. The three of us have a pretty subdued meal. They are both quiet and neither of them drinks. But my dad says he's feeling better and my anxiety drains away.

After dinner I ask Meryl to listen to my new tunes, and my dad settles down to a session in VR, and everything is pretty much back to normal. She likes the London Bridge one; the other, less so, and I stay awhile in the studio tinkering at it. There's something wrong with the transition, there's something dull and flat that I can't figure how to lift. I try one way and then another and the time ticks by, till I finally give up on it and go for a refill. The screen is off and the sitting room is empty. When I go up to our room Meryl is fast asleep and I guess my dad is the same. Well, it is knocking on midnight. I have a nightcap and creep into the warm bed beside her. She smells as sweet as a bunch of roses.

That's the last thing I remember, how sweet she smelled. I wake needing a piss at 4 a.m. and she is gone.

Gone gone gone, she is gone from my bed.

And this time I do know. What you know in the small hours is the truth, isn't it? That's why it hits you so stone-cold in the guts. It's the truth, with no pretty sunshine or birdsong to soften it, it's the cold dark truth and your body knows it. My wife is sleeping with my father. I don't even need to go creeping across the landing or listening at the door. I don't need to, but of course I do. And I hear what I don't need to hear; her sweet little rising gasps; his grunts, his groan. I go back to my room and I cry like a baby.

Day 8

No more sleep for me this night. I hear the running water, when she takes a shower in the guest room; I hear her creeping back into my bed at dawn. I hear her little feigned snores when I turn painfully in the bed, pretending to be wakening. I take my clothes and dress on the landing. The house is quiet as the grave.

Kay gives me a cup of tea but I can't stomach food. I go out in the auto and programme it to drive for an hour; I sit and stare at the early morning streets, the bots and deliveries, the dark tower blocks against the pale sky, the silvery sheen of the Thames and the darkness of the narrow streets. My dad with my wife. My wife with my dad. There's nothing much sicker I can think of.

I count up the days. He has six left. Could I send him back

early? Could I put the bastard in the auto and tell it to take him back to the clinic? And ring Butler and go, 'Here, we're done. Wake up the dude who owns this fine body, and send my old dad back to hell'?

What would I say to Meryl?

It's not his fault, it's hers. She's my wife. She knows who he is, she knows what she's doing. She said she was *sorry* for him. She said he was like a little boy. You can make every excuse in the book for him. If I had a twenty-year-old body and one week to live, I'd spend it fucking like a rabbit. And there is no one on earth more fuckable than my wife.

On the other hand – his son's *wife*? If it was me I think I might take myself further afield, and not foul the nest that sheltered me.

Well. He couldn't go out alone. I signed that I wouldn't let him. He couldn't go out alone so he hit on the one woman within reach. The woman on offer; *thank you for lending me your wife.* Right. I wasn't planning on that type of loan, Dad. She chooses for herself.

She's chosen for herself. So now I know where I stand. Classic cuckold, eh? The foolish fond old man, the sugar daddy who'll pay for his pretty young wife to play gardener in Cork and buy the fanciest clothes anyone will design for her, and go to the most exclusive gym in London. And he will foot every bill and be grateful for his weekly fuck. I'm her *old* man. And my dad is young. Why should she give a damn?

Oh Meryl, Meryl hon-eee. Honey pie, I loved you so.

I can't send him back. It would be murder. Parricide, even.

So what in hell can I do? I try to put the ducks in a row. Meryl and I are finished. Kick her out now? Then I'll have the old man all guilty and hangdog, with the added problem that there's no one to take him off my hands and I've got to spend six days with the cunt.

Pretend I don't know? Grit my teeth and get through six days, let him have a whale of a time and kick Meryl out when he's gone? That's the sensible option but I'm not sure I can stomach it. Not right under my nose.

I get out of the auto at Regent's Park and walk around. The sun's just coming up and there are joggers and health fanatics doing their stuff, and mist hanging over the silvery lake where Derren and I pedalled our boat so innocently and happily yesterday. There are little pointy yellow and purple flowers in the grass. Blossom on the bare trees.

I want to punch him. I want to slap her face and make her cry. I want to walk into the lake until the cold water closes over my head.

After a bit I'm just blank. Walking with an empty head. Walking across the wet grass. It's better not to think. Gradually I realise I'm not gonna know what to do until I do it. Why the hell am *I* out here in the early morning trying to figure out what to do, when this mess is entirely of their making? Let them figure out what to do. If they think it's so great betraying me, let them work out the next move.

I'm hungry. I head back to the road. When I let myself into the house Meryl's alone in the kitchen so it's easy.

'Where have you been so early, honey?'

'I went out to ponder why you think it's OK to fuck my dad.'

Her smile dies. 'Rich – Richard, it's not your *dad*. I know it's wrong but he's not your dad.'

'Oh but it is, honey. It's my dad's brain and my dad's memory and you know he's my dad and he knows you're my wife.'

She starts to cry. And then I'm crying too which is the last thing I want the cow to see. So I have to go and lock myself in the studio. And that's that. I don't know what else to do. She'll go and tell him, no doubt, and then they'll do whatever they do. The money he's cost me floats back into my head and I have to remind myself that he must not be damaged. Can I hide in here for six days?

It's the first glimmering of a solution. I have everything I need: music, VR, sofa, the studio has its own washroom. Kay can bring me food when I want it. Give them the run of the house while I stay in here. Let them wallow in guilt and fuck themselves stupid and go to his-n-hers gym, I don't give a toss. My obligation to entertain him is absolutely over. *She* can deliver him back to the clinic.

So that's what I do. One or other of them knocks at the door from time to time, but not with much conviction. Meryl tries to call me, but I switch off my phone. I'm in solitary, which is a damn sight better than being in the company of treacherous hypocrites. I listen to everything I've recorded in the last five years, and it's not bad, not bad at all. In the small hours I get Kay to bring me cognac and Gorgonzola and crackers, and sausage and mash, and ice cream. I eat, drink, play music, sleep. My life is reduced to its essentials. Fuck them. Maybe I'll never go out again.

I check out the latest VR and spend seven hours on a Viking rape and mutilation spree. And after that I'm primed. I could take him apart. God, nothing would give me more satisfaction, than to smash something heavy into that big innocent wide-eyed face. I don't care he's big, I can take him, easy. I wouldn't give him a chance, I'd take him by surprise, bash him when he wasn't looking. No need to play fair with a cunt like that. When I allow myself to imagine doing it – hell, it's sweet.

9.

LUKE

In the clinic, it's Jeanette who takes the call from Meryl Kahn. And Luke himself who goes with the medibot to pick up the injured body. Anton's conscious but woozy. The bot administers pain relief and diagnoses concussion, broken nose and two broken fingers. They remove him from the house with all possible speed, followed to the door by a weeping Meryl. No sign of Richard.

Back at the clinic Luke watches impatiently as the fingers are set. Then he pauses the bot and pulls up a chair to Anton's bedside. 'What happened?'

'He attacked me. I was trying to apologise – it was a mistake, it was never meant to happen, I don't know *how* it happened. Meryl was just so kind to me—' Anton begins to cry.

'Just tell me how you got hurt.'

'Richard. He wouldn't let me in and I was knocking and suddenly . . .'

It is tediously slow extracting the information from him. It seems Richard punched him square in the face. Certainly his face is a mess. There's a cold compress taped over the nose but one of the eyes has already swollen shut. A broken nose is not the end of the world, Luke tells himself, but it does look bad.

'Did you hit him back?'

'No, oh no.'

'How did you hurt your hand?'

'I fell. It was the surprise, you see. I wasn't expecting—'

Quite. He wasn't expecting his sixty-year-old son to break his nose. 'You probably put out your hand to break the fall.'

Anton nods once, then grimaces with pain and stops. Gradually Luke gets the full story. Richard K's dear old father has been screwing his young wife. It would be funny, if it wasn't for the damage to Joseph's body. When all his questions have been answered Luke anaesthetises Anton and removes his ID from the host. This is Gudrun's fault – with her special pleading, her 'we must bend over backwards to please dear Richard K'. Well now he can show her what arses they are, father and son both.

Joseph is the person who matters here. When he awakens, Luke will run his cognitive impairment tests on the boy, hoping fervently that there's no lasting damage. Leaving sleeping Joseph in the care of the bot, Luke retreats to his office. It's Jeanette's home time and he tells her she can go, the situation is under control. But he can't settle, and after a few minutes of agitated pacing he checks the time in the Caribbean and calls Mehmoud.

Mem listens sympathetically. 'When is Joseph due home?'

'The day after tomorrow. But even if there's no other damage, I can't send him back in this state.'

'Does he live on his own?'

'With his mother.'

'OK, why don't you contact the mother now? Tell her there's been a slight hold-up but he'll be home in a week or so.'

'He'll still look a mess.'

'You can think up some excuse, surely? Along the lines of walking into a door?' There's a laugh in Mem's voice and Luke finds himself giggling. 'And give him compensation,' Mem adds.

'Yeah, well Richard K will get the bill for that. It's quite funny to think of an old guy like him flooring a strapping young boxer.'

'It could have been a lot worse. Imagine if Anton had fought back!'

'This is Gudrun's fault. She insisted I let Anton stay in London. He should have been over there with you.'

Mem hesitates. 'I guess you shouldn't let her dictate over things like that.'

'What Gudrun wants, Gudrun gets.' Luke glances at the internal monitor and is reassured by the sight of Joseph sleeping, his stats flowing evenly and regularly across the bottom of the screen. 'How's it going over there?'

'All good. I'm giving each of them half an hour after their daily check-up with the medibot. Getting to know them, picking up feedback . . .'

'Any complaints?'

'Not really. There are a lot of questions, though.'

'Go on.'

'Oh, I think you can guess. Will the hosts know what their bodies have been doing? Are they really allowed to have sex? Is it possible to stay longer than two weeks? That kind of thing.'

'You can deal with that. *Are* they having sex?'

'I think two of them probably are.'

'And you've told them they're protected?'

Mem nods. 'The nearest thing to a complaint is, why can't they contact their families?'

Luke laughs sourly. 'Right. Like Richard K and his dad.'

Mem nods. 'It's hard for them to take in, though. I mean Katya, she's the oldest, she died before the year 2000. Her husband will have died, and quite possibly her children too. But you don't want to raise that because then she'll be desperate to find out.'

Luke shrugs. He can't be doing with this sort of thing. Lucky that Mem is there to be thoughtful and sympathetic; well done Gudrun. 'All their partners will have died or remarried, and their children will have moved on. What's the point of having a second life if you waste it online trying to find out if anyone remembers you from the first?' he says.

Mem nods. 'People are addicted to communication. I suppose they might cause havoc online, actually, being officially dead.'

'Quite right. Anyway, the dead have no news. And I don't think the living have any news which is relevant to the dead.'

Mem laughs. 'They belong in separate realms.'

'Exactly. Earth and the Afterlife. As per the world's original design.' There's a little pause.

'I'd better go,' says Mem. 'It's nearly lunchtime.'

Luke checks. It will be another hour at least before Joseph wakes. 'Shame. Well, if you must.'

'Luke, I want to thank you actually, before you go.'

'Thank me?'

'For this. This perfect job. Beautiful setting, fascinating research – and a five-star hotel thrown in. Not to mention the brilliant colleague.'

Luke finds himself smiling back. 'You enjoying the food?'

'Yes! The crab and mango salad—'

'Yes, I've had that. It is good.'

Mem raises a hand in farewell and switches off. Luke sits smiling foolishly at the screen until he notices his own idiotic reflection and jumps up to go and take a look at Joseph.

Joseph wakes at four in the afternoon. All his test results are within the range of normal. He's distressed to be injured, though, and Luke has a hard time convincing him he fell out of bed.

'Why didn't you strap me down, man? Why didn't you look after me good?' The offer of more money calms him but he wants to talk to his mum.

'I'm sorry, Joseph, it's not allowed. But I've spoken to her from the office and told her you're doing well, and that there's a slight hold-up, but you'll be home in a few days.'

'You tell her I'm hurt?'

'No. I didn't want to worry her.'

'Oh. OK. Can I have some food?'

Luke knows there's nothing fresh available because there shouldn't be anyone here to eat it at this stage in the hosting cycle. Fresh food will be delivered the day after tomorrow. But there's frozen, and Joseph agrees to burger and chips and ice cream, which are all in the freezer. Luke instructs Gemma to wait on the boy. Once she has cleared the tray, he pops his head around the door to recommend screen time. Joseph is not placated.

'She's a bot, isn't she, that Gemma?'

'Yes, a state-of-the-art nursebot.'

'Don't you leave me with her. My mum's told me about them. I want a human nurse.'

'You've got me. I'm the doctor.'

'You staying here tonight?'

'You'll be asleep, Joseph, fast asleep.'

'Don't leave me here with bots. I want a person looking after me.' The boy is clearly agitated, and Luke promises to stay – marvelling yet again at people's preference for erratic human care over competent bots. He helps Joseph select a sports channel and administers the boy's sleeping meds at 21.30.

Luke has spent a few nights at the clinic in the past, working on problems or waiting for results; but this time he is filled with impatience. The boy will sleep for ten hours and Gemma can give him everything he needs. But Luke can't bring himself to break his promise, after the damage that's already been done. He's detecting a new synthetic smell in his office, which is irritating because he's given crystal clear instructions on the types of cleaning product he can tolerate. It must be down to the suppliers. He sends a memo for Jeanette to investigate. He writes up his records then decides on a whim to call his sister Hilary. Gudrun asked after her. What's she doing? He hasn't spoken to her for months.

She picks up straight away. 'Good timing, bro! I'm trying to pay my bills – glad to be interrupted. What news?'

She looks astonishingly healthy, given the disgusting pap he last saw her eating in the name of food. Mind you, they all take supplements on the estates. Hilary told Luke that, when he asked her how it was possible to nourish athletes on the frozen ready-muck sold by the ubiquitous Lianhua chain. She's toned and tanned and bright-eyed, her hair severely pulled back in a pony tail.

'I'm at the clinic. Stuck here overnight, with a transfer that went a bit wrong.' He fills her in on the story and then remembers why he doesn't call her very often.

'What the hell, Luke? Are you insane? You let one of them out into the real world without a securibot? These are human beings you're dealing with, not guinea pigs.'

In his own defence he outlines the multiple reasons Richard K had for *not* damaging his own father.

'Uh-huh,' snarks Hilary. 'Glad to hear you defending your teenage heart-throb. And are the rest going well? The other Tourists?'

'Very well. They're all on Gudrun's island and she's got a nice new medic looking after them there.'

Hilary shakes her head. 'It's so weird. These are all her old friends, aren't they? Has she got an endless supply?'

'Well I haven't got an endless supply of hosts, so I hope not.'

'Where d'you get them from?'

Luke sighs. 'It's hard. Because they have to be really healthy. They have to be physically fit and ideally aged under twenty-two. The transfer is liable to be dangerous to an older host. Their hearts need to be strong.'

'Healthy youngsters in a digital world. There's a challenge.'

He's never sure if she's mocking him or not. But he ploughs on. 'I got the first batch online, through a medical research website. But you get a lot of time-wasters, and too many of them want to know all the details before they'll even turn up.'

'How unreasonable,' she says, raising her eyebrows. 'Considering you only want to pimp out their young healthy bodies to dead millionaires.'

'Shut up. This second batch, I recruited locally, via a boxing club – that's where Joseph came from – and a fitness studio. But local is—'

Hilary shakes her head. 'Never foul your own doorstep. How much d'you pay?'

'Gudrun pays. Ten grand.'

'There must be hordes of people who'd be happy to go off-grid for a fortnight for ten grand.'

'Young, healthy, good-looking people?'

'Even so.'

'Who can keep their mouths shut.'

'Sure.'

'Well, tell me where to find them.'

'I'll think about it.'

Luke glances at Joseph's monitor and recalls he has not yet asked Hilary anything about herself. She delights in telling him he's 'on the spectrum' and he won't give her that satisfaction. 'So,' he says hastily. 'How are you? How's life at Blackrock?'

'Thought you'd never ask.' She gives him a small sarcastic smile. 'Fine. We're busy. We're doing long jump, high jump, pole vault, hurdling – it's good. I'm hoping to get some girls started on javelin before the summer. A field would be fantastic, but you can't have everything.'

'Are you really going to stay there?'

'Why wouldn't I?'

'I thought you might miss London.'

She shakes her head. 'If you saw how limited these kids' lives are – how there's nothing for them to do but VR – then I think even stone-hearted you would have a hard time walking away.'

'Right.'

There's a silence and Luke wonders if he has asked enough and whether he can end the conversation now. Hilary is his big sister and she always makes him feel small. But she starts to speak again, then hesitates, and stops. 'Luke?'

'Yes?' he says warily.

'You know you're looking for hosts?'

'Yes.'

'The people who come to my gym – well, most of them are fairly young. And fit. And they're certainly skint.'

It takes a moment to sink in. 'Wow! Brilliant!'

'D'you think? You'd have to promise me, really guarantee, that nothing could go wrong . . .' She hesitates. 'Luke? Nobody's been hurt before this, have they?'

'Of course not.' It slips out easily. Octavia/Ryan was a special case, irrelevant to this conversation.

She nods. 'I just thought, well, it's not as if they have jobs to beg time off from. They're the other end of the country to you. And that amount of money would seem huge, up here.'

'It's perfect.'

She laughs. 'You've turned into Robin Hood after all!'

'How so?'

'Giving to the poor. Taking from the rich, Gudrun, and giving to the poor estate kids.'

'Interesting. Cos if you think of *time* as the valuable commodity – rather than money —' He is remembering Mehmoud's elegant analysis, the day they first met. 'Then it's the other way round. Taking time from youngsters who'll only waste it anyway, and giving it to the time-poor.'

'Time-expired, you mean. How many do you need?'

'Six. I do them in batches of six.'

'Six is a lot, Luke.'

'Well how many do you think you could ask?'

'Maybe two or three, to begin with?'

Luke can see that three would be less noticeable than six. Three is a good number. 'Hilary?'

'Yes?'

'It needs to be confidential.'

'I'm not stupid.'

No, she's not stupid. She's a genius! 'I'll send you the contract and the info we used with the last batch.'

'OK.'

Before they even finish, Luke's thoughts are leaping ahead. Back and ahead. Didn't Octavia congratulate him on sourcing hosts from an estate? Ryan and Paula. *The impoverished young,* she called them. And Paula has built a dance studio on her estate. Paula, like Hilary, will know fit hungry youngsters. Paula can provide the other three.

Luke is so pleased with this development that he's pulling on his jacket and heading out before he even remembers Joseph. Ah, Joseph! He checks the boy's stats, double-checks the bot, and goes out anyway. Just for a breath of air. He'll be back in an hour or so, and Gemma is set to page him if there's an emergency. There won't be an emergency, the emergency's been and gone, and now he's had a solution to the hosting problem handed to him on a plate.

Deptford High Street is busy with overnight deliveries but the pavements, as usual, are empty. Luke is propelled by a need to catch up with himself. It's the same impulse he feels after an international flight. He needs to feel the journey through making step after step after step, to physically understand the changed scenery and the distance travelled.

He heads for the river. It's full tide and the water is deep and black and swirling, with gleaming highlights where London's orange glow is reflected back down from the overcast sky onto ripples and snags in the current. The biting wind has dropped and the air on his face feels warm with promise. Warm like the evening on Paradise Island. Warm like Mem.

Turning back, from shadow to light to shadow, from street to darkening street, he walks himself into a trance. There's the glowing rainbow sign of the club where he took Octavia, a lifetime ago. His head is as empty as the street when he pauses to unzip his too-hot jacket. And opposite him is the dimly lit doorway of the boxing club. He's been walking for more than an hour so he must have gone in a circle. But he grasps immediately why he's here; touches his pass against the securipad, and runs downstairs through the layers of sickly-sweet deodorant and sweat to the locker room. He can see the noticeboard from the doorway and yes, his card is still there. Two tall black guys are getting changed and packing up their stuff. One of them says, 'Night.'

'Night!' Then they're gone and the room is empty. Three tacks to remove, and the card is his. *Volunteers needed for medical research. Must be aged 18–22, in good health, and available full-time for three clear weeks. Good rate of pay. Ring -------*

He slips it into his pocket. As if it was never there. It feels like a sign that he can move on, with Hilary's volunteers. With Paula's. With Mem?

He hurries back to the clinic and lets himself into the softly lit, silent building. Like a waiting spaceship, he thinks, a bubble of the future alighted here in the dingy streets of Deptford. Joseph sleeps on, no events. Back in his office Luke realises he forgot to get food – the Vietnamese on the corner is his diner of choice – and makes do with a burger from the bot. As he crams it into his mouth he acts on his other, equally imperative need, and puts through a call to Mem.

'Hi.'

'Wow. You keep late hours!'

Luke shrugs. Mem is wearing a white hotel dressing gown and his skin is darkly golden. He's sitting in a pool of shaded light, Luke guesses, from a desk lamp. He looks like the romantic lead in a film.

'Luke? Is Joseph alright?'

'Yes, yes, he's fine. He's asleep.'

'Good.'

There's a little silence. Luke takes another bite. He realises he should say something. But then Mem speaks. 'The night's long, isn't it, when you're on call for a patient?'

'Yes.' Luke laughs in relief. 'That's it. Exactly. But am I keeping you from bed?'

Mem shakes his head. 'Something came up at dinner, actually – I was going to message you but it's easier to talk. They were asking about their contraceptive implants . . .'

Luke finishes his burger, wipes his hands carefully, and settles to watching the fine movements of Mem's delicately curved lips.

'. . . the question of what else is in their systems, via implants or their morning meds.'

'Vitamins,' says Luke.

Mem laughs. 'These people are cleverer than that.'

'Uh-uh. I know.'

'So now they're speculating about mood-enhancing drugs. And Katya – the one who was a doctor, remember? – after dinner she asked to see a pharmaceutical list of the ingredients.'

'Tell her you've asked me.'

Mem looks at him quietly.

'And I've forgotten to reply.'

Mem does that head-waggle thing, which Luke always thought was an Indian gesture, but which seems perfectly suited to Mem and the moment. Luke understands it as, *With all due respect I'm ambivalent on that but you're the boss.*

'I shouldn't ask you to lie,' he says. 'But—'

'But you don't want them to know what you're giving them.'

'What's the point? I mean, they're enjoying life, they've got a limited time. If they start agonising over whether their pleasure is real or drug-enhanced . . .'

Mem nods. 'It's one for the ethicists.'

'Maybe.'

'No, really. It is. Like a decision to have pain relief. The doctor can offer, the doctor can recommend. But at the end of the day the patient should chose.'

'Mem, this is so far removed from normal medicine that – I mean, did they choose to come back at this time? In these bodies? To this place? For this duration? They've got *no* choices beyond what to have for lunch. It would be hypocritical to pretend they have choice.'

Mem smiles. 'I disagree. You could give them a choice over those elements of the drugs that are not essential to their physical health—'

Luke interrupts, '—but *are* essential to their mental health? You think it would be a good plan for someone to spend their fortnight in catatonic depression, because they know they're about to die again?'

'I don't know.' He laughs. 'I really don't know, Luke. I mean, this will all be subject to ethical scrutiny once it's market-ready, won't it?'

'I suppose.'

'So I'm just playing devil's advocate.'

Luke nods. 'That's good. It's good to have someone clever to talk to.' The memory of Octavia flares for a moment.

Mem grins. 'It *is* good. I'm glad you called.'

'Me too.' Luke hesitates. 'Mem?'

'Yes?'

He doesn't know what to say and blurts out, 'I'm looking forward to seeing you again.' But Mem doesn't recoil. In fact he smiles, and his smile is like a flash of sunlight.

When Luke finally drifts off to sleep on his comfortable office sofa, the warmth of that smile heats his dreams.

10.

MARY

All the long, long time my son Joseph is away at that clinic my brain's turned to mush.

Then comes a beep from a man as if Joseph's doctor. The TV is blaring and I have to ask him to repeat again each single thing he says. I'm too busy looking under the cushions for the remote. That tricky gadget is ever lost when you want it. Eh-eh, he's telling there is a hold-up with Joseph coming home. So I ask what, is he sick? And the man says no, no, nothing serious. He is planning keep Joseph under observation another two–three days before he can pop home. Since I'm not wholly stupid I know observation is ever for a reason. 'Even me, I am a State Registered Nurse,' I tell him. 'I can observe him good at home.' But he doesn't listen me, just tells 'a short delay' again and my son will be home soon.

'But why are you delaying to send him?' Then I ask speak to Joseph himself but the doctor is already saying goodbye, just. He hang up before I finish and number withheld, no surprise to me there.

Eh-eh, what can I do nothing but worry. Worry even more, till I lose track of how many days Joseph is lost and how many extra already passed like that. I go about as if a bot doing all my chores on automatic. At night I wish for sleep to take me over like a hen. But sweet sleep is lost too. Then cometh the day.

I'm watching that nonsense gameshow with the remote in my hand. I ever hold it ready since that doctor call. And I hear the front door open. I hit *pause*. There's a woman in mid-air with her yelling mouth wide open and jumping into the pool which sometimes contains the crocodile and sometimes the treasure chest. I have that stupid image fixed in my head thank you very much, as I haul myself up out of my deep chair and put my legs on the ground. 'Joseph? Joseph?' My clumsy hands fumble to open the door, slow as slow.

'I am the one!'

'Joseph, you OK? Oh! Sorry, I am sorry.' My child's face is a funny shape, puffy under his eyes. His nose looks fat. And his arm in a sling. My eyes glued on him.

'Me I am fine, Ma. How are you?'

'Oh my sweet Lord, what they done to you?'

'Nothing serious. Just a couple of broken fingers.'

'Is it fighting you're coming from?'

He looks at me like I'm stupid then and I have to admit it's somehow not the brightest question. 'The doc says I fell out of bed.'

'Hospital bed? They have sides you can pull up. That's pure negligence, no patient ever needs to fall out of bed!'

'I guess they forgot to pull up the sides.'

'Eh-eh. Your nose, bambi—'

'Yeah. Boxer's nose!' Joseph grins and somehow I can draw my breath deep again. He is OK. I hug him from the side on account of his sling.

'Let me take a good look at you.' I lead him in the kitchen and sit him down and I can see into his face. His eyes are shining brown as fresh brewed coffee. He laughs at me.

'You expect my eyes to change colour?'

'Eh-eh, I don't know. Where did they put that thing? In your head?'

'Right here.' He pulls up his shirt and shows me a neat little bandage under his armpit. Clean, no redness or swelling and looks like one tiny incision was made, just.

'This one here?'

'Yup!' And he grins at me and pats his belly. 'Seems I even put on a little weight, with all that fine food.'

'Can you remember?'

'Nope. They injected me and pow, I was gone.' He looks like Joseph and he talks like Joseph. And now he jumps up and yanks open the fridge and starts to hunt food like Joseph. 'Eggs. Cabbage. Chillies. You fancy making me a Rolex, Ma?'

'You demanding for warm food?'

'I'm hungry.' He laughs. 'Hey, you even have tomatoes! They got nothing but burger and chips in that clinic.'

'They pay you?'

He fumbles his phone out of his pocket single-handed and pass the thing to me. 'Already in my account.'

'Tell me, just.'

'Ten grand, like they promised.'

'For me I think they owe you compensation for that fall.'

'You're on it, Ma. Guess how much?'

'You already got that too?'

He nods. 'Another five.'

'Hundred?'

'Thou.'

Well, I ha-ha'd at that. Five grand for two fingers that will heal as good as new and a kink in his nose? It's almost a shame he didn't suffer ever more damage.

Sweet Jesus forgive me for thinking such wickedness. Eh-eh, I'm so glad I don't know what to say. 'OK, the Rolex, you want green peppers in?'

He laughs again. Lord, I love that sound and brings balm to my soul. 'Been shopping? You counting on me popping home tonight?'

'No.'

'Why all this new food on a Friday?'

He's teasing me but I am perplexed. 'I ever think you're not coming back to me at all, Joseph. I thought you were lost for good.'

'Hard to believe. With you sitting in and the fridge full of my favourite things?'

'Even me I don't know how that happened. I went shopping but I never imagined you here to eat it.'

He laughs again. 'OK please.' He walks to check his screen and I cook for him.

It's been a month now since he came back to me. I changed my opinion on this possession thing. Joseph is kawa; healthy, happy, doing fine. My boy is extra bossy, but I don't complain cos that goes hand in hand with extra ambitious, just. He's enrolled at college and ever studying hard. He calls on his taata with an A* paper and his dad has agreed to house him for his course. I paid six months' rent up front. And we're planning a trip to Uganda come the summer, so Joseph can see his ancestors' country. Fifteen thousand pounds is mob money but we can surely spend it.

When I say that to my boy he replies, 'Could be more where that came from.'

'What? You can do this thing again?'

'I can ask.'

I think, why not, just? Now I know it's no kind of juju.

I am still puzzling my head over the soul of that dead man, though. How can a soul of the departed pop back to earth? I ask myself if the *memory stick* as Joseph terms it, comes without the soul? Can a mind return to life and the soul ever abide in Heaven with our Lord? I know Death uncouples body and soul, so is mind part of the body just? Somehow that makes sense, with the brain being physical. I have seen grey matter in a patient's skull, but never a soul. But can a man be alive without his immortal soul?

All this worry nearly makes me to go mad and I stay behind after Sunday service to quiz Pastor Jenkins. He preaches a rousing sermon on *I am the Resurrection and the Life* and when we sing the final hymn, as if the church catch fire.

Hail the day that sees Him rise, Alleluia!
To His throne above the skies, Alleluia!
Christ, the lamb for sinners given, Alleluia!
Enters now the highest Heaven, Alleluia!

Arms waving, feet stamping, tears coursing down our cheeks.

He hath conquered death and sin, Alleluia!

While we're singing and calling upon our dear Father, I feel my mind expand so wide I can even somehow understand that soul/body conundrum. But as if a flickering will-o'-the-wisp. As soon as my thoughts grab it, it vanishes. So, when the congregation departs I ask Pastor Jenkins. 'When our Lord Jesus was lying in that sorrowful tomb, and the stone rolled across to shut him in, you think his soul went to Heaven?'

'He rose again on the third day,' says Pastor.

'But before the third day. What happened on day two, just?'

'On the second day, the mortal remains of our dear Lord lay in the sepulchre.'

'But his soul? When he died on his cross, bless his sweet name, didn't his soul fly straight away to Heaven? The soul of Jesus Christ our Saviour cannot be stuck in some dark cave three days?'

The Pastor look at me over his spectacles. 'Why you asking, child?'

'I'm asking to know if, after the soul departs, it can come back.'

'In the case of our Redeemer, yes. And that is the miracle of the Resurrection, Mary. He took human form for our sakes, was crucified, dead and buried. But then he ascended into Heaven.'

'And then he reappeared to the disciples.'

'Indeed.'

'In his real body, isn't it?'

'That's right. *And while yet they believed not for joy, and wondered, he said unto them, "Have you here any meat?" And they gave him a piece of broiled fish, and of a honeycomb. And he took it and did eat before them.* Luke, chapter 24, verse 43.'

Oh, how clear I see it all on a sudden! My boy was patting his stomach and telling me, *Seems I even put on a little weight.* 'So, a soul can go up to Heaven and then return to earth, just?'

'The soul of Jesus Christ our Saviour, certainly.'

'How about Lazarus?'

He looks at me, puzzling his face.

'I mean, Lazarus was dead. So when Jesus raised him up, did the soul of Lazarus jump down from Heaven and pop back inside his body?'

'Our saviour said, *He that believeth in me, though he were dead, yet shall he live.* But is something troubling you, Mary?'

So, I put my trust in Jesus and tell him about my boy doing medical research and lending his body to a dead man's mind. And how I am ever worrying about that corpse's soul.

He listens to me patiently but with that little crease between his eyebrows that tells me he is displeased. When I finish, he asks me if my boy is home again?

'Eh-eh! yes, and rich. They paid him just like they promised.'

'Will you ask him to come and see me, Mary? Ask him to come today – as soon as possible.'

OK, now Joseph is not a great one for church. Lord knows I try and when he was a youngster I made sure he never cut a Sunday. But even me I can't force a grown man. You can bring the donkey to the water, but . . . Pastor sees me hesitate and he leans forward and takes my hand. 'This is important, my child. Your boy needs guidance. Our heavenly Father has more love and forgiveness for one sheep that goes astray, than for the whole flock that stays obedient.'

'He's not astray, Pastor,' I tell him. 'He's no churchgoer, but the Lord knows my boy is not astray.'

Pastor Jenkins smiles and pats my hand three times, which tells me he's ready to move on.

When I open the door to the flat, the air is thick with the sweet stink of ready meal. I ever tried to teach my boy some cooking. He's happy enough to eat *my* cooking but as if lazy when it comes to turn and turn about. His turn to make Sunday lunch and he's microwaving two packets of pap. But I hold my peace cos even in a good mood I have my work cut out to make him visit the Pastor.

'Why does he want to see me? Look, Ma, I don't interfere in your religion and you shouldn't interfere in mine.'

'You not practising any religion!'

'Exactly.' Oh, that boy sometimes too cocky for my liking.

'He needs to see you, Joseph. After lunch you go.'

'Why? What you been telling him?' He's busy shovelling that muck into his mouth and then all on a sudden he stops. 'You didn't tell him how I earned that money?'

'Eh-eh, I asked him about the soul of the man who dwelt in your body. One Christian to another, chatting religion.'

'You what?' He stares at me like I turned hyena, then he slams his fork into his meal and it splatters all across the table. 'You crazy? You want to give all that money back?'

'Get the cloth and wipe that up now-now. A pastor is confidential. As if a doctor.'

'I signed an agreement! I should never have told *you*, only you nag the living daylights out of me. What bit of SECRET don't you understand?'

'Hush your foolish mouth. The Pastor wants to talk with you, he's not about to go tale-telling all around Deptford.' But even me I am troubled now because what *does* the Pastor want to say? That it's wrong-doing, that Joseph must ever desist from this 'hosting'? We are already welcoming his payment from the next time.

Joseph is madder than a nest of hornets and he storms off,

where only God knows. I doubt to the Pastor and maybe that's for the best when in such a filthy temper. Which reminds me – cos he left without putting on – he never went back to that clinic to ask his new red jacket. I only bought that jacket in December and contains top-quality down. Why he forget to fetch it home is beyond me.

So I clean the table. And then I take a good look at my kitchen and the splashes of chilli sauce on the wall above the cooker. The crumbs and fluff down that narrow crack between washing machine and under-sink unit. You pay enough and you can buy a domestibot with attachments for every single thing. Ours is OK but we have the basic model, just. Sometimes it's good for the soul to fill a bowl with honest soap and hot water and do some scrubbing. I put a wrapper over my hair and I roll up my sleeves and clean that kitchen until as if brand-new. I stop fretting about Joseph or where he's gone. Even Pastor Jenkins or what he wants with Joseph. I concentrate on spots and stains.

Joseph comes bouncing in before I even finish. Grin as if the Cheshire cat. 'What you got to grin about?' I ask him.

'He don't believe it! Your clever Pastor thinks this whole story was invented by me, to pull the wool over your eyes!'

'Why? Careful, the floor's wet.'

He perches on a chair. 'Because, Mother, I am a criminal mastermind. I've made a fortune drug-running. Or maybe scamming bank accounts. And you are so gullible you have swallowed a ridiculous sci-fi tale which I have invented, to explain the source of my ill-gotten gains.'

'He thinks you spun me a tale?'

'Yup. And he told me not to take advantage of your innocence!' He helps himself to ice cream and swaggers off to his room with it, cock of the walk. Pretty soon his music starts thumping loud enough to make the walls shake. Well. I make a cup of tea and take the comfy seat. Eh-eh, let me also put my aching feet up on the stool.

OK, this is a good ending and Joseph stops being mad at me.

Plus, no danger of Pastor Jenkins asking some high-up in the church that thorny question I quizzed him, re souls returning after death. What if that set them thinking could be Body Tourism against God's will? As if it caused any harm. Our Lord commands: *Thou shalt not kill*, and *Love thy neighbour as thyself.* If ever you stick to those precepts you will surely reach to the place of the righteous.

The point I'm somehow not so happy is Pastor Jenkins's opinion of me. He really thinks me so foolish? So innocent? To have a criminal for a son and to believe the crazy lies he tells me? I think the Pastor owes me more respect than that.

Sometimes I think of the mzungu who inhabited my boy's body for two weeks. Eh-eh, perhaps he was old and bedridden for years as if on the geriatric ward, and died of misery and despair. Then I feel proud we can give him such a happiness to enjoy that fine young body and taste again the sweetness of his youth, bambi. I thank our heavenly Father for these blessings to us all.

11.

PAULA

It was easy being pregnant, I never had any of that morning sickness or backache or heartburn. It was like my body was totally in control. Mum took to Paul, and he and I slept together every single night, either at his or mine. I didn't hardly show till the sixth month, and I kept on with the dance no problem. In fact it wasn't being pregnant that made me stop – it was money.

The thing was, even with Mum's help I couldn't make the studio pay. There was too many bills; insurance, heating, lighting, water. It was eating up my ten grand. I bought ballet shoes and leotards online and sold them on but somehow I never made a profit. I had to pay Charmayne and Meghan for teaching, and they stopped my benefit cos I was running a business! So I had to pay my own food and rent. I didn't know about accounts and profits and losses and expenses, or paying tax, or any of that stuff. We'd been open a year, and suddenly there was nowt to pay the insurance with. Insurance was steep, of course – a studio like that in such a shit area – and I just couldn't risk it. So I had to close the doors. There was nowhere to turn, nobody has money on Coldwater – course not, or they wouldn't be there.

Now I was home all day I was ratty with Mum, so she went out a lot visiting her friend Mr Woodhouse. He was a crabby old bloke she met in the lift one time. He was the type of person who always pretends he hasn't seen you until you say *hello*. But she reckoned he was only shy, and very chatty once you got to know him. I said to Paul, maybe they'll get married and she'll stay there, then you can move in with me!

It was the end of May and roasting hot. I was heavy as a hippo with the baby, and nearly two weeks overdue. I remember Paul fetching me a bag of ice cubes from Lianhua and crushing them in a towel so's I could press it to my cheeks and neck, to stop myself from burning up. The baby wasn't coming and the studio was broke and I was beyond fed up.

Then Luke Butler gets in touch. Last time I heard from him was when I sent him pictures of the brand-new studio, to thank him. So when he congratulates me on my 'delicate condition' and asks me, how's it going? I can't help bursting into tears. Then I have to find some tissues and try to pull myself together, and he's not saying anything but tap-tap-tapping a pencil on his desk and the noise is going through me. 'Please don't!' I say, and he looks up like he's surprised to see me, and asks what's wrong?

So I tell him all about it – how I'm rubbish at making any money, and now I've got all these students and I can't even pay the bills. And he says, 'Well I rang to ask if you could help me out. Maybe we can help each other here.'

It's a long conversation and he's pretty hesitant, but what it boils down to is, he's got his Body Tourism on the road again, he can guarantee no one will get hurt, and he's looking for new hosts.

I can't believe he's asking me. After what happened to Ryan. It is totally beyond belief.

And he says he understands that and quite right too, but he still goes on talking. He knows there will be some of my dance students who'd make fantastic hosts. They'll be fit and young and strong, and they'll be eternally grateful for the money. Just because there was a terrible accident once, doesn't mean other people can't benefit from Tourism. He's not going to pressure me, but will I at least sleep on it? Because if I can see my way to recommending three hosts, he could take care of the dance studio bills.

I'm so mad when I come off the phone that I think I've pissed myself. (Which would be no surprise cos a monster-sized baby is not good for anyone's bladder control.) But it turns out my waters have broken.

Baby Ryan was born with the help of Paul, my mum and a nursebot. He was a beauty, with a mop of dark hair like Paul and the most perfect tiny fingers you ever saw. I couldn't take my eyes off him. Oh, that really was love at first sight! It was sweet to see my mum with him, with tears in her eyes, and even sweeter to see him in the arms of his daddy Paul. But sweetest of all to have him warm and solid in my own arms and to whisper to him, 'We made you, baby! We made you all by ourselves.' He latched on like a good 'un and, I know I was lucky, I never had a scrap of trouble feeding him.

Having a baby of my own suddenly made me curious about how did my mum manage with me? When I asked her, she laughed. 'Badly, is the answer, Paula. Very badly. I was only eighteen and my grandmother who I was living with wanted me to have an abortion. But that made me even more determined to have you.'

I thought she might tell me something about my father but she wouldn't budge an inch on that. She did say she left her grandmother's the day she got her first pay packet off Parks and Gardens, when I was still a tiny little squirt.

'Did she help you look after me?'

'Certainly not. You come from a long line of very stubborn women, my girl.'

Well, I realised then that I was pretty lucky to have both her and Paul to help me. I got some time off between feeds. I think I was high on the excitement of having the baby – I wanted to be up and doing, right off. I wanted to start dancing again and get my figure back. I let myself into the studio and paced about like a tiger in a cage. It was empty as my fridge on a Friday. How could I open it again? I couldn't open without insurance, I couldn't get insurance without money. Luke Butler's was the only cash on offer.

I started my post-natal exercises and did them on my own in the studio every day, rebuilding my fitness. I just about drove myself round the bend, trying to come up with other ideas for raising money.

It was the last thing in the world I wanted to do – send kids from Coldwater down to that evil clinic. And what did my head in as much as that was, I couldn't even tell anyone. I couldn't talk to Paul or my mum about it, I couldn't break my silence.

It was a great sack of stones weighing me down, every time I locked up that cage and walked away from the empty studio. Kids from my classes were messaging constantly; Yay! For the baby, and When are we starting dancing again?

It got so I knew I would agree and I begun to hate myself for it. I tried to run it past Mum, cos she knew the studio finances. I told her I'd had an offer from the clinic, to pay bills in return for recommending some kids for medical trials. Didn't tell her what, of course. She thought it was OK, 'as long as he can guarantee there are no risks'. Well that was no help to me, cos I knew from bitter experience what his guarantees were worth.

It was shit but what could I do? I twisted and I turned but there weren't no other way to go. It took the sweetness out of everything. At last I called Butler from the studio, where I was on my own, and told him how much cash I needed and how I wanted safety guarantees. And he said yes to everything. I done my deal with the devil. He asked for a boy and two girls and it was agony. Should I send students I really loved, or three who were pains in the backside? And how could I explain why I chose them? It'd be a great thing, to them, because of the money. Everyone else would be jealous.

That time were so bitter, with all this, it brought back the bad days after big Ryan's death. Yet my little Ryan was such a beauty I wanted to dance with joy. I was so confused I started forgetting things and losing things – my keys, my phone, my jacket. Mum called it 'new baby brain' and told me it was normal, but it wasn't and I knew it. I just had to get through it, get it over with, get life back to some kind of normal again.

In all this poor old Paul was getting a raw deal. Which was another thing that made me hate myself. He was such a lovely guy and he was proud as punch of baby Ryan, and he wanted to be with me. He wanted to come to the studio and watch me do my exercises. He wanted to sit by me when I was feeding Ryan. And I couldn't stand it – I needed some space. I was constantly giving him the brush-off and he was upset and afraid something was wrong, like did I have post-natal depression and did I need some meds? And all I wanted was for him to go away and leave me alone. I didn't want his love and kindness cos I knew I was behaving like a complete shit and the only love that wasn't complicated was baby Ryan. All he needed was his milk and a cuddle.

In the end I chose Asmara, Baz and Sarah. The girls because I reckoned they were more mature than most, and would be able to handle the money. Baz – well, if I'm honest, he came more into pain in the arse category. Anyway, all three of them were cock-a-hoop about being paid.

I reopened the studio four weeks to the day after baby Ryan was born, and taught sitting down for the first couple of weeks. The students were as keen as I was to get the place going again. As the clinic dates for the three volunteers came nearer I got more and more jumpy. I asked them back to the flat to sign the secrecy agreements and let them see I was signing exactly the same as them. I couldn't warn them – I couldn't tell them anything. I had to pretend I were as ignorant as them.

The eighteen days they were gone (cos they all travelled up and down together) passed slower than the slowest days of school when I first come to Coldwater. Staring out the window, getting nothing but *Poor effort* and *Repeat* from the bot, till I was bored senseless. Dreading break cos I'd be sitting on my own, practically wetting myself cos I was afraid of the bullies in the toilet – god, every minute lasted an hour. That's how it was when those three were down London. My only relief was baby Ryan. He yelled when he was hungry, he yelled when he was wet, and those yells connected me. When I fed him and changed him and cuddled him, he smiled. Simple. I didn't want nobody in my life but him.

It was weird when they finally did get back. In a way, an anticlimax. Cos they were all happy and excited about their money. They were like, 'Aren't we lucky!' And, same as when I come back from London, everyone wanted to know what happened and what did they have to do? And hit on them for loans. They were good, they never let out a word more than 'medical research'. Some of the others in top class wanted to know, could they do it too? I had to fob them off with, 'I don't know if any more will be needed', and act like it was nothing to do with me.

Asmara and Sarah were proper organised about their money. They planned to set up a dance school of their own and make it pay. They moved to Sheffield to stay with Asmara's uncle who was in the police. God knows if that worked out but at least they didn't come trailing back to Coldwater. Baz bought a motorbike – maybe he bought more than one. He and his mates took to racing around Coldwater. Which some people complained about the noise but to me it was a sign of life, at least, in that dead grey place. It started a fashion, and a few of the VR zombies unplugged their selves and dug out old bikes from god knows where and joined them.

For me that year was all about baby Ryan and the studio. I kept him with me as much as I could. I used to breastfeed him in the studio and put him to sleep there in his little buggy. Sometimes my mum would beg a go with him and I let her take him for two or three hours. Once he was weaned, she sometimes kept him in her room overnight. Paul went from being proud to being like a sullen kid himself. He was jealous. He wanted sex before I was ready and then he tried to suck my breasts. 'That's Ryan's!' I told him. 'What you doing? Stealing your own baby's milk?'

'Your tits were all mine before,' he whinged.

'Actually they're all mine, and my milk is for Ryan.'

He sulked. I tried to talk to him but it never solved anything. We'd get happy and relaxed for an hour or two but next morning he'd be just the same. He said I loved the baby more than him.

'Well of course I do. That's how it's meant to be. If mothers didn't love their babies to bits they wouldn't look after them properly and the human race would die out.'

'I love *you* more than *him*.'

'It's not a competition! It's different kinds of love, it's not rationed.'

'Yeah it is. He gets more than me.'

I was very irritated, I s'pose because what he said was pretty much true. I did prefer the baby's company to his. I did enjoy breastfeeding Ryan more than sucking Paul's cock. I did feel wide awake and happy when Ryan smiled at me, and suspicious and weary when Paul grinned. I dunno. I think it's normal.

Anyway, Paul was the fly in the ointment that year. He didn't ask to look after Ryan like my mum did, and it made me mad he didn't ask, so I didn't offer. I was glad we hadn't gone to all the hassle of moving in together. Between us the result was that he never hardly saw the kid and he resented that too.

Looking back – oh, looking back I can see only too well where I went wrong. But what I should say now, what I should admit, is that when Paul stopped pestering me and started spending time in VR instead, I heaved a sigh of relief. I was sad and angry too, because I did love him. I missed him. But being mean to him was almost like a way of punishing myself for all the lies about the clinic. I'd chosen to cut myself off from Paul by taking Luke Butler's money and signing that secrecy agreement. I didn't deserve Paul anymore.

Baby Ryan came to the studio with me every day. People learned to move around him, and anyway he was always happiest right up next to the mirror, pulling faces at himself and patting his own hands' reflections. The students loved him, he was like a chubby little mascot. In Advanced, Nadia especially was soft on him. Before that I never took much notice of her. Her dancing was precise without being showy, she was quiet like Asian girls sometimes are. But she was a natural with a baby, and she had no inhibitions. She'd kneel in front of him and get him to clutch her middle finger on each hand. Then he'd pull himself up to standing. She made daft faces and talked nonsense at him, shuf-fling backwards all the time, and that's how he took his first steps, trying to catch up with her, laughing his head off. When she asked could she babysit, I nearly bit her hand off.

By the end of that year my beautiful little boy was walking and had a smile that could melt your heart. I'd got my figure back and we had waiting lists at the studio. The summer show we put on for the parents was better than what you see on TV.

Then Ryan grew up a bit more and started charging about and yelling, and he tripped a couple of people up. In Advanced he wouldn't let Nadia dance at all, he just wanted her to play with him. My mum of course was only too keen to take him off my hands but I was worried for her because her knee was bad. She'd had to stop teaching completely.

'What if he runs away from you?' I asked her. 'You won't be able to catch him.'

'Why would he run away?'

'Just for the hell of it. He's a kid!'

'He'll come back when I call.' I didn't think he would. I looked into the estate nursery. There were kids plugged into educational games, kids clustered round a screen singing along, kids using play equipment with nannybots monitoring their safety. It wasn't awful. But my mum went mental. 'You going to give up care of your child to a set of robots?'

'They're specially designed to give him better care than most humans, Mum.'

'You honestly think a machine can give better care than a person?'

'Yeah. Better care than that dopey female who looked after me when *you* went to work. Alice whatshername. All she did was plonk us in front of videos. At least he'll get some variety at nursery.'

'I had no choice. I didn't have anyone else to look after you. *My* mother was dead.'

'Oh play the violins.'

'Paula, I beg you, let me look after him. He won't be bored, he won't run away. Let's at least try it for a couple of weeks.'

Well I couldn't argue with that, could I? She was still knitting like mad. She made all Ryan's jumpers. But her knee was bad and it meant she couldn't go fast. In fact she did nearly everything sitting down. She seemed to get a lot of pain. I suppose it took that, the worry about her not being able to look after Ryan safely, to make me really focus on how slow she was.

'Mum, what meds are you on now?'

She pulled a face.

'Mum?'

'They don't do any good.'

'You mean you're not taking them?'

'Look, I keep moving, that's the main thing, keeping going.'

'Seriously, you are off your head. I'm coming with you next week to see the doctor.'

'It isn't a doctor anymore, it's a bot.'

'In charge of the whole clinic?'

She nodded. 'They've upgraded them. They're supposed to be more efficient than humans.'

'Fuck's sake. Well I'm coming with you to ask about your treatment.'

'I'm perfectly capable of asking for myself.'

'Clearly not, Mother.' I knew I was being sharp with her but it was plain daft – she was turning into a cripple and refusing to take the meds which might give her some relief. She and Ryan and I queued with everyone else on Thursday morning and I have to say the medibot was pretty impressive. It checked her out and scanned her legs and produced two printouts, one for meds and one, new dietary supplements. She was all set to leave then, so just as well I was there. 'My mum says these meds aren't strong enough.'

After a bit of processing it said, 'A replacement right knee, arthroplasty, is the optimum solution for advanced osteoarthritis. The protective cartilage on the ends of your bones has broken down due to excessive wear. This is caused in turn by your favouring the right leg over the left, which is almost certainly due to earlier damage to the left ankle. Arthroplasty is available for an average cost of eighteen thousand pounds to members of BUPA, Health First and Happilife.'

Mum and I looked at each other and burst out laughing. 'I don't have health insurance,' she told it. 'You're on an estate here, you know.' It printed out another prescription, for tranks. When we picked up the drugs she scowled at the boxes. She'd never been into taking tablets, not even paracetamol for a head-ache.

'Mum, I understand, but will you give it a try? If you get less pain, surely it's worth it?' I was glad she was having Ryan, because it gave her a reason to need to be mobile. Plus he was a distrac-tion from her own aches and pains. And at the end of the day, I was glad for him, because he did love being with her.

She didn't like being told, though, so no surprise she found something to niggle at, tit for tat. 'What are you paying Nadia?'

'Nadia?'

'For babysitting.'

'She doesn't want anything. She only has him now and then, nothing regular.'

'You should pay her, Paula. You know she has to look after her father?' They lived in our block but I'd never even seen her father. Mum launched off on how he's got dementia and needs care 24/7.

'I can pay *you* for childcare, Mum. We should sit down and work out the hours.' I thought that's why she said it. But no.

'Don't be ridiculous. I don't want paying, of course I don't. But I know Nadia gets her neighbour to sit with him when she's out, and that won't be for free.'

'A human sitter?'

My mother raised her eyebrows at me, as if to say, yes, not only are you so debased you want bots to look after your child, you also think they should care for the elderly.

Well, they do. And I've never heard any complaints. Obviously when people are past it and go into the Bin, the care's pretty basic. So they say. Since you can't even visit, who knows? But if you get homecare by a nursebot it's probably OK, in my opinion. Not my mum's though. Anyway, I gave Nadia some cash the next time she had Ryan, and she tried to give it back, until I told her to buy something nice for her dad's tea. Then her eyes filled with tears and she gave Ryan a bear hug, and slipped the money in her pocket. So I was glad that I knew. Though it didn't stop me from being annoyed my mother was always right.

Then comes what I've been dreading – a call from Luke Butler. The first time, I blocked it. I was planning an intermediate class, I'd just finished rejigging the list of barre exercises and I was moving on to floor work, when up pops his name.

I switched off my screen and went to lean my head against the window. Nothing to see but the next two towers, Heseltine and May, tall and dark and grey, blocking our light. The corner of the clinic, and the empty tarmac down below.

He was still paying the insurance. And there was nothing else to pay it with. It wasn't much good pretending I had a choice. I told myself, look, it was OK for them three I sent before. It was all good. He's done what he promised and made it safe. But somehow it sickened me more than it ever had before. I looked at my hands gripping the window frame and I imagined another person, touching things with my hands. Touching things I didn't want to touch. Pressing my fingers, my skin, onto something I would never touch.

You don't know what they do while you're asleep. Better not imagine. But once you start imagining, it's hard to stop.

I tried to be like my mum, sensible, brisk. I know what she would say. *What the eye doesn't see, the heart doesn't grieve.* And that's the truth of it, I just gotta shut my eyes and hold my nose. I thought, anyway, I don't have to call him back. Maybe he'll ask someone else. But as soon as I switched on he was there again. Same as before, he wanted three volunteers – and soon. Could I get the paperwork to him this week, and could they go down London the week after? OK. Sooner it's done, the less time I have to fret.

This time I asked Charmayne, Meghan and Abdul. I thought it made sense to ask older ones and give some of the others a chance to teach their classes. Once it got out they were going, I was fielding a lot of questions. *Can I go, Miss?* And parents wanting to know about it, and everyone suddenly thinking, OK, we want a slice of the pie. I tried to play it down, I tried to hush it up, and it was gnawing away at my insides like a rat.

I blocked it the best way I know, with work. Mum took over with Ryan and I started to plan a really big show for Christmas. I wanted an up-to-date story that was relevant to the kids' lives, and I spent ages trying to decide on the music. We'd been practising to *The Nutcracker* and *Cinderella*, so I was thinking fairy tales, and I hit on doing a modern version of *Sleeping Beauty*, where Sleeping Beauty is in VR and won't come out of it for anyone. The littlies and middle-band kids could be in her VR. I imagined rigging up a big rectangular frame that the audience would watch them through, and weird costumes and lighting, sort of fantastical. It was good because they could practise separately, in their own classes, to tunes they already knew, and then their dances could just slot in. I'd work with the top class on the adult characters – Sleeping B and her parents and courtiers who were trying to wake her before the prince arrived. I wanted modern music; something edgy and unsettling – and I remembered the music Paul used to listen to.

I sent him messages and tried to call him, but no reply. I hadn't spoken to him for days. He never came round my mum's anymore, and I didn't go to his. Well, there wasn't any point, it was boring. He never saw Ryan from one week's end to the next.

He didn't answer the door so I let myself in. A bit of me was scared. What if he was ill? Or worse? But I could see, straight off, as soon as I opened the door, that he was OK, sitting there in his VR glasses. Needless to say he was deaf to the world. His

room stank so I opened the window but he never noticed. I had
to shake him and pummel his back, to get him to realise I was
there.

'What d'you want?'

'That's not very friendly.'

He shrugged. 'I'm busy.'

'No you're not. Listen, I'm looking for some music.' I started
to explain but he was away with the fairies. 'Paul? Paul? Shall I
make us a cup of tea?'

'Not now. I'm in the middle of something.'

'Well can't you stop for a chat?'

'I don't come and interrupt you at your studio.'

'But that's different, that's—'

'No it's not.' And he put the glasses on again. I waited but he
wasn't bothered if I stayed or went, he was in another world.

It hit me hard then, what I'd lost. He used to light up when I
came in the room. All the time I was pregnant, and when Ryan
was little, he couldn't do enough to help me. He was always
trying to make me comfortable, fetch me things, cook me something tasty, cheer me up with a funny story or play me a new
track he'd just heard. I knew it was me that drove him away. And
now he was one of the zombies. I remember thinking there must
have been something subconscious made me fix on that *Sleeping
Beauty* story, cos it was him, wasn't it? I knew I needed to wake
him up, just like the Prince would wake Sleeping Beauty. Cos I
did love him.

In the end my mum helped me find the music I was looking
for. She googled a composer called Philip Glass and played me
some of his opera. It was just right, edgy and repetitive and right
for lots of sharp staccato movements. I got down to practising
with the top class.

Nadia fell into step beside me after one class, and asked could
she talk to me? It was raining so I told her to come up to mine
for a coffee. But she shook her head and said she couldn't leave
her dad any longer, and they only lived on the ground floor.

'So should I come with you?'

She hesitated. 'Would you mind?'

When she opened the door it was the smell that hit me – incontinence and curry, not a great combo. A fat woman was parked in front of the screen, and a hunched little Asian man, Nadia's dad, looked up at us from his wheelchair and smiled.

Nadia dealt with it in five minutes flat. She sent the sitter packing with a sharp reminder that changing her father was part of the job; she pointed me to the kettle to make coffee; and she took her dad to the shower room and cleaned him up.

Then she introduced me to Faisal and he shook hands and asked me courteously, how was Nadia's dancing coming along?

'Very well.'

'She takes after her mother. She was as light as a feather on her feet.'

Nadia smiled at him and turned to me. 'I know you must be busy. Forgive me. But I want to ask you, next time you are selecting volunteers for that clinic, please would you consider me?'

It was the last thing I was expecting. I thought she was going to ask if she could look after Ryan here, or if I could help her father in some way.

'We need the money, that's why I'm asking.'

'Nadia, no,' said her father quietly.

'Please, Dad, I have to ask.' He bowed his head. 'They're saying my father should go to the Bin and I – we—' her voice broke.

'I have vascular dementia, and I can't get myself onto the toilet,' her father said softly. 'It is probably time.'

'It's not time! It will never be time!' she cried. 'I want to pay for proper care, here in our flat.'

I had a vision of me and Mum one day. One day it would come. Would I let them take her to the Bin? But this was not simple. 'Nadia, you would have to be away for more than two weeks.'

'Yes. I'd arrange sitters. We'd manage, wouldn't we, Dad?'

He smiled sadly.

'I know I shouldn't ask, probably everyone has good reasons why they need the money. But I haven't annoyed you by asking, have I?'

No, she had not annoyed me by asking if I would put her down for a dangerous experiment she might never come back from, while her poor old father sat in his own mess being ignored by Mrs Lazy-sitter. I felt ashamed – for myself, for her, for him. Ashamed there was nothing better on offer. 'Of course I'll put you forward, Nadia, if they ask me again. I don't know if they will, mind you.'

When I got home I googled 'vascular dementia'. It was a depressing read.

And then it happened again. There were three of them off down London. But only two come back.

I heard about it before I even opened the studio that morning. Meghan had an accident in London. A tragic, fatal accident. She must have been distracted by her phone, cos she just stepped in front of a trans, and she died on the spot. Right. When Charmayne and Abdul come in for their class at 12 they were proper down-cast. In shock, really. The others asked them what happened and they said they didn't know, they didn't see, she went out on her own.

I knew it was the same story as Ryan's aneurism. But what could I say to them? The secrecy agreements had us all tied up, and no doubt they'd been given an extra wad of cash to keep their mouths shut about Meghan, same as me with Ryan.

It was Charmayne who come to see me at home, next day. She was in a pathetic state, big dark bags under her eyes, face like a ghost, frightened little voice. Well, she and Meghan were mates from day one. 'Promise you'll never tell anyone, Paula,' she whispers. 'But I really need to ask you something—'

'I know, love,' I told her. 'They killed Meghan, didn't they?'

She cried then, poor girl, and it took me a good while to calm her down. She didn't know for sure Meghan hadn't come back, but when she asked to see the body they wouldn't let her. They told her it was too badly damaged.

'It doesn't make sense,' she whispered. 'None of us went outside that clinic. You couldn't even *go* out, the door was locked at night. I know that cos I tried it.'

She had a rough night before her own Hosting, panicking about the whole thing. She was afraid and she seriously thought about leaving. 'I was frightened to leave on my own, but I was mad at myself for being such a wimp. So I decided to just go outside and see how it felt to start to walk away from all that money. And my door was locked.'

'Did you see Meghan in the morning?'

She shook her head. 'It was all so quick in the morning, the bot just came in my room and gave me the injection before I had a chance to speak—' She started to cry again.

'What do you want to ask me, Charmayne?'

'If this has happened before. If you knew we could die.'

A bad question for me. What could I do but shake my head and lie?

'But now, will you stop recommending people?'

I felt like a complete shit. 'If I stop, Charmayne, Mr Butler will want to know why. What'll I tell him?'

'Tell him, cos Meghan died.'

'But he'll say that was a road accident, could've happened anywhere, it's no reason to stop kids hosting.'

'But—'

'But. Yes, I know. And you know. And so does Abdul, I should think. But we've all signed secrecy agreements, haven't we? So if the clinic finds out we're stopping because they let Meghan die, they'll know someone's talked.'

She hadn't worked it out, she was in too much of a state. I got out my own contract and read it to her. '*Any leaking of information, no matter how trivial, about events and research taking place at the Clinic for Body Tourism, pertaining to the subject or to any other individual, will result in civil prosecution*

and automatic forfeiture of all fees and monies paid to the subject.
You'd have to return your money and you'd probably end up in
court.'

'But it's murder.'

I hadn't thought of it quite like that. But she was right. And
I realised the cat was out of the bag. If I went on recommending
kids to the clinic, the fact of Meghan's death – even if they
believed the story about the road accident – was enough to cast
a shadow over the whole thing. And who's to say Charmayne,
or one of the others, wouldn't crack and tell more people that
Meghan had died because of the research? Char had already
broken her contract by telling me. I needed to be honest so I
explained to her that the volunteers weren't the only ones getting
paid. Butler's money was keeping the studio open. 'You can have
my money,' she said. 'I don't want it, it's blood money.'

'Oh, Char, don't say that. What can I do?'

She was staring at me and her eyes were fierce. 'When you
went to that clinic – did Ryan really die from natural causes?
From that haemorrhage thing?'

'Yes. Yes! Why would I lie to you?' I swear, I thought my heart
would beat its way out of my chest. She kept glaring at me and
I could feel myself getting redder and redder. But then her eyes
filled with tears and soon they were streaming down her face.

I hugged her then and we cried together, for the mess and the
sadness of it all, and for being caught like fish in a net with no
escape. Charmayne put me to shame. I mean, she was where I
was when Ryan died. But I kept my gob shut and built my studio
and put it all behind me. And now another kid had died, you
might say, because of me. Because of my studio. Because I recom-
mended her.

I made us a hot drink. I didn't know what to do. In the end
I just hugged her again and told her I would work something
out – and she needed to give me time. If I beat my brains against
it long enough, I'd find a way through. When she left, a load of
stuff was churning in my head. The studio, and how it had all

come from Luke Butler's money – in the beginning, to build it, and now to keep it open. His money was the reason my life turned out like this: his money did what I wanted. Plus Paul, and baby Ryan. Was it my fault Paul had become a VR zombie? I knew it was. I'd turned away from him after the baby was born and he didn't have anyone else. I felt sick and selfish and responsible, and then I came down with a proper dose of flu.

Sometimes you can't separate out what's in your head and what's in your body. My body was heavy and unbalanced and I couldn't dance, and nothing could shift my headache. My spirits sank so low I even considered opening the window and stepping out.

Days and nights ran into each other and my mum and little Ryan were there looking after me.

Eventually my temperature came down and I lay in bed weak as a kitten and watched them. I didn't want to talk. There was nothing to say. I watched how little Ryan helped my mum. When she needed to get up, he brought her stick. When they were going out to the shop she give him the bag to carry. They were proper partners.

When she brung me my dinner I thanked her. 'I don't just mean my dinner. I mean thanks for all your help with Ryan.'

She smiled. 'No problem. You see, he didn't run away.'

'I've been thinking. Maybe I should close the studio.'

'Why?' She sat on the edge of my bed. 'What's this all about?'

So I told her. That's to say, I told her what Butler's clinic was really doing, and what happened to big Ryan. Which I should have done long, long ago.

She sat quietly and listened to it all and when little Ryan came mithering she gave him some paper and her special pen and told him to draw Mummy in bed, and there was peace and quiet for me to finish the sorry tale.

'I wondered about big Ryan, whether something had gone wrong,' she told me. 'It was such neat timing. I mean, why should his aneurism burst when he was there? I wondered if they had caused it.'

I shook my head.

'But swapping digital memories into youngsters' bodies? I know they've done that with synths. But – into *you*, Paula?'

'Didn't harm me.' There was a silence then and I listened to Ryan's pen scribbling over the paper.

Eventually she said, 'I'm amazed it's possible.' She passed me a tissue. 'Don't cry,' she said. 'The studio's done some good, whichever way you look at it. It's brought life to this wretched place.'

'And death.'

'Oh, Paula, what a mess.'

I reached out and took her hand. It was warm and polished and bony, and strangely comforting. We sat like that for a bit, quiet and peaceful, and then she said, 'Would you like to move away?'

'From Coldwater? How on earth would we do that?'

'I don't know. But let's pretend you could. Would you?'

'Well what about the studio? What about all my dancers?'

'I know. But this awful business of sending youngsters to the clinic . . .'

'I've got to find a way to stop it, haven't I? I can't just walk away.'

'No,' she said. 'You're right. I'm glad you think that.'

'Mum?'

'Yes?'

'Will you ring Nadia for me, and ask her can she take over all Meghan's classes? Tell her the pay.'

'Of course.'

'Thanks.'

When I got a bit better I sat up in bed and read to Ryan from the little books Mum had borrowed from the nursery. He knew the names of all the animals; pig, sheep, cow, duck, dog, cat. I thought how strange it was he's never seen any of these and perhaps never will, but still he knows their names and what they are. Like fairy, dragon, wizard, goblin, they're just things in a story. The world is full of stuff he'll never see and that's the saddest thing. What if he has to live on Coldwater all his life and never go anywhere else? What if he turns to VR? How could I bear it?

At least that didn't make me cry. It made me angry. Feeling angry, I got better. I was ready to try and do stuff differently. I was ready to make things change.

12.

ELSA

Lindy's death is as random and insane as were the accusations against her. There is a passage of time which is experienced by Elsa as a film screened by a lunatic projectionist, fast-forwarding through a blur of people and places, then freeze-framing odd moments. Standing alone in her – their – bedroom in the early morning light, rigid with distress at the silence in the house. Realising that Lindy's disappearance has also occasioned the disappearance of the drones; that their constant buzz is something she can miss. Opening and shutting the door to Lindy's wardrobe, once, twice, twenty times – with what intention? To clear it? To bag the clothes for charity? And simultaneously seeing in a split second on every hanger a time, a place, a sound, a smell, a mood, an embrace, a day of their life together, so that opening the door is an explosion and she has to shut it again fast, to stop her brain from bursting. The lawyer ('obviously the case will be dropped'), the families of the other bomb victims enlisting her to share their *Defiance of Terrorists*, which Elsa cannot do because the bomber died in the blast and anyway she has always had a sneaking sympathy for the NOBOTS campaign. Not for terrorism, obviously, but she'd be content to never see another edubot. And then there's the cremation (what was in the coffin? Not the head. Was there enough to cremate?) and the curiously stilted expressions of sympathy – her own paranoia, undoubtedly – the flowers, the cards, the chaos in her house and the kindness of friends bearing food and wine; flashing past quickly, quickly.

And her own guilt. Pulling the bedroom chair in front of the mirror and sitting staring at herself. At her greying hair, her double chin, the crow's feet around her eyes and the mean thin lips. You're glad she's dead. You wanted her dead. It's easier for her to be dead than alive, and no one will ever love you again. She knew you thought her guilty, and that's why she's dead. Her grief at your suspicion called down that tragedy upon her. There's a reason why Lindy was on that trans at that moment on that day in the whole of London. Her sadness drew the bomber closer, like a magnet. You were the one person who should have stood by her. How can you pretend you couldn't make her speak to you? How hard did you try? Why didn't you prostrate yourself and weep, why didn't you creep through her window in the small hours and touch her hand, why didn't you refuse to eat or drink or sleep until she answered you? How could you let that silence continue for so many terrible days? It's your fault she's dead.

And then, the opposite. Relief at owning the house again, relief at the thought of returning to work and activity that will consume her time and energy sufficiently to blot this out. Relief that the case will never come to court and that Lindy's name (and her own) will not be publicly smeared; relief that that gnawing suspicion can be ignored.

Time jerks forward, stops, unspools, stutters forwards again. The police return tablets and phones – all clear. Jim offers her early retirement but why would she want that? She wants to immerse herself in work again. There are kind messages and cards from parents, describing Lindy as a wonderful teacher and a really special person, all of which seem as horribly double-edged as Elsa is to herself, mourning a beloved partner one moment and rejoicing in the removal of a perverted monster the next. The fact that Lindy has died is perhaps proof that she was guilty; death has come to spare both Elsa and Lindy herself from the vilification that lay in store. Death has come as the least worst option.

She swings between memories of before and after the Fall; of passionate, honest, laughing, loving Lindy, and the grim and hateful creature she became.

Once Elsa is back at school, working with a new deputy, furiously busy with the new curriculum and tests, and the IT headaches created by the introduction of second-generation edubots and the budgetary implications of roof repairs; once she is back, leading that life she has always lived, she settles into the knowledge that Lindy was guilty. She must have been. All that couldn't have happened for no reason; a child, no matter how disturbed, does not invent an accusation like that. The evidence proved the child right. Elsa has lived in blind ignorance of Lindy's nature for years. Where ignorance is bliss, 'tis folly to be wise. She can castigate herself and she can be broken-hearted at her own lack of perception, she can feel hurt and betrayed by Lindy, but at least she can be clear now. There was one terrible wrong-doer in this, and that was Lindy. And so she must banish Lindy from her heart. She will never trust another person, or imagine herself to love them, ever again. She will never again open herself to this kind of betrayal. Lindy abused a child, and in that action also abused Elsa – her trust, her loyalty, her love.

Elsa has been back at school for two months when the phone call comes. Jim, phoning at 5.30 p.m. She is in her office, completing the forms for SATs returns. As she speaks to him her eyes are still engaged with the figures onscreen. 'Have you heard?' he asks.

'Heard what?'

'About Jade F.'

'No and I don't want to.' She has been relieved to find the child gone from the school and never mentioned.

'Her father has just been found guilty.'

'Her father?'

'It's on the news right now, he's just been sentenced.'

'But . . .'

'I thought you would want to know, Elsa. He's got a custodial sentence. It was the father, when the child accused Lindy.'

'I don't understand.' The green figures on the screen are slipping and blurring.

'I don't know the details. But the girl was being seen by a

psychologist, wasn't she? Presumably that didn't end with Lindy's death. And maybe Lindy's dying pushed young Jade into telling the truth.'

'So her own father was abusing her.'

'Yes.'

'Not Lindy.'

'Not Lindy. As we always knew. I'm only sorry poor Lindy isn't here to see her name cleared. I know none of us ever for a moment imagined . . . but still it's a relief to have it out in the open, that the story was a fabrication.' His voice goes on, but it sounds quite far away. Elsa is trying to open up her head to the fact: Lindy was innocent. Lindy was innocent.

'Elsa? I'm sorry, I'm afraid I've upset you. Well, it is upsetting, all that trauma for you and Lindy, and then the tragedy of her death. I'm really very sorry. Are you alone? Would you like me to come over?'

'No. Thanks. I'm just a bit . . .'

There's a pause. 'Yes. You can understand, in a way, why the child needed to blame someone else. If it was her own father.'

'Yes. Thanks for telling me, Jim. Goodbye.'

Elsa switches off the computer and goes home.

And now there is no escape. Lindy was innocent. And she – Elsa – said, *there's no smoke without fire*. She made her innocent beloved understand that she suspected her of a vile crime. And now her beloved is dead and she can never make it right. There are not enough tears in her head to wash this away. There is no escape from her own guilt. If she had been supporting Lindy properly, Lindy would not even have been on that trans when the bomb exploded. It is Elsa's fault that Lindy is dead, and that her life was bitterly unhappy before she died. And there's no way to right this terrible wrong.

Jim and his fellow governors fully understand that Elsa needs more compassionate leave. And now she is crying properly. She is grieving for both of them, for their lost innocence.

*

Time passes. At a snail's pace, and crammed and cluttered with every kind of practical difficulty. Elsa can't sleep, which means that sometimes in daylight hours, through sheer exhaustion, she drops off over a meal or at her screen. She falls off her chair; she spills scalding coffee on her bare legs and fails to treat the burn, which in turn refuses to heal. She becomes such a clumsy fumbler she drops glasses, her phone, her earrings, cutlery, pieces of food. Everything seems to be broken and there are sharp things on the floor. The vacubot sucks up all sorts of bits then starts making a weird rattling noise. Once it stops working, the kitchen becomes properly squalid. Friends come to help. They bring food and flowers and games and sympathy, and none of it is any use. Since Elsa doesn't sleep, day runs into night runs into day and she loses sight of mealtimes and snacks randomly on whatever is in the fridge. She eats strange-tasting yoghurt and gets food poisoning. When she is not crying, Elsa is silent and furious. Also her house smells. Gradually, friends give up on her. When Jim visits because she has not answered the final warning messages about her return to work, she tells him to go away. Which he correctly interprets as her resignation.

One day somebody speaks to Jeanette, a cousin of Lindy's, who works at a clinic nearby in Deptford. She's fond of Elsa but has not visited her for a long time; the mutual friend paints a lurid picture of Elsa's decline, and this sets Jeanette thinking. She visits in January.

'You can't go on like this, Elsa. It's been over a year.'

'So?'

'So. Lindy would never have wanted you to destroy your own life like this. You've got to move on.'

'Leave me alone.'

'Elsa, I've come to tell you something.'

'What?'

'Wonderful news, actually.'

'If you're about to tell me Jesus loves me it would be wise to save your breath.'

'He'd have a hard job right now, to be honest.' Jeanette grins and the ghost of an almost-smile crosses Elsa's face. 'But it's secret,' Jeanette tells her.

'Whatever.'

The story Jeanette tells is so incredible it is almost certainly true. The memories and character of cryogenically frozen brains can be stored in digital form and downloaded into living bodies, young volunteers whose rightful owners have been temporarily put to sleep. Jeanette knows because she works on reception at the clinic where they do this. 'Helen told me how low you still are, and I realised – I don't know, I hadn't put two and two together. But you . . .'

'But I what? What?'

'Well they froze Lindy, didn't they? After the bomb.'

'Froze her? Oh. Yes. I think they did. I couldn't understand why.'

'Insurance. They were covering their backs.'

'I don't understand,' says Elsa.

'The bomber—'

'He was from NOBOTS. I used to support them.'

'Yes, NOBOTS. Well, he got someone at Transporto to switch off the scanner. Didn't you see the news at the time?'

Elsa raises her eyebrows and Jeanette has the grace to blush.

'Sorry. The mechanic went straight to the police. He'd been naive. The bomber convinced him he was only going to use the bomb to negotiate. And all the mechanics were afraid of being replaced by bots.'

'So?'

'So this guy's confession made Transporto liable. And they paid all the medical bills, to save themselves from being sued. Including cryogenics. To offer a little hope.'

'Lindy's dead. Hope won't bring her back.'

'Our programme could.'

Elsa begins to understand. 'You mean, her head—?'

'Her head is all you need. Her brain.'

'So what are you saying? You could get Lindy's brain installed in a young living body?'

'Not permanently, obviously. For two weeks. And not her brain – her consciousness, in digital form.'

'With all her memories?'

'With all her memories.'

'She'd know me?'

'She'd know you fine. You wouldn't know her, because she'd look totally different. But anyway, you probably wouldn't see her because they send them to this amazing tropical island where they can live in luxury having the best of everything.'

'Could I go with her?'

Jeanette hesitates. 'I don't know. I mean, this is totally secret. I'm not allowed to talk about it at all. But maybe, I thought, you could look into it.'

'How, if it's secret?'

'It's secret in that they don't want the media to get hold of it. It hasn't passed all its ethical whatsits yet. But you're a special case. Firstly, Lindy was an innocent victim of a terrorist outrage. Secondly, you're obviously still experiencing a lot of trauma and grief. You're ideal subjects.'

'Well what do I have to do?'

'Make some innocent enquiries. Have you got the contact details of the company that's frozen her?'

'Somewhere.'

'Right. Get in touch with them and ask about the options. They know all about this, but they're not going to tell you if you don't ask.'

'They'll put me in touch with your clinic?'

Jeanette smiles. 'Yes.'

When she has left, Elsa goes online and scrolls back through hundreds of unopened messages, to the date of Lindy's death.

She moves the cursor through the subject headers and when she locates it, she knows immediately what it is. The subject header says *Your Loved One.* She clicks to open and there's a flowery little essay about how her loved one is being preserved in optimal conditions until the time is ripe. There's even technical info about temperature, humidity, and electrical back-up systems. There's a client helpline. Elsa's built-in pedant objects that the client, surely, is Lindy? But she rings them immediately.

Jeanette was telling the truth. Once they've got the ID from the message, and her assertion that nothing on earth could be more precious to Elsa than to restore Lindy to life, they note her number and tell her the clinic will get in touch. Elsa lays her phone in the centre of the table and paces around it. She is shaking. If she can speak to Lindy. If she can say sorry to Lindy, and tell her how much she loves her . . . It would be worth anything.

Slowly, slowly, it comes to pass. The stumbling block which emerges after an online application, is her desire to spend time with the new Lindy. A message informs Elsa that the new Lindy can be told that Elsa has requested her return. It is even possible for Elsa to meet her for an hour at the clinic, on the morning of the day she is due to fly to Paradise Island. But Elsa is not allowed to go with her.

Elsa requests a meeting with the man in charge, Luke Butler. The clinic, just off Deptford High Street, is close enough for her to walk there. With its curved walls and dead-eyed windows it looks futuristic and rather sinister. When the bot shows her into Butler's office, he jumps up to greet her. He's younger and taller than she imagined, and strangely ill at ease. 'Your partner died in that bomb on the trans. It's exactly the kind of situation Body Tourism should be helping with.'

'Well I hope so.' Elsa sits in the big blue chair and he retreats behind his desk. 'The thing is, I need to see her.'

'You must remember she will look completely different. You won't be seeing the person you knew.'

'I have read the information.' Don't be sarcastic. You've got to get him on your side. 'I'm sorry,' she says, 'it's just I really need to spend time with Lindy. Much more than one hour.'

'An hour is the maximum. We can only cater for people who return on Paradise Island. It's not possible for them to stay in London.'

'Then please can I go with her.'

He's shaking his head. And Elsa is shaking hers, because to have this flicker of hope extinguished is more than she can bear.

'I need to be with her. I need to explain a terrible, terrible betrayal.' Suddenly to Elsa's intense embarrassment, tears are pouring down her cheeks and snot slithering over her top lip. She's trying to sniff it up and choking on it. 'I'm – sorry, sorry . . .' She can't get her tissues fast enough, and long strands of snot slip from her chin to her chest. He thrusts a box of tissues at her. Between them they drop it. Elsa howls.

She's aware of the man fussing about, getting her a cup of tea, checking his screen, avoiding looking at her. She fights for control. 'I'm so sorry.'

'It's alright,' he says, fidgeting with a pencil. 'You're very upset. Do you want to tell me why?' He's not being kind: the question is simply matter-of-fact. And Elsa realises she does. She hasn't told anyone, ever, because what would be the point? Why reveal to any of their friends or relations that she suspected Lindy of that foul crime, that Lindy spent the last weeks of her life knowing that Elsa believed her capable of such perversion?

Pressure builds up behind a secret. It's like a capped oil well. The oil is there, amassing force, roiling, swirling, swelling. And when it blows, it blows. Elsa can't hold back, she tells him everything. Then there's a silence.

She gathers herself, blows her nose, glances up at the man. He's hunched over his desk still fiddling intently with his pencil. He looks up suddenly, nods, and pushes back his chair. 'I'll just . . . I'll be back in a minute.' And he leaves the room. Well. What an exhibition she has made of herself. Still, she feels better for it. Lighter. Even if it doesn't make any difference, at least she's said it.

Luke is uncomfortable. Not knowing what to do, he takes himself to the toilet. People weep. They spill over, when they should contain themselves. They expect certain kinds of response, a pat on the back or even a hug. He dislikes it. On the other hand, it is becoming clear that for some users of Body Tourism, exile to Paradise Island is unsatisfactory. Richard K, for example, wanted to be with his father. Ha-ha. And Octavia wanted to be in the real world. That doesn't end well, it's no longer an option. But is there any reason why he couldn't send this woman to Paradise Island with her partner? She is giving off a distressing odour. He recognises it as the scent of anxiety/depression; he used to detect it on his mother from time to time. A no-hope smell.

He processes the question. Is this anxious teacher likely to create trouble on Paradise Island? He thinks not. Will she pull out if he refuses? Probably. Which would be a shame because this was Jeanette's request and Jeanette has been an exemplary employee; discreet, versatile, and offering human kindness in those situations where Luke knows himself to be lacking. She has worked for him since before the clinic opened.

There's no reason for not trialling this. And it's time he showed Gudrun who's boss. While she's lining up overprivileged ancient bitches like that Chloe Esterhazy, he's finding Tourists who *deserve* the experience. Giving life back to someone who lost it far too young; healing grief; doing good. Just like Robin Hood. He has nothing to lose by letting Elsa go to Paradise Island with Lindy. It is a relief when she nods, shakes his hand, and leaves without another word.

Elsa puts the house up for sale. She'll never get back into teaching now. There's an army of unemployed and highly skilled teachers chasing every vacancy. Without a job she no longer has London entitlement, and anyway she can't afford the mortgage on her own. She will get the standard pension and can apply for single person's accommodation, a flat or room in one of the retirement blocks outside the city.

Clearing the house is weirdly easy, now she knows what's happening. Now she can open Lindy's wardrobe, where all those memories, those skirts and trousers and dresses hang, and simply bundle them into sacks to go to the estates. The new Lindy won't need or fit these clothes. They're no more than the shed skin of a snake, the drift of hair lying waiting to be swept up by the hairdresser at the end of a morning's snipping. The shelves of teaching materials and records, digital and print, can go straight to recycling; Lindy's video games; the old-fashioned china, the bedding, the lamps, the cutlery, all to charity, saving herself just one of each. Her own clothes . . .

It is only her own clothes that give her pause. Not because she is especially fond of them. If anything, the opposite. The smart head teacher trousers and jackets have been her uniform for the job, not an expression of her own taste. She could gladly bundle them into sacks. But now she is brought up against three obstacles. One, she will need clothes for the remainder of her life and will not have the income to buy them. Two, she is going to a tropical island for a fortnight and has nothing suitable; and three, suddenly, all in a heap, she realises Lindy will be young and she will be the only holidaymaker aged fifty. Her hair will still be grey, her waist thick, her breasts drooping, her chin almost double. She doesn't have the right clothes or body, and she will look hideous.

There's an afternoon when Elsa scours the internet looking at all the cosmetic sites she and Lindy used to hold in amused contempt: laser surgery, skin tightening, fillers, wrinkle removers, peeling, tanning; hair colouring, hair thickening, hair rejuvenating serums; eye brighteners, teeth whiteners, blemish removal, liposuction, eyebrow threading, lash lengthening, skin softening, follicle removal, lip plumping. Before and After pictures portray wrinkly sixty-year-olds next to themselves grinning out of peeled-back selfies apparently twenty years younger. *Show respect to your family and friends – stay young! You owe it to them to keep looking good! You owe it to yourself!*

What vanity. Even if she could afford it, which she can't. She's going in order to lay her heart bare to Lindy, to confess her own terrible suspicion and to beg forgiveness. Not to try and compete with the beauty of the young. If Lindy can forgive her, that will be more than she deserves. Trying to beautify herself might suggest that she dares to hope for affection, or even love. She has no right to these.

Ruthlessly she sorts her clothes into three piles: Estates, Keep, and Island. There are some summer tops, there are a couple of cotton dresses. She adds light trousers and her rusty black swimsuit to the pile. That's it. In a flash she remembers giggling helplessly with Lindy over 'rusty'; one of them was reading a nineteenth-century novel and there was a description of a 'rusty black dress'. Neither of them could imagine it, and the black swimsuit, and indeed all black garments, were afterwards referred to as rusty. Now she's grinning.

Nevertheless, on the morning she is due to meet the new Lindy, she changes her clothes four times. She has not been able to sleep, and her breath is coming so fast and shallow it is almost a panic attack. If Lindy remembers everything, as Jeanette said she would, then maybe she won't even speak to Elsa. Maybe she will turn her back. Elsa has rehearsed what to say so many times that she has absolutely no idea what words will come out of her mouth. Gibberish, nonsense; she is not in control.

At the clinic, Jeanette gives her a big hug. 'I've just been talking to her, to Lindy, the new Lindy. She knows when and how she died, and that you asked for her to be brought back.'

Elsa nods. Her questions stick in her throat.

'She grasped it very quickly, Elsa. And she told me she's really looking forward to seeing you.'

Really looking forward. A securibot takes Elsa's luggage; a nursebot precedes her along a corridor and stops at the third door. Sitting on the bed is a slender black-haired girl. She jumps up at the sight of Elsa. 'Elsa!'

'Lindy? Is it really you?'

The girl nods.

'Oh, Lindy, I'm so sorry. I'm so, so sorry.' Faced with this waif-like stranger, Elsa can scarcely keep her balance, and has to steady herself on the door frame. The girl moves forward quickly and takes her hand.

'Sit. Come and sit down.' She guides her to a chair, and kneels in front of it. 'Have you been ill?'

Elsa looks at the beautiful worried face. The eyes are green, the skin flawless. She looks nothing like Lindy, and yet there's a quiet certainty which is entirely Lindy's. 'Not ill, exactly. Just – heartbroken, grieving for you.'

The girl shakes her head. 'For nearly two years, Jeanette told me. Oh Elsa, it's enough.' She reaches out tentatively to Elsa's hair. 'I've turned you grey, you poor thing.'

At the soft touch of her fingers, tears start to Elsa's eyes. 'Not you. My own stupidity, my own cruelty . . .'

'Hush! Stop it.'.

Elsa cannot keep looking into those clear green eyes. She bows her head. 'Can you forgive me?'

'Please don't cry. There's no need.' She scrambles to her feet. 'Look, I'm here! I'm fine.'

Elsa blows her nose and forces herself to look up. New Lindy is smiling down at her.

'See? Nothing to forgive. Give me a hug.'

Elsa hauls herself to her feet. 'Well there's plenty to forgive. But I'd like a hug.' She wraps her arms around the slim body, and the girl's soft warmth presses against her, and it is both like and unlike hugging Lindy.

'Your quest is over,' new Lindy whispers in her ear. 'Game over. New start.'

Talking is easy. Lindy wants to know everything that has happened since her death, which, with interruptions for the trip to the airport, and Elsa's panic that she has forgotten Lindy's passport ('But I have my host's – look!') takes quite a while. They are airborne by the time Elsa gets to Jade's father and his guilt. Lindy's face goes white.

'Do you know where Jade is now?'

Elsa shakes her head. She watches Lindy's young face as tears fill her eyes and she grimaces with the effort of containing them. The seats next to them on the plane are empty. 'It's alright,' Elsa whispers, closing her hand over Lindy's on the armrest. Lindy shakes her head impatiently. When she's regained control she speaks in a low, savage voice. 'I would kill him. If I could, I would kill him.' There's a silence then, the first real silence between them as the chasm of the past yawns open. Then the trolleybot brings drinks and snacks, and they toast one another with inflight champagne and smile wryly at their confusion of sorrow and joy.

13.

PAULA

Money was the issue. Money, money, money for the studio. If I could find a way to get some, I need never speak to Butler again. I wanted more than that, though. I wanted to get *him*. Charmayne was right, it was murder, and when she said we should go to the police I thought, it's not a stupid idea. She and Nadia had done a brilliant job of keeping classes going while I was sick, and I gave them both a £50 bonus to say thanks.

I was back on my feet and teaching again, and warming to the idea of the police (fuck it! What's Butler going to do? Confiscate my studio? I don't think so!) when I get a call from someone with a posh voice. She calls herself Hilary, she's from Blackrock. It takes me a bit to remember, she's the one Big Brian did the work for before he came to me, building an indoor athletics track. Bony and too thin, I'd say, but her face is young.

'Oh,' says I, 'so you know Luke Butler.'

'I do. That's what I want to ask you about.'

'Fire away.' Now I was sorry I'd mentioned him.

'This is confidential,' she says. 'But you will know that as well as I do. Luke has a clinic.'

'Right.' I was afraid I was going to be in trouble.

'I've been recommending a few volunteers for his research.'

'Right.'

'Like you have.'

My mind froze. Is this some kind of trap? 'Did he tell you that?'

'He did.' She gave me a sad little smile and I suddenly thought, oh, I can trust you.

'I've sent him six.'

'Me too.' She chewed at a fingernail and then she looked at me straight. 'Can you tell me, Paula, have they all come back?'

She knows, I thought. But I asked, 'Have all yours?'

'Yes.'

'Well two volunteers from Coldwater never came back.'

'Oh!' Her hands flew to her mouth. She was properly shocked. 'Two! I knew you lost one, but *two*—!'

'Ryan and Meghan.'

'When? I mean, I've heard something about Meghan. But the other one?'

So I give her a potted history. She seems a lot more interested in Ryan than Meghan, but maybe that's just cos she didn't know.

'Four years ago – you must have been the very first set of paid hosts. And it was all hushed up?'

'Course it was. Haven't you been asked to sign a secrecy clause?'

'Yes. I just didn't realise . . .'

'So how d'you know about Meghan?'

'I – well, one of my volunteers was in the same group as Meghan.' Hilary starts brushing some crumbs or something off her shirt, like I'm even going to notice. 'She told me. She was upset.'

Like Charmayne, I thought. Though that wasn't quite right cos Charmayne was Meghan's friend and this other girl didn't know her. But I don't know why I was niggling.

'Listen, Paula,' she leaned right forwards so she was practically popping out my screen. 'We have to stop this. We have to get it stopped.'

'I agree,' I said, and then it sank in. Someone on my side! Someone in the know, someone who understands it all – at last! My heart did a pirouette. Well, then we talked. We talked about my dancers and her athletes and what a difference it made to the kids on the estate, to have anything at all worth doing.

'People here are on the scrapheap from the day they're born,' she said. 'I don't think the rest of the country has any idea.' We talked about how we were both desperate for cash to keep our places open, and what a big deal the clinic money was for the kids. It was so good talking to her – like talking to Mum only she understood quicker, cos she was in the exact same trap as me. Stop sending volunteers, and the money dries up. Send them, and risk another death.

'Some of mine are already signed up and due to go next week,' she said. 'I don't think I can stop them at this stage, they're too excited about the money. But I swear, these will be the last volunteers from Blackrock.'

'Yeah, I feel the same.'

'If Luke asks you for more volunteers, play for time. Say there's an outbreak of flu or something. And I'll get back to you very soon. I'm going to work out we can do.'

'Sure.' I trusted her. She was clever and I could tell she knew a lot more than I did. My energy came flooding back and I decided to try and put a few other things right in my life. I researched VR detox programmes and messaged Paul that I was coming round to cook him dinner if he unplugged for long enough to eat it.

He did unplug when I arrived. My heart ached for him cos he looked so pale and skinny, like a ghost of the Paul I first fell for. He was weird and jumpy and kept staring over my head into the corners.

'What you looking at?'

'Nothing.'

I could see he couldn't settle. 'Paul! Talk to me. What's up?'

'It's dark, isn't it? Is there something wrong with the lights?'

Nothing wrong with the lights. I put the curry in the microwave and told him to just sit down with me. I told him I was worried about all the VR he was doing. But he couldn't sit still and began to pace around the room, staring wildly at the ceiling and the walls. 'Paul! Listen to me. Hey, how long is it since you been out?'

He didn't know. He'd been living on supplements or ordering ready meals delivered from Lianhua. He told me he wasn't hungry.

It was a dull grey sort of an evening but not dark yet and not raining, so I helped him into his coat and took him down in the lift. Outside he looked little and hunched and frightened. 'It's OK, Paul, you're safe, you're with me.' I held his hand.

'It's too big.' He gestured weirdly at the sky. The clinic was closed up so I took him under the porch there and he crouched down against the wall at the back, as far away from open space as he could get. I squatted down next to him.

'Paul, this is no good. It's messing with your head. Look, I can try and help you come off it.'

He didn't say anything, just stared out like he was expecting the world to come and kick him in the teeth.

'Paul? If you detox you can see Ryan, and play football and that. He's getting big now. Takes after you.'

He did look at me then, as if he was surprised to see me. 'Paula?'

'Yes?'

'Paula.'

'Will you let me help you?'

After a bit he said, 'OK. But I need to go back now.'

I was pleased. I thought I'd got through to him. But as soon as we get in through the door he goes to put on the glasses. 'Hey! Wait – have some food!'

'I've just got to – there's something I have to do . . .' his voice drifted off, he fiddled with his armband and I'd lost him. It was a start of sorts, though, and I promised myself I'd call in every day and just keep trying to prise him out of it, to the point where maybe he could see for himself it was worth doing. Ryan, the time with little Ryan would be the carrot. And for me – well, seeing the old Paul again would be the carrot. It hit me in waves, what a precious thing I'd lost.

My mum was still having trouble with her knee. But it never stopped her looking after Ryan. Sometimes she'd take him to visit her friend Mr Woodhouse, and Ryan loved that. He'd come home with stories of Mr Woodhouse's toy soldiers, and his picture books about aeroplanes. When Mum told me Woodhouse served more than forty years in the armed forces I begun to think more kindly of him.

Often she just stayed in the flat and looked after Ryan there. She used to play a lot of music. I'd come back from the studio and they'd be drawing monsters or building a tower, and Bach's clavichord or Chopin's *Nocturnes* or the Beatles or Richard K would be playing. She liked every kind of music, she knew all about it, and I thought that was great for Ryan. He was already an impressive little dancer! Her parents used to be musicians, real ones. Her mum played oboe and her dad violin, and they were in an orchestra together. They died in an accident before I was born but because of all the music when she was a girl, she knew all the classics. She was always able to find me tunes and extracts that were perfect. I don't just mean actual ballets like *Swan Lake* or *The Nutcracker*. Piano music by Mozart and Chopin, crazy violins by Berlioz, and folk dances from olden days. I told her the sort of thing I wanted, sometimes I gave her the timing, and she just knew where to find it. She kept up to date too, for the Street classes. Cos the kids loved dancing to current hits, plus the back catalogue of hip-hop, grime and rap. Street was popular with the lads and often they asked for bands or singers I'd never even heard of. And for Modern we were using golden oldies, rock and pop from when I was a teen, and from my mum's youth too. Richard K was a staple – we both liked him, and with him there's always a really strong beat so you can do some quite complicated choreography and not lose them all.

Mum and I were close then, we were getting on better than we ever had before. Maybe it was cos I'd told her the truth about what happened at the clinic. I told her about Hilary from Blackrock as well, and she was glad for me: 'Two heads are always better than one!' She was dead curious about how it felt, being a Host. 'Can you tell you are being directed by someone else's brain?'

'I told you, Mum; I got no memory of it. Not even like a dream. It's just blank.'

'But when you woke up,' she persisted, 'didn't you feel even a tiny bit different?'

I remembered the pearly nail varnish and the faint scent of some expensive skin product. It made me think of flowers, those little white flowers that used to come on the bush Mum grew in a tub outside our flat, before we come to Coldwater. It was a lemony smell but sweet with it. I asked her what it was.

'Philadelphus. Orange Blossom. Why?'

'Nothing. It doesn't matter.'

She went quiet for a bit, counting her stitches, then she goes, 'I think it changed you.'

'How?'

She kept on knitting steadily, not looking at me, a little frown on her face. 'It's hard to say, isn't it? Because your boyfriend dying like that would be a big enough thing on its own. That's what I thought did it. But now I know what happened to you . . . I think it made you more determined.'

'That's not exactly rocket science, Mum. I mean, Ryan died and I got a shedload of money.'

'Yes, but the way you thought it through, and managed to keep it a secret, and battled to get the studio up and running.'

'You saying I couldn't of done that before?'

'I don't know.' She put down her knitting and looked at me finally. 'Honestly, Paula, I'm not being funny. I don't know.'

I was prickly with her because no one wants to think they've been altered or brainwashed or whatever you might call it, do they? Been 'improved' by some clever dick taking over their faculties. No. And if I've done something good I'll take all the credit, thank you very much.

But it set me thinking about how Baz used to be, before he went to the clinic. He was in Meghan's class before mine and she asked me to move him cos he was a proper loudmouth with her, always giving her cheek and answering back and leaping about when she wanted him to stop and listen. 'Sack him,' I told her. 'We've got a waiting list now.' But she said no, he had the makings of a top-flight dancer, it was just hard for her to keep a lid on him in that group.

So I moved him up and kept my eye on him, and Meghan was exactly right. The boy had more energy than a flipping nuclear reactor. Hyperactive, probably. But strong and graceful and really alive to the music. When they were all doing floor work, he was the one your eye went to. Then as soon as I had something to say to them, he was off. Clowning about, behaving like a kid of ten when he was eighteen years old. He was an ideal candidate for Luke Butler anyway due to his physique. I was as frightened and worried for him as I was for the girls, but I will admit it was easier teaching that class while he was away.

He came back calm. To begin with I thought he was tired, which is an effect it does have and not surprising. But he actually listens quietly while I explain what I want them to do; he's stopped attention-seeking. Fair enough, thinks I, he's getting plenty of attention for his antics on his show-off motorbike. But now we're doing extracts from *Firebird* for a little show and he's asked me can he write some words for the 'Supplication of the Firebird' when she's begging for her life? I told him don't be daft, it's a ballet not an opera. But last week he hangs about after class and comes up to me with a bit of paper where he's written a song. 'I know we can't sing it,' he goes, 'but you could put it on the programme. It's the Firebird's lament.' Well I read it and it's good. It's a proper poem. Hey, what do I know? It's a proper poem far as I'm concerned. It makes me feel sad and happy and mixed up all at once, just like the music does. So I told him I *would* use it in the programme.

'When did you start writing poems?' I asked him, joking like, and he sort of shrugs then goes, 'When I come back from London?' Like *he* was asking *me*.

It still makes me uncomfortable though, thinking about how I might've been changed by it. Even if it is in a good way.

14.

ELSA

It's not until they're in their hotel room that the real conversation can take place. They check the view (banana palms, hedges of bougainvillea in red, gold and purple; and beyond, the beach and turquoise sea). They note the screen, the wine and fruit, the bed. Elsa settles in a big green armchair and Lindy sits on the end of the bed facing her.

'Oh, Elsa,' she says. 'New start – but where do we begin?'

'I've had longer than you to think about this. I've tried to plan what I'd say – played and replayed the scene guessing your reactions, trying to get it right—'

'I'm here.' Lindy smiles. 'Speak your mind.'

Elsa takes a deep breath. 'You wouldn't talk to me.'

Lindy rocks back on the bed, hugging her knees to her chest.

Elsa ploughs on. 'I would have given my eye teeth to bite back those words. The smoke. The fire. Derek's words. I *knew* I was wrong, I knew full well, but was there *any*thing I could have done to break through after that?'

Lindy rocks back up to face her. She hesitates, seems to reach for an answer, and then discards it. Her cheeks flush pink. Elsa is struck to the heart by a vision of young Lindy – the real young Lindy, back when she first met her at teacher training – flushed with embarrassment, painfully picking her honest words. This, this new Lindy, this stranger's body, is expressing Lindy's battle to speak true, in precisely the way that her own body did when she was young. How sharp it stings. Elsa wants to fold her arms around her and press her to her breast.

'It was like schizophrenia,' says Lindy. She raises her eyes to meet Elsa's. As she speaks, her voice gathers confidence. 'A weird kind, because it wasn't me, it was *you* there were two of. Before and After. And not just you but the whole world. Like I had walked out of bright sunshine into the dark. Into a dark mirror-world, where everything was distorted. I tried to help Jade and the result was that poisonous accusation. And then all the other children, Gary and Peter and Andrea and Bethany, who I loved, who I've worked with since they were five years old – all of them and their parents saying those terrible things about me. Everything I'd done and worked for became hideous.'

Her voice trails off; she's staring fixedly at the floor, as if she can see right there the faces of the children who betrayed her. Elsa restrains her impulse, which is to lean forward and touch Lindy's arm, to reassure her. Lindy hasn't finished. How often during the bad time did Elsa cut Lindy off, hug her and tell her it would all be fine? How often did she forget to wait for Lindy to unravel the difficult skein of truth? She castigates herself for a know-all, a platitudinous oaf who has trampled on rare, fragile growth. Who has always thought she knows best. She knows nothing. Lindy glances up at her and starts again.

'And my friends, everyone I knew, was cut off from me. I didn't want them to know what was happening, of course I didn't. I asked you to keep them away and so you did. But it was as if they had abandoned me. Everyone abandoned me, and I was shunned, like the monster Jade said I was. And the thing is—' she pauses, formulating the thought; 'I don't know if this happens to other people, but because I knew I was innocent, I began to feel that everyone around me must be wicked. I was in that distorting mirror-world and people who had been my friends were now my enemies. I had to believe that because the alternative was to admit that I was guilty.'

'Oh, Lindy!' It slips out, tears are sliding down Elsa's cheeks. Lindy glances at her kindly and gives a little nod.

'And you,' she says, 'Elsa, you were my rock. My one fixed point. You still believed in me. It was foolish of me but I invested everything in that, all my hope – I'm so sorry this is hurting you, but I must tell you the truth.'

Elsa nods wordlessly.

'So when you said that, when you said, *there's no smoke without fire,* and I realised that you too were in the dark world and that your love also had turned to poison . . . The only way – the only way I could carry on was to tell myself you were evil too. You were distorted and ugly, like everything else in the world I'd fallen into. I had to hate you.' She looks into Elsa's eyes and Elsa sees her own grief and loss reflected there; their joint grief and loss shared, back and forth, in the direct stare between them.

Lindy sighs. 'It's primitive, isn't it? Kill or be killed. It's a really basic instinct. In my dark world everyone betrayed me, everyone hurt me. And you – this is the schizophrenic bit – you who had been the most loving person in my life before – you became the most wicked and treacherous, after. And I tortured myself by thinking about the old Elsa, and what she used to say, and how she loved and protected me, and why she had turned into this hateful creature.'

'Yes. I was hateful.'

'You weren't, you were in an impossible situation too. But I had no resilience. I mean, silly little things – you talking to the lawyer, you opening the blinds so the drones could film me, you going through my room when I was out—'

Elsa closes her eyes in shame.

'No, you were being sensible. But I thought you didn't care how I felt.'

Elsa shakes her head then nods. No. Yes – it's all true. But she didn't mean any of it, and she thought Lindy would surely know that and brush it aside because of course it wasn't important. What was important was getting character witnesses and building a good defence and trying to be normal . . .

'It was wrong of me,' Lindy continues in her low, hesitant voice, 'but I guess I had no objectivity left. I put all my energy into hating you!' She gives an apologetic little laugh. 'It was really quite mad. I didn't want to stay in the house with you so I went out and walked round London. I didn't want to see anyone I knew. I walked up and down the river, right down to the Thames Barrier, and up to Vauxhall. I walked in Southwark and Walworth and Deptford. I tried to avoid the main streets because there are so many bots. Hardly any people walk, did you know that? I mean, there are joggers and cyclists, and at rush hour humans walk to and from the trans and the Tube, but that's all. They keep their heads down looking at their phones with their earplugs in, they side-step you neatly without ever looking up. No one sees you, no one hears you, so you walk the streets like a ghost. Invisible, watching this mass of digitally connected creatures rushing about its business. It was the same dark perverted world I'd been catapulted into, where everything was wrong and hateful. I wore my shoes out. I bought new shoes and got blisters that bled, and the hurt of that pushed me onwards when I started to slow down.'

'Oh, Lindy!'

Lindy shakes her head. 'It's strange to talk about it. I thought I was being stoical, but really I think I was half-mad. And getting on that trans—'

'Yes, the trans.'

'Thing is, I wasn't using transport. I was walking to my limits and back, forcing myself as far as I could go. So getting on that trans was very odd. It was late afternoon, and it was so hot! D'you remember how hot it was? I'd drunk all my water and I was looking for somewhere to refill my bottle. And the air was so dry and gritty it was hurting my eyes. I was going along Fleet Street heading towards the Strand. I noticed a trans at the stop a long way ahead of me. No one getting on or off. And I thought, that will pull away in a minute. But it didn't. I got closer and closer and still it didn't move and I could see it was going to Wandsworth and I told myself, OK, I'm not hurrying. But if it's still there when I reach the stop I'll get on and ride across the river at Vauxhall. At least I'll be out of this horrible hot wind. I kept doing that when I was walking, making bets or bargains with myself – if that pigeon flies away before I pass the lamp-post then I'll be convicted, if that deliverybot goes into the café then one person will smile at me today. I climbed on the trans and the scanner didn't beep so I thought maybe it wouldn't go at all.'

'They'd switched it off. They were from NOBOTS, the people who planned it.'

Lindy laughs. 'Really? Well, I'm glad I died in a good cause.'

'I don't know how you can laugh.'

'I'd rather laugh than cry. Anyway, there were other people on the trans, patiently waiting in the lovely cool of the aircon. I went up to sit in the front seat upstairs, so I could look down the river as we crossed Vauxhall Bridge.'

'And you never knew – you didn't see—?'

'Nothing. No bang or flash or pain or fear. Honestly, Elsa, nothing.' She grins. 'Never even knew I was dead till they woke me up in my new skin.'

'I suppose the dead don't know. I mean, how can they?'

'It's a comfort, eh?' Lindy jumps to her feet, suddenly broken free of the weight of her story. 'Can we go try the sea? A paddle at least. Let's see how warm it is.'

But Elsa is still processing. 'I should tell you my side of the story. What I did was indefensible.'

Lindy comes and kneels by her chair, takes Elsa's knobbly hands in her own smooth slender fingers, and looks up into her face. 'Else. Please. We were both in that bad world, and you did nothing wrong.'

'Yes I did, I should never have—'

Lindy lays a warm finger against her lips. 'Hush. Anyone would have suspected me. I suspected myself.'

Elsa smiles, despite herself.

And Lindy laughs. 'It's over. We can talk another day. But for now, isn't it enough?'

'For now. OK.'

'So shall we go down to the beach?'

They move together to the window. The sea is darkening; the sun, low in the sky behind the hotel, is casting elongated shadows of buildings and palm trees reaching like dark fingers down towards the water. 'What time did they say dinner?'

'I'm not hungry. Are you?'

'Not really,' Elsa lies.

Lindy touches the screen. 'We can get room service. Look, you can have anything you want.'

'*You* can have anything you want. I have to pay for mine, so maybe a bag of peanuts.'

Lindy laughs. She is quicker than old Lindy, she's as light as air. She should be with other young people.

'But don't you want to meet the others?' asks Elsa. 'Everyone'll be introducing themselves.'

'Why would I want to meet the others when I've got you?' She moves laughingly close, rubbing her nose against Elsa's. 'Idiot.'

'Idiot yourself.'

They are kissing. Lindy's right hand is cupping Elsa's throat in the way that she does, and her left is moving down Elsa's back, pressing her body to her. A wave of desire floods through Elsa. 'Lindy – Lindy,' she mumbles. She should tell her to wait.

'Hush. Come to bed now.'

'You don't – you don't have to . . .'

Lindy is leading her to the bed. 'Come here. Oh, Elsa,' her voice is a whisper, 'oh, my darling, touch me.'

Elsa lowers herself onto the bed and their clever fingers are unbuttoning and unzipping and slipping between garments to find warm sensitive skin. There is no mistaking: Lindy wants her as much as she wants Lindy. Elsa lets herself go.

Afterwards they look at each other and laugh. Elsa brushes Lindy's hair out of her eyes. 'That was alright.'

'It was indeed, thank you ma'am.'

'But is it *you*? I mean, sex is your body. Does it feel different in a different body?'

Lindy considers. 'I don't know how to tell. It feels amazing. But sex used to feel like that. I mean, I recognise the feelings.' She begins to laugh.

'What?'

'What if this body belonged to a virgin? Then when she gets it back – don't you think she'll have some kind of physical memory, of what we've been doing?'

'No way of knowing,' murmurs Elsa lazily.

'You could find her and ask her. *You* could. I couldn't.'

'But I'd think she was you and she wouldn't be. It would be tragic.'

'Tragic. I'm hungry now, what shall we order?'

They do not get to the beach that night, but they get there early in the morning, walking through the hotel garden which is fragrant with angels' trumpets and frangipani. The sun is rising out of the sea and the sky is primrose yellow, pale and luminous, shading to near-green before it becomes deep clear blue at the zenith.

When they do talk about the dark time again, there's been a shift. A lifting, a lightening, a leavening, a loving. Elsa has been transported to a world beyond her wildest hopes. Lindy forgives her and loves her still, and the vileness of the dark time recedes. It doesn't vanish – how could it? – but it takes its place as one year among the many of their intimacy, and there are other memories to unravel and explore. There's the energy and optimism of rediscovering each other, and the poignancy of the shortness of their allotted time. Let the distress be boxed, let it not invade the precious present.

15.

GUDRUN

Paradise Island becomes more deserving of its name by the day! It's such a joy to see these young people. These old heads on young shoulders. I can't keep up with them, of course, but I've been over to the hotel several times this week to chat with old friends and Mehmoud (what a treasure that man is!) and hear them speculate about the future of all this. I'm in absolutely no doubt that it has a future, but the how and the what of it are outside our ken. Last night my dear friend Katya, in the guise of a strapping young Amazon who can't be a day over eighteen, was advocating an Anniversaries package. So, for a couple's fiftieth wedding anniversary, for example, their family and friends could buy them a spell of Body Tourism together – the pair of them in young bodies again. 'Imagine!' she said, with sparkling eyes.

There was ribald laughter, of course, but Mehmoud – who is always thoughtful – raised the tone by reminding us that physical attraction plays a large part in young love. In different bodies, our couple might find there is no spark at all. 'Even if both the hosts are young and conventionally attractive, it doesn't mean they'll necessarily fancy one another. What about pheromones, and early conditioning? Never mind colouring and body type.' And then they all really engaged with the topic. There is a wonderful sense among them that they are pioneers, road-testing something which may ultimately be within reach for all; working out the positives and negatives – but somehow lightly, with the bounce and resilience of youth added to their wisdom.

Oh they make me feel old! But this is a truly marvellous development, and Luke deserves all the praise he will surely get.

Mehmoud and Katya even coaxed me into the sea, last night. I haven't sea-bathed for nearly a decade. But Katya helped me change, so deftly and gently that it really was no effort. Then the pair of them took an arm each and led me down the beach and into the water. Oh the delicious cool of it! and the firm sand under my feet. They helped me keep my balance out to waist-depth and then Katya held me while I lay back in the water. It supported me and I floated, weightless as a spaceman in his capsule, and all the aches and pains in this old body melted away.

Katya seems to understand everything I feel and know exactly what I need before I even know it myself. 'Of course I do, Gudrun,' she told me. 'I've *been* your age, I know it inside out.' And then we fell to imagining what wonderfully empathetic carers Body Tourists will make, when Luke finds a way to extend the two-week deadline.

Age does have its pleasures, even though they may have to be experienced at one remove. I'm finding the developing relationship between Luke and Mehmoud highly satisfactory. Mehmoud is a perfect fit for Lukey, as I knew he would be. He's a cautious, patient perfectionist with impeccable social skills and heartwarming levels of empathy. As a team, both romantically and in their work, each supplies the other's deficiencies. And imagining them together physically may be naughty but I find it irresistible; golden brown skin with snowy white, jet black hair with dirty blond, dapper matinee idol looks and Luke's arresting skinny height – oh yes, my dear Gudrun, your matchmaking skills are still absolutely up to scratch!

The auto brought me home to find a message from Hilary; a typically annoying one at that.

Hi Gudrun, Do you have any idea what my dear brother is doing with your money? Even if you do, I'm guessing you don't know the whole story. Did you know two of the youngsters he's used for hosting have died? Two deaths out of how many people in his foul experiment – twelve? Eighteen? It's a high proportion of failure either way.

Luke isn't like the rest of us – you know that as well as I do. He gets so obsessed with his precious research that he seems able to brush off any inconvenient results that don't tally with his own idea of success.

But you're financing this, which probably makes you accessory to murder. Did he even tell you? He kept it secret from me; in fact he outright denied it. But I've got proof.

I don't want to harm him. At the end of the day, he's my brother, warts and all. But this research has to be stopped. You're the one who can stop it, all you have to do is pull the plug on the money.

Please do that, Gudrun. If you don't, I'm going to the police.

Hilary x

I thought that final kiss a charming touch.

She's right, he does tell lies. He told me he'd lost one, a young woman, Meghan something. Not two. And I shall have to take him to task over that. I will not be lied to. I should like to know if Mehmoud knows – surely he must? I need to make it clear to him that I expect his head to rule his heart; his loyalty to me comes before his loyalty to Luke.

Hilary's righteous indignation is stopping her from seeing the bigger picture. What are two deaths, in the scales against the benefits Lukey's invention will bring to humanity? To sacrifice your life in such a cause – well, it has dignity and meaning, it's heroic. Luke probably doesn't see that. He's hushed up the deaths because he's afraid someone will try to stop him. But if we celebrated them, named new buildings after these young people, credited them with being stepping stones along the way to a new and better kind of life; well, I think Luke would find himself swamped with volunteers.

And whoever made an omelette without breaking eggs?

16.

PAULA

Charmayne and Abdul hung around in the locker room till all the others had left, after Advanced. It was the end of the day and that room always smelled sweaty by then. I was tired, and I thought I might have pulled a muscle in my calf – I was getting nasty twinges. My mum would massage it for me, but it was nearly Ryan's teatime and I'd promised to pick up some food from Lianhua before I went home.

'Come on you two,' I said.

'We want to talk to you.' It was Abdul. He was usually very quiet.

'Another day?'

'Now, please,' said Charmayne.

The penny dropped. 'Sorry, Char. With being ill I just . . . I've been meaning to talk to you.' I didn't know how much Abdul knew and I glanced at him.

'I told him everything you said.' Charmayne's voice was sharp.

'OK, let me just—' I messaged Mum I'd be a bit late and to give Ryan the pizza in the freezer. She hated giving him frozen shit but I knew the fridge was practically empty. I led them back into the studio and we sat on the bench at the far end. It was good to be able to rub my calf and I was hoping maybe it was just cramp.

'I've been to see Meghan's mum,' said Char. Oh my god. Why the hell hadn't I been? Yes I'd been ill but why didn't I go the day I heard the news? Before I could gather my wits she was hurrying on. 'I didn't tell her. I mean, I told her what Mr Butler told us to say, about Meghan being knocked down. But

Abdul and I think people should be told.' She glanced at Abdul, who nodded then quickly looked down at his feet. He spoke softly.

'If you ask for any more volunteers, we're going to tell them. The people you pick, we're going to tell them Meghan died because of that research.'

I couldn't think what to say.

'We don't care about the money,' said Char. 'If we have to give it back cos we broke the stupid secrecy thing. We don't care. We don't want anyone else to go to that clinic.'

Words flooded back into my head. 'Listen, I've been talking to someone. Hilary, who runs an athletics centre in Blackrock. She's been sending hosts to the clinic too, and she's going to help us get it stopped.'

They stared at me.

'Char, I'm so sorry you had to go to Meghan's mother. I'll go and see her myself – tonight. Can you give me her number?'

'How?' asked Abdul. 'How are you going to get it stopped?'

'I – I imagine we'll go to the police. I'm just waiting for Hilary to get back to me.'

'Why wait?' Charmayne this time.

'Because she's working out the best way to, to deal with it.' I could see they thought it was lame. 'I'm not messing you around,' I told them. 'I agree with you. This needs to stop.'

'Well why are you just carrying on like normal?' said Charmayne

'What d'you want me to do? Close the studio? As soon as I hear back from Hilary I'll let you know.'

They were both quiet for a moment. Then Charmayne said, 'If you don't do something by Friday I'm going to tell everyone in Advanced. OK, Abdul?'

He nodded. And they got up and went, without saying goodbye or even looking at me.

It made me feel sick. I mean, I've had run-ins with kids before, of course I have. When someone gets moved up a class and their mate wants to move up too, or when they start bitching over who'll get the biggest role in a show. Lots of kids – and their parents too – think they're better dancers than what they are. I can handle that. But this . . .

That night I called Hilary. She didn't look happy to see me.

'I'm sorry, Paula, I've been waiting to hear from Luke's funder.'

'Funder?'

'Who pays for his clinic.'

'You know them?'

She nodded. 'Gudrun. She's very old – maybe she's losing it. I expected a reply before now.'

'Maybe she doesn't care that people died.'

'Maybe. Anyway, obviously she's no help, so I think the next step has to be a press release.'

'Aren't we going to the police?'

'Well, I've been thinking about the bigger picture. It's not just that Luke is doing something dangerous, it's that people on the estates can only ever earn money off shady stuff like this clinic. I've been writing a blog about it all and it's helped to clarify things for me.'

'OK,' I said.

'It's a *political* issue, it's about grotesque inequality.'

'I don't think we can fix that before tea,' I said, and she grinned at that.

'No, but if we put it in a press release we might get a better result than just the clinic being closed down. Because we both know that when Luke gets arrested, our funding dries up.'

'You think we can get money from somewhere else?'

'I don't know. But I don't see why not. It's worth a try.'

'But Butler will deny it. He'll say Ryan died of an aneurism and Meghan got knocked down.'

'You can't just gloss over deaths. He'd need a signed death certificate for both of them, stating cause of death. And not just signed by himself, the lying little toad.'

I laughed at that because it was like she was talking about a naughty kid, not a clever scientist. She smiled at me laughing then she said, 'Paula, I ought to tell you something. Since we're in this together. Luke's my brother.'

'Luke Butler?' I was gobsmacked.

She nodded.

'Well do you . . . are you . . .?' Accusing your own brother in public might be a bit of a problem, is what I was thinking. But she jumped in right away.

'No. Luke's always been like this. Incredibly clever but he just doesn't do normal emotions. I mean, anyone else, if somebody had *died*, they'd stop the research. And put proper checks in place. They wouldn't just pretend it hadn't happened. When our parents died he—' She broke off and shook her head. 'You don't need to hear all this.'

'It's OK,' I told her. She was so clever and sorted, it was strange to see her upset.

After a moment she rubbed her arm across her eyes and said, 'Yes. It's OK.'

Something was really puzzling me. 'Why d'you live on Blackrock? I mean, if you're his sister and you know his funder—'

'Choice.'

'Choice?'

'Choice.'

I must have looked gone-out because she laughed at me then. 'I spent my first thirty years living a life of incredible privilege. So now I'm trying to – I don't know – pay back, a bit.'

'But if you've got money . . .'

'I haven't anymore. Big Brian's got it. I paid for the athletics centre; building work, equipment, the lot. I'm skint. Which is why—'

Which is why we were both in the same boat, needing her brother's money. 'OK,' I said, 'I get it.'

'I'll send you my draft press release tonight, let me know what you think.'

The document she sent me set it all down. Under point one she told all about the clinic and how hosts come from the

Northern Estates, and how they have to be young and fit but two of them have died. She told about how we had been frightened into silence by signing a secrecy clause. And then it said, point two:

This is about more than just a few no-hope kids being collateral damage in the development of a post-life experience. This is about us and them. The poor, powerless and young vs the rich, powerful and dead. They've taken the wealth and the jobs and the country. They've locked us in Estates where we don't live, but survive, addicted to VR and junk food; poorly educated, poorly fed. And we have only one thing left that they want – YOUTH. How can you enjoy your wealth and power in an old decrepit body? Or worse still, a dead one? But they can use their wealth to rent young bodies and inhabit them. While they're enjoying those bodies, the young owners lose the use of them. The old are buying youth and the young are losing their final asset. If you fast-forward twenty years, don't you think every single teenager will be selling months of their youth to rich dead people? And the Northern Estates will be battery farms for them. Brilliant economics! It keeps rich old people happy and it keeps money in circulation on the Estates. Youth is monetised. Win-win.

If we want to stop this, if we want to save young lives and give them purpose, we have to work together and win many more supporters to our cause.

I was pretty impressed and I showed it to my mum. She nodded like she'd known all along. 'Bright woman, this Hilary.'

'Yes,' I said.

'So what's the plan?'

'We're going public, and see if we can get the clinic closed down.'

Mum nodded. 'And beyond that?'

'What d'you mean, beyond that?'

She tapped the screen. 'Your friend is saying more than that. *If we want to save young lives and give them purpose, we have to work together and win many more supporters to our cause.*'

'Yeah well, she's trying to run before she can walk.'

Mum put down her knitting and used both hands to massage her knee. 'No one here has got any power. I've known that since we came here. Since before then. But this could give a – a voice, to kids like Ryan.' We both looked at him. He was crouched on the floor playing with a heap of pebbles he'd picked out of the gravel. He liked to make patterns with them, a circle of browns with blacks and greys inside, or alternating rows of blacks and browns. As soon as he got them all in place he started again with a new design, very precise and finickity. My mum had given him an ice-cream box to keep them in.

'I'm not stupid,' I said. 'I don't want him banged up on Coldwater all his life. But the first thing to do is make sure he never gets a chance to be a host for one of Butler's stiffs.'

'Of course. I'm not disagreeing with you, Paula, I'm just agreeing with your friend that this is part and parcel of something bigger.'

It felt like she was lecturing me and that makes me stubborn. I had a three-year-old son. But she was still the only grown-up in the room. 'Right,' I said. 'Bigger.'

'It's the old, old story, isn't it? Rich v. poor.'

I laughed. 'You think Hilary's gonna get the whole political system changed?'

'Sounds like she's going to try. Which no one has done for a very long time.' She said it like she was accusing me of something. Or maybe she was accusing herself. I didn't want her to put too much on Hilary. If you aim too high you get nowhere. I just wanted it to be out in the open about the clinic and the risks, because that was tangible. And I wanted something to show to Char and Abdul, as soon as I could.

'She's sent me a link to her blog,' I told Mum. 'I'll forward it. Then you can tell her yourself how much you like her ambition.'

Ryan laid Mum's stick on the carpet and began to line up his pebbles along it. I saw her watching him. She liked her stick within reach. I got down on the floor with him and passed her stick back. I showed him how to make a maze with his pebbles. She was quiet counting her stitches, then she suddenly said, 'I saw Paul.'

'Yeah?'

'He looks terrible.'

'Where d'you see him?'

'Clinic queue. He said you'd told him about a VR detox.'

'I didn't mean meds!'

No reply.

'Mum? Did he say anything else?'

'He asked after Ryan.'

Now I had to be mad at myself because I'd been too busy to go back to his since that failed curry evening. 'What d'you want me to do?'

'Couldn't you take Ryan round to see him?'

'I could but what good would it do him to see his father plugged in to VR?'

'You don't give Paul a chance. And the boy should see his father.'

'Oh, here we go. Like I saw mine?'

'That was different.'

'How? I was a child. I must have had a father.'

My mum sighed theatrically. She's never even told me my dad's name, much less introduced us.

'I don't think it would be good for Ryan,' I told her.

'It would be good for Paul.'

She was right there and I knew it. If Paul was making the effort to get himself down the clinic then he must have been thinking about what I said. 'Alright. I'll get in touch with him. OK?'

Mum never said anything, only nodded.

*

Hilary told me she was sending the press release out to all the media next day. I kept checking, but I didn't see it anywhere, not a single word about it on any of the news sites. I wanted to send a link to Char and Abdul. By next morning, when there was still nothing, I called Hilary to ask if I'd missed something. She told me, no.

'We're not important enough,' she said bitterly. 'You don't get in the news unless you've got a celebrity on your side.'

'We need to go to the police.'

'God! Richard K!' She clapped her hand over her mouth. Her eyes were staring.

'What about him?'

'I know how to get the media onto this! Hah! Why didn't I think of it before?'

'What you on about?'

But she wouldn't tell. She said she needed a couple of days to clear it, whatever great mystery it was. It annoyed me to have yet another delay, and I ended the call. I forwarded the press release to Char and Abdul even though I knew it wasn't enough. Then I messaged Paul to say I would bring Ryan to visit him next day.

When we arrived he really had gone to town. The place was clean, there were biscuits and juice on the table, and he'd dusted off a couple of his drums and put them ready in case Ryan wanted to play them. Which of course he did, and it was brilliant for everything except conversation. I sat and watched as Paul showed Ryan how to hold the sticks and what to do, and listened while he tried to copy rhythms Paul clapped out for him. Ryan picked it up straight off. He played Paul's rhythms then he played a load of his own, so loud I thought my head would explode.

It was bitter-sweet, watching Paul teaching him and laughing with him. Paul was thinner than ever, but he'd got something back. Something of his old sparkiness. I found myself thinking, *you're still a good-looking feller, old boy*, and even hoping he might glance up at me and smile. I thought, *what if . . . ?* and stopped myself for a fool. Because it would be too good, wouldn't it, for me and Paul to be a couple again and a storybook mum and dad for our boy? I still fancied him rotten though, and that's the truth.

So. Visit a success. Tomorrow, says Paul, maybe Ryan can stay on his own, just for a couple of hours? Fair enough, I thought, no point in me sitting here like a lemon listening to that racket. I was already running ahead, imagining Paul might look after him one or two afternoons a week, which would spare my mum's legs and/or leave me time for a shower and proper tidy-up after my last class. There was a tiny bit of me thinking, yes, and when Paul brings Ryan home I'll offer him a drink, and maybe we'll get talking again, like in the old days. Like I said, I was running ahead of myself.

Ryan's dead keen to get back to Paul's – to get back to the drums, I suspect, but that's OK. So next day I drop him off at 2 p.m.

But when I go back for him at 4, Paul's flat is suspiciously quiet. I wonder if one of the neighbours has maybe complained about the drumming. The walls are pretty thin, and some people keep their headphones on all the time on account of that. You can programme them to *Rural tranquillity* which I personally am not keen on. It's like listening to nothing – well, I suppose it is silence – but then all of a sudden there's a rustle of wind or chirp of a bird and it makes me jump. I'd always go for music, myself. Anyway, there's no answer when I knock and my heart skips a beat. Has Paul run off with him?

I know that's not true. And when I let myself in there they are, sitting side by side, both in glasses, both in VR.

Well, I went mad. Wouldn't you? The *first* time he has the boy on his own and he gets him into VR. As if there won't be enough temptation and peer pressure when he gets older, as if I won't be fighting him turning into a zombie all through his teens.

'You *bastard*!'

Paul took off his glasses, all sweetness and light, and went 'Hello, Paula.'

'What the hell d'you think you're doing?'

'He was asking me about it, he wants to know why people think it's so good. So I just—'

'So you just thought you couldn't even keep your fucking head out of it for one afternoon while he was with you!'

'No. No!'

'Ryan!' I pulled off his glasses. 'We're going.'

'Mummy, I want to—'

'Yeah yeah. Like your dad.' I didn't want him to hear me swearing at Paul and if we'd stayed I could have really let rip. So we left. Paul was properly upset, nearly crying I would say. But so he should be. I marched Ryan home in silence.

That night I got a message from Paul and I was still so mad I deleted it. But while I was trying to get to sleep I found myself wondering what he could possibly find to say for himself, so I called it up out of the Trash.

Dear Paula, I am sorry you are so upset. I didn't mean any harm. Ryan's a great kid, and you are a wonderful mother to him. He told me you said VR is really really bad and I saw that was making him overly curious. So I took him into a kids' game, DINOSAURUS, for five minutes, so that at least he knows what it is. You can take a look. www.dinosaurus.com It's pretty standard stuff, ages 4–6. Then he won't go building VR up into some great forbidden thrill. We were literally looking at it for five mins, just wandering around looking at the different types of dinosaur, when you arrived. Forgive me. I was trying to do what I thought was best for Ryan. I don't want to fall out with you, Paula. I'd like us to be friends again. Paul xx

Well, I cried myself to sleep.

In the morning my mum said she needed to talk to me. I went

201

and sat opposite her, across the tiny table. Ryan was running around bashing a balloon against every bit of furniture in turn, including our backs. It gave me a headache, but I didn't want to start telling him off again. I thought it was about the studio bills cos she was the one who handled them and I knew we must be running low again. But no. She'd found some medical website offering a miracle cure for knee injuries. And there was a description that exactly fitted her bad knee, and she'd decided to go ahead and pay for it.

'Mum, those medical sites—'

'I know, I know, I've checked it properly.' Of course she had, she was my mum, she'd been warning me about online scams since I was a kid.

'OK, but how are you paying?'

'That rainbow shawl I knitted, I got a hundred and fifty pounds for it. And prepaid orders for three more. It's all done and dusted.'

'Have you got to go away?' I was thinking about childcare, of course. But she shook her head.

'No, it's an injection then some kind of heat treatment and straps. I have to keep my weight off it for three weeks, and I was thinking that might be perfect for giving Paul a chance to help out with Ryan.'

If I knew how to do a hollow laugh I would've done one. It sounds like it would be great, doesn't it? Empty and sort of echoey. But I don't know how to make that noise. So I said, 'OK.' I would have to put Ryan in nursery, and leave him to the care of creepy nannybots. And I would have to make damn sure I didn't overrun at the studio.

Mum was looking at me with a little frown. 'You sure?'

'Of course.'

She heaved a big sigh and I realised she must have really been bothered about asking me. 'You're right, it's sensible,' I told her. 'I mean, if you don't do anything, your legs will only get worse.'

'Yup. Don't want to end up in the Bin any earlier than I need to.'

'Mum – I'll never let them put you in the Bin!'

She smiled. 'Nice of you to say so, but we all come to it in the end.'

'No!'

'You know they've taken Mr Woodhouse?'

I didn't know. I had no idea. 'When?'

She shrugged. 'I don't know exactly. I took him some rice pudding at the weekend, and when I called round next day for the dish, there were domestibots in there clearing it out for a new tenant.'

'Oh, Mum, I'm sorry.'

She shook her head. 'He'd been going downhill for a while.' Ryan's balloon popped and he started bawling. I took him up onto my knee for a cuddle. He was heavy and hot and sticky and I thought, I don't ever want to let you go or have you get old. I wish we could stay like this forever.

'It's given me the push I needed,' Mum said. 'The parcel's been in my drawer for the past week. I'll open it tonight and get started.'

17.

LUKE

Luke has spent the afternoon in the gym. He is back in the flat and deep in a chess tournament against his computer when Mem calls. The AI always wins because its algorithms enable it to learn from Luke, but he's enjoying looking for illogical and unpredictable moves, trying to catch himself out.

'You're early. Call you back after dinner?'

'Luke, we've got a problem.'

'Can't you handle it?'

Mem is sexy, Mem is the nearest thing Luke has found to a soulmate, but at work he's less independent and robust than Luke would wish. Since his return to Paradise Island with the Body Tourists, he has called Luke repeatedly with pedantic queries, interrupting Luke's solitary routines.

'One of them has disappeared.'

'Shit.' Luke's concentration is shattered. He looks up to Mem's anxious face on the screen. 'Who?'

'Chloe Esterhazy. You sent her over on Friday and I think she must have got herself onto the return flight yesterday. It was the same pilot. Apparently she chatted to him in the cockpit on the flight out.'

'What the fuck?'

Mem nods. 'I've tracked down cabin crew from the flight out but—'

'The pilot?'

'Didn't go home.'

Luke calculates. Yesterday's flight would have landed at Gatwick at 11 last night. 'Why didn't you tell me before?'

'I didn't know till this morning. She went for a nap in the

afternoon then excused herself from dinner, she left a message she was having an early night. I don't go round and check they're all tucked up in bed.'

'Why not?'

Mem rolls his eyes. 'Sarcasm, my love – beyond you. You're going to have to chase her at that end.'

'But how?'

They kick this around for a while, but the question is answered as soon as Luke switches on his news feed. A young woman with a sub-machine gun has gone on a shooting spree in central Oxford, killing thirty-two people before being brought down by a police marksman. CCTV images of the shooter's face are flashed across the screen with requests for public help in identifying her. Luke can do that easily: Jill Bailey, the most recent hosting recruit sent to him from Blackrock, by his sister. And no sooner has he made the connection than a message pings in from Hilary.

Murderer! Monster I'm calling police right now

He stares at the jumpy images of screaming shoppers and tourists; drones, emergency vehicles, bodies, blood. Mem's distraught face resurfaces on the screen. 'Yes,' he tells him. 'I've seen. It's a mess, isn't it?' There's a bit of his head – maybe the bit that was so intent on outflanking the chess AI – that is wondering if this is a new trial of his research, and whether he might be able to turn it around so that it works in Body Tourism's favour. Gently, Mem puts him straight.

They agree that Mem will tell Gudrun, but what happens next is hard to plan. Mem wants to tell the other Tourists and bring all five back to London. But they have not had their full two weeks – Luke counters that it's not fair. Why should they have their time cut short?

'Because thirty-three people have died! The clinic will be crawling with police soon enough, and you've got five hosts to restore.'

'Well they're not going to stop me from doing that, whenever the Tourists come back to the clinic.'

'No but won't it be better to get it out of the way as quickly as possible? Plus I can come back with them, and we can face the music together. Otherwise you're on your own there.'

'What's the worst they can do?'

'Charge you with murder.'

'Do you really think they will?'

'Luke, I'm coming. I'll go and see Gudrun now, and aim to get them all onto a flight this evening. See you.' And he's gone.

After pacing around his flat a few times and eating several handfuls of salted cashews, Luke returns to the unfinished chess game. It's the only logical thing to do.

18.

PAULA

There were all sorts of stories about why that woman Chloe lost it and went on the rampage. People said her husband had left her for a model younger than their daughter, and that her parents owned a firearms company and brung her up to be a crack shot, with a cabinet of guns in the sitting room, and loads of other tittle tattle that didn't alter the facts one jot: thirty-two dead plus another Host, the third.

And then everything happened so quick it was hard for me to keep up with it. Hilary identified the host as Jill Bailey, who was one of her best sprinters. She went with the police to see the girl's parents. Poor things, Hilary told me they'd seen it all onscreen but never even recognised their own daughter as the shooter, and they couldn't make head or tail of it. Jill's parents weren't the only ones. The media went berserk with questions about what was Body Tourism and who was responsible and was it Chloe or was it Jill, and how was any of it even possible?

Hilary warned me the police'd be coming to take statements off me and the dancers who'd acted as hosts, and she suggested I have a chat with them to make sure we were all telling the same story. There was only three of them. Asmara and Sarah were gone to Sheffield, Meghan was dead, the only ones left were Baz, Charmayne and Abdul. I asked them to come round and when they arrived I could hear Charmayne through the door before I even opened it –

'—just as easily have been one of us who ended up shooting thirty-two innocent people!'

Baz said hello but Abdul just stared at the floor. Charmayne didn't stop for breath.

'That's down to you, Paula, thirty-three dead bodies. If you'd done what we asked and gone to the police as soon as Meghan died—'

'I know. Look, Charmayne, I know, believe me. I wish to god I'd spoken out.'

She threw herself onto the sofa. I asked Baz if he knew about Meghan, and Char leapt in, 'Course he does, everyone does now, everyone knows it was a cover-up.'

'Paula didn't *make* us volunteer,' Baz said quietly. 'And we were all glad to get the money.'

'Right. And so was she. Didn't think of that, did you? Paula getting paid for pimping us out. How much did *you* make out of it?'

'The money was to keep the studio open. That's all I ever wanted money for,' I said.

'You knew we could die. And you never even told us the danger. You lied and lied.'

'Paula?' It was Abdul, but he still wouldn't meet my eyes. 'When you and big Ryan volunteered – how did he die, really?'

There was a horrible silence. My throat was so tight I couldn't speak. Charmayne stood up. 'She's a murderer. You going to sit here and let a murderer tell you what to do?'

'Be quiet, Char,' Baz said. 'If Paula's got some advice for us about dealing with the police, I'd like to hear it.'

I swallowed and managed to unstick the sides of my throat. 'Thank you, Baz. All I wanted to say was, be completely honest. Forget the secrecy clause, tell the police the truth about everything you know.'

'Including you!' said Charmayne.

'Of course, including me.'

She flounced out followed by Abdul and, after a moment's hesitation, by Baz. And then I started getting messages, a steady flow of messages from students, angrily calling me names or asking questions that brought tears to my eyes. *How could you, Paula? Why didn't you tell us?*

I didn't want to burden my mum cos she had enough on her plate with trying to fix her knees. But I had to talk to someone who'd at least listen to my side of the story and not jeer at me, and I didn't know who that could be apart from Paul. If he was in VR he wouldn't answer, but if he wasn't . . .

I kept thinking of his text, *I'd like us to be friends again. Paul xx*. He didn't have to put two kisses. Maybe I'd got it wrong about him showing Ryan VR. Like I got it wrong about not telling my dancers the dangers in going down to London. Like I got it wrong not going to the police when Char and Abdul first asked me to, and when thirty-three lives might have been saved. Like I was just basically wrong about everything I tried to do.

So I forced myself to call Paul. He asked me what the matter was and that made me cry. Then he asked could he come round? He sounded so timid I was even more ashamed. I managed to say *yes please*, and *I'm sorry*, and before I even had time to wash my face, he was there. He was so sweet to me – and honestly, I didn't deserve it. So then I told him the whole sorry story, starting with the truth about big Ryan's death. I told him about sending my dancers to the clinic, the secrecy clause, the payments, Meghan's death, and Hilary.

When I'd finished he just sat there, staring out the window at the dark, and never said a word. Eventually he went to the bathroom and I heard the tap running. He came back with a warm towel that he'd wrung out, and he wiped my face with it so gently I would have bawled again, if I'd had a single tear left. Then he kissed me and said, 'It's late. D'you want a midnight snack, or shall I put you to bed?'

I laughed at that. He made us cheese on toast which we munched in silence, listening to our own crunching and all the little ticks and creaks of the night-time building. Ryan coughed and turned over in his sleep, like a pebble being chucked into that pool of silence, making ripples. Then it slowly reformed around us again, calm and quiet spreading through the flat and the building and all the land around.

We begun talking again, in whispers. We talked about what would happen, how the clinic would close down. That was a great weight lifted off my shoulders. But I'd lost my dancers and that was like daggers in my eyes. All that anguish and hard work, and lives – Ryan's life, Meghan's life – all that had made one good thing, the dance studio. And now my students hated me.

Paul was shaking his head. 'Listen,' he told me. 'Slow down. You need to close the studio for a while, but not forever.'

'But—'

'But nothing. What happened when you had the baby and the studio was closed for a few weeks?'

'They all wanted me to open it again.'

'Exactly. And so they will this time. Cos you're the force and the energy behind it. And if you're not there making it happen, they'll start to think about what they're missing.'

'Someone else can run classes. Some of them already do.'

'Yeah but without you it'll fall apart. And anyway, what's the first thing they're going to need?'

Well I knew the answer to that one. 'Money.'

'Right. And when there isn't any, they'll ask themselves, where did Paula get it from? Then they'll understand a whole lot better why you were dealing with Luke Butler.'

'But I lied to them.'

'Of course you did. Cos if you'd told them your boyfriend Ryan was killed by the clinic, you'd never even have got a studio built at all. You made a deal – your silence in return for a dance studio. And it was the cleverest thing you ever did.'

'Wickedest, more like.'

He grinned. 'You know what, Paula? This is a fantasy I've been having ever since we split up. A dream that one day *I* would be able to help *you*.'

I didn't understand. He leaned forward and took my hands. 'Of course it was clever. Cos nothing you could do would bring Ryan back. So at least you got a studio out of it.'

Things began to shift in my head and a shaft of memory

opened, shining back onto me standing in Butler's clinic and shocking myself by saying, 'I want a dance studio.'

Paul was right. If I hadn't asked I would of got nothing. 'But I should have told them the risks. When they volunteered for hosting.'

'Maybe. But who's to say they wouldn't have done it anyway? Ten grand is quite an incentive.'

I shook my head and after a moment he nodded. 'OK. But you give it time, and I honestly think this will come right.'

'Haven't got much choice, have I?'

'Nope.' He grinned at me, and I tried to laugh quietly and that made us both laugh so loudly that we woke Ryan up. The three of us ended up together in my bed with Ryan in the middle like jam in a sandwich.

And there we were when we woke up in the morning – three in a bed, a proper little family. It felt like it does when snow falls in the night and everything's different. The light's brighter, the muck is covered in pure white, the air tastes clean and dry and the world is new. Paul made us breakfast in bed. Then Ryan spilled his juice all over the duvet so that was a step back to normal. I had a hollow like a hangover inside me but it wasn't till I was cleaning my teeth that I remembered why. The studio. My dancers.

I picked up a voice message from Nadia softly telling me she would not be able to teach dance anymore. When Paul saw my face he asked if he could listen, so I replayed it for him.

'Can I give you some advice?' he asked.

'OK.'

'Close the studio right now. Send a message to everyone just saying closed till further notice.'

'Without giving any reason?'

'They'll all know soon enough. You don't need to suffer death by a thousand cuts, Paula.'

'Shouldn't I go down there and talk to them?'

'No.'

Ryan was messing with the cushions, piling them on the floor and jumping off the sofa onto them. 'Put them back,' I told him, 'you'll hurt yourself.' So then he starts dragging his chair across the floor making that horrible scraping noise.

'Ryan! Stop it!' shouts Paul. So I switched on the screen and passed Ryan his headphones. Kiddy TV exploded onto the screen and there was a minute's silence then Paul said, 'Really?'

'What?'

'You know what.'

'It won't do him any harm. I'll take him down to visit my mum in a bit.'

Paul washed up, and brushed the crumbs out of the bed and put a clean cover on the duvet, while I just sat there like a lump. Then he came and sat down opposite me at my little table. 'Can I talk about VR without you getting mad?'

'If you want.'

'It's a lot more educational than this—' he jerked his head at the screen. 'Cos Ryan can be active in it, as opposed to totally passive.'

'I know.'

'So what's the problem?'

'For god's sake, Paul! How have you spent the past couple of years?'

'OK, it's a bit addictive—'

'Don't make me laugh.'

'You said you'd listen.'

'I'm listening.'

'You think it gets you hooked on games and porn. But it's real people, Paula. In *Parallel Worlds* I've got real friends, loads of them, all over the world. It can translate Japanese and Korean for me and we're building stuff together, cities, civilisations.'

'But it's not real, Paul. It's a game.'

'The friendships are real. The ideas are real. We are really communicating.'

'But why can't you communicate with people in the flesh?'

'Because it's superficial. OK, say you meet someone at Lianhua. You say, *Hi, how's it going?* And they reply, *Fine.* You talk about the weather. You blather about what you watched onscreen last night, which was probably crap anyway. But in VR, we're trying to redesign the world and invent new politics.'

'Yeah, but when people *really* sit down to talk, when friends really talk and listen to each other—'

'How often does that happen?'

'You saying there's no boring chat in VR? No bragging, no bullying, no bullshit?'

'You can cut out those voices. You can chose who to talk to, you're not stuck in the room while someone bores your arse off telling you their digestive problems.'

'Is it better than talking to me now?'

'It's more democratic.'

'Than me?'

He interlaced his fingers with mine. 'I already know I want to talk to you. But new people, well, everyone's equal in VR. Because you don't see their real face or hear their real voice. A white sixty-year-old man is equal to a black twelve-year-old girl is equal to a twenty-year-old guy with spina bifida in a wheelchair is equal to – I don't know – a supermodel. People don't judge each other on appearance.'

'Right. And the sixty-year-old man pretends to be fifteen so he can groom the twelve-year-old girl.'

'No. Occasionally, maybe, but the point is basically people are decent. They want to think and work together. And all this ageism, sexism, racism just gets in the way.'

'OK. But how can you make *that* connect with *this*? With life on Coldwater?'

He looked down. 'I dunno. It's really hard. VR is more fun, people are kinder and you learn more. The scenery's better and the colours are brighter. It's hard not to see this as just – dreary.'

'So why don't you stay plugged in?' My eyes strayed to Ryan who was curled in the corner of the sofa sucking his thumb in a television trance. What was the difference, really? And why was I being shitty to Paul again, when all he was doing was trying to help me understand?

'It boils down to escapism in the end, doesn't it?' he said.

'And trying to keep people quiet. Trying to keep a lid on them.'

He glanced at me questioningly and I pointed at Ryan. Paul grinned. 'I'll take him down to the playcage, while you have a shower and get dressed. Then you can take him to see your mum.'

'Hilary told me the police will probably turn up today.'

'No problem. Ryan can come round to mine. Practise a bit of drumming.'

'Yeah. Like last time.'

'Sure.' He grinned his best Paul-ish grin. 'Virtual drumming's much kinder on the neighbours!' I watched while he teased and coaxed Ryan away from the screen and into his coat. He's a really good dad, I thought. They were halfway out the door when he stuck his head back in to ask for the code for the playcage. 'If a man's allowed to know it.'

'You're not a man, you're a parent,' I told him. And gave him the code.

While I was having my shower that new-snow feeling came back. Ryan was safe with his dad. I didn't have to rush because of being afraid he might be up to mischief on his own in the other room. I had all the time I wanted. And I didn't have to keep leaning on my mum. I didn't have to send any of my dancers down to that hateful clinic ever again. And the studio might be stood closed and empty, but it was there. It wasn't going to melt away. Paul was right. One day probably we'd all be ready to start again.

19.

RICHARD K

The Oxford shootings? A terrible tragedy. Definitely. But I have to say when they began to spill the beans about what's gone on in the miraculous clinic for Body Tourism, I was tickled pink. Nothing's given me greater satisfaction than seeing that long streak of piss Luke Butler being bent double and stowed in the back seat of a paddy wagon. I hope they put him away for good.

I was edgy when the DI came to question me, I freely admit. Cos as far as I know, the punch I landed on my benighted father's revenant was never drawn to the attention of the fuzz. Butler made me pay, I had to cough up £5,000 damages, but it was all done without benefit of the strong arm of the law. And I certainly don't want them poking around asking questions about that now. Presumably the young stud has learned to pull with a broken nose just as effectively as with a straight one. I certainly don't want him getting any ideas about litigation for GBH.

I needn't have worried. The old inspector was a consummate arse-licker; he even brought a repro LP for me to sign for his wife. The colours are crap compared to the original but I didn't tell him that. And when I let slip how much I paid to bring the old man shuffling back onto this mortal coil, he nearly popped.

'It's research!' he told me. 'The only way that clinic can get away with any of this is by claiming they asked for volunteers for research. If you pay for something, as a consumer you have rights.'

Ah, rights. Very nice to hear I have some rights, after all the shit that's gone down. But first he wanted to know who I paid and where's the evidence?

So I told him about Gudrun and her offshore account, and

then he was visibly un-chuffed. 'Didn't you pay anything to Luke Butler? Or to the clinic? Were you ever given an account with the clinic?'

No and no; and it doesn't take a genius to see how clever they've been there. And I certainly wasn't going to mention the damages, which was a payment direct to the host anyway. Joseph something, I recall.

'But did you discuss your payment with Luke Butler? Was he aware of it?'

The honest answer was no. I assumed, obviously, that he did know. But that wicked old crone Gudrun is perfectly capable of creaming off all the profits for herself, I don't doubt.

'What about the others?' I asked Sherlock Holmes. 'Did the other customers pay Butler?'

He shook his head, and that made me think I'd been taken for a mug. 'Can I get a refund?'

He didn't know.

Anyway, since I paid, I have rights. As a consumer. So I've got Samuel the lawyer dropping in this morning for a bit of a chat about it. I reckon I can claim damages for trauma. Firstly, there's the trauma of seeing my old man black-faced. That'll need clever handling, to not sound racist, but it's *not* racist and when all's said and done that's what I pay Sam for, to be clever. Then there's the trauma of him hitting on my wife, under my very roof. If that's not traumatic I don't know what is. And that leads to the seriously damaging trauma of ruining my relationship with my dad's memory. Parents are sacrosanct. Where would the human race be, if we couldn't sit around waxing sentimental about our deceased forbears, and fondly remembering childhood escapades and words of wisdom imparted? Instead of which, my image of my dear departed father has been rudely shattered and reconfigured as a predatory sex maniac. How much will a shrink charge to fix that?

And finally, there's the lasting and highly expensive trauma of my wife's divorce settlement. Cos I couldn't live with the bitch after that and she said some spectacularly vicious things in court. I could claim for character assassination. Yes, I definitely need compensation for the pain and heartache she inflicted. None of this would have happened, if my old man had remained decently dead and buried.

'You could probably claim for loss of earnings,' was the advice from sycophant detective. But that's the one loss I couldn't claim for, since the divorce had the opposite effect and jacked me back up into the charts for two glorious months. Nothing sells records like dirty linen, washed in public. And the media loved everything about that case, but most of all the mystery identity of my wife's lover. Hacks paid exorbitant amounts to all the humans they could find on our street, in search of info about strangers and visitors and likely candidates for lover boy. But the tall black guy with the distinguished overcoat is the one person no one can track down. Ha-ha. I found his red puffa in the wardrobe the other day. I cut it to pieces and fed it to the kitchen garbage disposal.

Seriously, Meryl is a loss. She is a loss. I loved her as much as all my other wives rolled into one. And there's nothing cuts a man down to size more than his wife taking a lover young enough to be his son. She sure was sweet. My ho-ooneey.

Nothing to be done. I'm leading a pretty quiet life these days. I see young Derren a couple of times a week; fool around for days at a time in my studio; spend a fair bit of time in VR. This busting of the Body Tourist clinic has been the most exciting thing that's happened in a while.

20.

ELSA

Lindy's good humour and quiet courage, the day before her second death, silence Elsa's grief. 'You're doing really well, love,' she tells Elsa, as Elsa packs her case. And, with a wicked grin, 'Thank you, Mario!'

As gravely as if she were in church, Elsa recites the response; 'But our princess is in another castle.'

'Exactly.'

You do not howl and cling on to a person who is facing non-existence with such fortitude. Elsa and Lindy have had their extra time, and the best way to honour Lindy now is to try and emulate her calm strength.

On her lonely way home Elsa feels herself almost in suspended animation, experiencing the world through glass – up until she hears the news. Oxford shooting, thirty-three dead, Luke Butler's clinic closed down for good. It makes her cry, which is mad since she has not yet cried for new Lindy.

But maybe these *are* tears for Lindy; for that door into impossibility which swung open at just the right moment, and has now swung shut again, sealing the barrier between the living and the dead.

When a detective questions Elsa, she seems rather disappointed to learn that Elsa did not pay to bring Lindy back, that the experience was wholly positive, and that no one was hurt or injured. The media is so overwhelmingly negative about Body Tourism that Elsa's strict sense of fairness kicks in, and she messages Mehmoud, the kindly doctor in charge on the Island. His reply is instant:

If you feel able to make a statement showing the good side of Body Tourism, it would be greatly appreciated by both Luke and myself. I agree, it is heartbreaking that this work should be terminated.

Elsa busies herself, in the empty shell of her old home, writing, cutting, recording and re-recording, until she finally has a short speech she can bear to send to Mehmoud.

My name is Elsa and my partner Lindy died two years ago in a London bomb outrage. They were able to freeze the victims. It was very hard, because she had been accused of a terrible crime, and then she died violently and suddenly without anything being resolved. And afterwards she was revealed to have been completely innocent. I so much wanted to see her and tell her that her name was cleared, that I couldn't sleep. I thought about her every minute of every hour of every day, I would have given anything to bring her back.

Then I had the tremendous luck to hear about Body Tourism, and Lindy's mind was implanted in a healthy young body. Thanks to Mr Butler's kindness we got a special dispensation for me to go with her to Paradise Island. I will tell you one thing about her. She loved games – video games, computer games, the kind of game where if you lose you're dead, and then if you want to keep playing, you come alive again. So how fitting it was for her to come back to life, and have a second go.

We were happy. We were so happy to see one another again, it was wonderful. She looked different but she was my Lindy through and through, with perfect recall of her old life. And when I told her what had happened and how she had been completely exonerated . . . well, we both had to cry then, because it had been such a terrible blight on our lives. I had to apologise for ever doubting her for a moment, and she helped me to understand how isolated and desperate she had felt. We were able to make up – completely and unreservedly – and that's the best thing, isn't it? To be fully open with the person you love.

Only two weeks, yes, and it goes in a flash. But we had a chance to put right everything that had gone wrong; it gave us our lives back, if you can understand me, even though we only had them for two weeks. We talked all day and at night we cuddled up together like in the old days. And what I want to say is, don't let anyone tell you this is all bad, because of what that dreadful woman did in Oxford. This is good, especially if you lose someone suddenly, without the time even to say goodbye or to say sorry, and 'I love you'. It's a time machine that can give you your happiness back. So, I just wanted to go on record saying a big THANK YOU to Mr Butler and his marvellous team.

It is more personal than she intended, but in the end she decides that makes it more honest. She's not a scientist, she's not an ethicist, she's not qualified to pronounce on the rights and wrongs of the process. But she can talk about her and Lindy's experience. And a lot of people who have absolutely no idea what that experience is, nor any other qualifications for talking about it either, seem to be pontificating about it non-stop, online.

Mehmoud sends a brief, grateful reply. He has been let out on bail, with restricted screen time. He's sending her speech to someone who can post it online.

Elsa spends the next day on her own, testing the flavour of Lindy's absence. How can a person die? How can warmth and humour and knowledge and experience and love just – vanish? Where is Lindy now?

The time they have had together on the Island has been all that Elsa hoped for, and more. But it doesn't answer the intractability of death; its implacable finality. Body Tourism plays at having power, but death wins in the end, always.

Elsa is curled up on the sofa in her half-cleared house. The shelves are empty of ornaments and books, and smeary with dust. There's a pile of packed boxes heaped against the wall. Her mind is still, with the calm that comes after continuous company and intense experience. She's alone. Slivers of memory flicker in the stillness like swallows darting over a pool: the smell of freshly baked bread in this house, the day they came to view it. How cynically she and Lindy grinned at one another, recognising the oldest cliché in the book – if you really want to sell a house, make it smell of coffee or baking bread. They bought it nevertheless, proving a cliché is a cliché because it's true.

She remembers the ache of cold in her wet feet, when Lindy jumped across a swollen winter stream and she tried to follow. That niggle of humiliation. She remembers leaning together against a sun-baked church wall in the stillness of Todi siesta time, and feeling the sudden vibration of the bell tolling 3. Heat, stillness, shimmer of sound. She remembers the silky touch of Lindy's – real Lindy's – cascade of coppery hair, falling across her naked breasts. And clasped hands slick with sweat, rejoining as linked little fingers. The taste of damp and peat in the Galway holiday house. Pushing their feet between clammy sheets on the unaired bed, and clinging together for warmth.

The peace of concentration in this room when they sat together over reports. Or as she worked, the reassuring sounds of Lindy cooking, the slow stir of the wooden spoon, the rapidly chopping knife. She remembers sitting in the darkened theatre near the end of *Death of a Salesman*, unbalanced by tears sliding down her cheeks. And Lindy's warm hand finding hers. The exhausted smell of school at the end of the day: dinners, hot little bodies, hand soap and heated plastic. The pleasure of switching off the edubots, and together heading out into the evening air. The sight of Lindy's lost contact lens balanced on the side of the plughole like a gravity-defying drip; its feather-lightness on her fingertip, Lindy's grateful smile. Turning a corner in a Hepworth exhibition and seeing Lindy as a stranger might; transfixed, intent, reaching out her hand to stroke a bronze flank.

They are come and gone in an instant – fleeting memories. But where do they go when Elsa dies? Nobody will know them. They will be extinct. And there are so many, a lifetime's worth, packed in her synapses.

You can't keep it.

You can't keep it.

Let it go.

And now she's thinking, my brain is like my house. Full of stuff accumulated over the years. I can clear the house, but I can't clear my brain. It's packed with Lindy. I can't start over. Maybe that's why we have to die.

She is adrift, aimless, floating on the rising tide of her past. It's alright, she can give it time, and let it take her where it will.

21.

PAULA

I'm still trying to finish my wretched statement for the police when Hilary calls. The police didn't stay more than ten minutes – just told me to write it all down, everything that happened, in my own words, about Butler and the clinic and my students and the money, with dates and times. I've got to send it to them. It would've been a damn sight easier if they'd asked me questions. I'm not a writer! I told them, I'm not flipping Charles Dickens. But the woman just laughed.

Anyway, here's Hilary, looking knackered and wanting a chat. 'It was so grim with Jill's parents, Paula. I can't get it out of my head. She was their only child and they just – they worshipped her.'

'I'm sorry.' I'm sorry and I still haven't been to see Meghan's mum. What the fuck is wrong with me?

'I'm thinking we should start a fund in her memory. And in memory of everyone who's died. And use it for other estate kids.'

'How?'

'Depending on how much we raise – we could use it to pay for athletics and dance, for a start.'

'You mean to keep the gym and studio going, to replace Butler's money?'

'Yes.'

'I had to close the studio. My dancers are all mad at me.'

Hilary frowns. 'They'll come round. Anyway, we could use it to pay for other activities, taking them off the estates. Mountain climbing, scuba diving, seeing the outside world.'

'You have to be pretty fit to do stuff like that.'

'Well we'd train them, silly. Or pay someone else to. The money would be about improving chances for youths on the estates. What do you think?'

'You reckon we'd raise enough for that?'

'Paula, it's been in the news everywhere. OK, people are upset about the Oxford victims. But there's a second wave of sympathy now. People are going, *Why did those poor youngsters take such a terrible risk?* They don't know about life here, they have no idea.'

'Right.'

'I've been getting a lot of hits on my blog – a *lot* – so I've done some proper research. Look, Paula!' She opens a screenshot for me:

81% of children born on the estates have never been off them.

90% of children born on the estates have never seen the sea or a live animal.

The suicide rate among young men on the estates is double that of the outside population.

Average life expectancy is 67 years (compared to 90 years outside).

Rate of VR addiction is estimated at 70%.

When I see it in figures all I can think of is my little Ryan. No, no, and no again. 'Oh, Hilary!'

'Exactly. I've already posted up three lovely pictures of Jill running. It will be easy to add some text to show people what a great kid she was – and talk about her optimism, and her innocence . . .' Hilary's having a hard time getting her words out and I can see she's tearing up.

'It's OK,' I tell her. 'It's OK to be upset, Hilary.'

She buries her head in her hands.

'Look,' I say, 'it's a great idea. And I can help you. Now the studio's closed I'll have time on my hands. We'll fundraise. We'll make sure no one ever forgets Jill Bailey.'

Hilary sniffs. 'Thanks. I want – I just want something positive to come out of it, at the end of the day. You know they're charging Luke with murder?'

I nod. 'Is that a problem?'

'He never intended anyone to die. He didn't set out to kill anyone. I think intention has to come into it, for murder.'

'But all those people are dead.'

'Isn't it manslaughter?'

'Have you spoken to him?'

She shakes her head. 'Gudrun's got him a hotshot lawyer who's advised him not to speak to anyone.'

'Gudrun's the funder, right? Won't they be arresting her?'

Hilary laughs. 'No, they won't get hold of her, the wily old fox. She's safely tucked away in some tropical tax haven, she's much too clever to get caught.'

I think about Luke Butler on the day of baby Ryan's birth, when he asked me to find him some hosts. He knew what he was doing. He didn't care about big Ryan getting killed. 'I can understand you feeling sorry for him. But when I think about the deaths – Ryan being dead, then Meghan, and him just merrily carrying on . . .'

'You think he wanted them to die? He was working to *help* people, to make them happy, to give them a second chance at life.'

'Yeah, but—'

'But what?'

'He wasn't even that bothered, when Ryan died. All he was bothered about was covering it up.'

Hilary sighs. 'That's why he won't get off. Cos he doesn't wear his heart on his sleeve.'

I'm remembering when she first told me now, about Luke being her brother and covering up the deaths. *He's incredibly clever but he just doesn't do normal emotions.* She was saying it was bad, back then, she was calling him *a lying little toad*. But now she's upset, what can I say? 'No, he doesn't wear his heart on his sleeve.'

'He *wants* to do good. Deep down, I know he does.'

He may be her brother and fair play to him, but from where I'm standing, the amount of good he's done is precious little. Time to change the subject, I reckon.

'What do we have to do to set up a Jill Bailey fund? How can I help?'

Hilary takes a gulp of water from the bottle on her desk, and nods. 'OK. I think we need trustees or a board or something so can I use your name and address?'

'Sure. You can use my mum's as well. She's always telling me what a bright woman you are.'

'Really?' Hilary perks up. 'What have you been telling her?'

'Oh, she reads your blog. She agrees with everything you say.'

Hilary laughs. 'You must introduce us sometime. Put her on next time we talk.'

'I will. See you, Hilary.'

'See you, Paula. Take care.'

22.

GUDRUN

And so my two dear boys are in jail; Luke for the rest of his life, I regret to say. I can see that the public needs a scapegoat, but it really is not as if the poor boy pulled the trigger. It is deeply regrettable that they can't find anyone else to blame for the Oxford fiasco.

Mehmoud was skilfully defended, and his newcomer status, taken together with his subordinate position at the clinic, largely exonerated him. He's been sentenced to five years, but we expect him to serve less than half of that.

I've picked up a few requests to *help the police with their enquiries*, but I can't see much to be gained from that. A private island rather comes into its own, when the long arm of the law starts reaching for one. They've closed down the clinic, of course, which is a dreadful waste of an asset.

But I think Hilary will come round. My proposal to her is nifty, though I say so myself. I'm advocating repurposing the clinic as a treatment centre for VR addiction, where they can rescue some of those poor lost souls from the estates. She bemoans their plight often enough in her blogs; it would be churlish of her not to assist in a cure. And her marvellous Jill Bailey Fund has raised more money than anyone can possibly spend on dancing and athletics. Paying for state-of-the-art rehab for VR addicts would be a use that donors can really get behind.

Which would, in turn, help me recoup the fortune I spent on Luke and Mehmoud's lawyers. What goes around comes around. Providing VR rehab will satisfy my philanthropic instincts; and frankly, the need for it is only going to increase, so it will certainly turn a profit.

When Mehmoud comes out, I shall have work for him. The UK media have kicked up a fine old stink about all this, and frightened Parliament into passing several retrograde and shockingly prohibitive laws. The insertion of digital memory into organic material is banned. The number of legal and ethical hoops researchers must now leap through before they can even begin to work has been increased to a ludicrous extent. It spells the end of organic/digital research in the UK, and has sparked a new brain drain of the nation's top scientists.

The UK was unlikely to be a big player long term, I must admit, given the size of the potential market for these developments. This has not been the publicity I intended for Luke's brilliant work, but it is publicity nevertheless, and it has been reported worldwide. My lawyers have been discreetly fielding a number of enquiries from Big Pharma about the programme, its success rates, its technical specifications, the pharmaceutical regime, the time parameters of Host/Tourist inhabitation, and so on. The Chinese have been the first in with a bid, and very handsome it is too. But I've instructed my lawyers to hang fire, and see what other offers we get. We can probably bump them up.

I am most inclined to go with the Chinese, because they have the intelligence and the technical expertise to properly value Body Tourism. They know how to look to the future and are therefore unlikely to allow the research to be derailed by foolish notions of morality or sentiment. I can't imagine it will be difficult to extend the Tourist/Host habitation beyond the paltry two weeks Luke was limiting himself to. The Chinese will undoubtedly be able to persuade Hosts to volunteer for longer spells; one hears that the lives of their prisoners of conscience are scarcely worth living. What will it be to them to host for six months, a year, or longer?

In fact, Body Tourism could improve the lot of humanity in yet another way, by reducing prison populations, using all who are young and healthy enough, for long-term hosting. What humane regime would not pay handsomely for that win-win solution?

Once the time is no longer limited – what joy Body Tourism will bring! Immortality, in vigorous young bodies. All thanks to Lukey's cleverness and my own skill as puppet mistress. Though I say so myself, the game has been well played. Truly, *Death, where is thy sting?*

ACKNOWLEDGEMENTS

I should like to thank the following for really helpful critical feedback on earlier drafts of *Body Tourists*: Mike Harris, Lesley Glaister, Wendy Rogers, Laurie Harris, Marina Vickers, Edmund Copeland, and my editor at Hodder, Emma Herdman.

Special thanks to Atuki Turner for advice on Ugandan English! Thanks to Simon Ings for commissioning the original story, to Clive Brill for the radio drama, and to my agents Charles Walker in London and Georges Borchardt in New York, for all their hard work.

Jane Rogers